DANGEROUS PLAY

DANGEROUS PLAY

EMMA KRESS

Roaring Brook Press

New York

Published by Roaring Brook Press
Roaring Brook Press is a division of Holtzbrinck Publishing Holdings
Limited Partnership
120 Broadway, New York, NY 10271 • fiercereads.com

Library of Congress Control Number: 2020919570
ISBN 978-1-250-75048-8

Our books may be purchased in bulk for promotional, educational,
or business use. Please contact your local bookseller or the Macmillan
Corporate and Premium Sales Department at (800) 221-7945
ext. 5442 or by email at MacmillanSpecialMarkets@macmillan.com.

First edition, 2021 • Book design by Aurora Parlagreco
Printed in the United States of America

10 9 8 7 6 5 4 3 2 1

For my mom, Susan, and my dad, Jack, who helped me believe
I could change the world.
For my daughter, Mazie, and my son, Max, who will.

ONE

THE AIR FEELS DIFFERENT OUT here—wilder, freer. In a few minutes, our girls will jump out of windows and leap off roofs all over town. Ava already has. She'll be here soon. I could leap off this roof, swing around the elm branch, and let go into a tight flip before landing on the ground. It would totally get a 10 from the German judge.

But the soles of my shoes stick to my bedroom floor, and my hands hold tight to the window frame. I'm not Ava.

And I don't do rooftops.

I tuck my head back inside, shut the window, and head to my parents' room. I lean my note on Dad's nightstand but send one of his pill bottles rattling to the ground. So much for subtle.

Sure enough, his eyes open, narrow and cloudy. "Sorry," I whisper, grabbing the bottle. "Go back to sleep."

"Hey, Zoe. Mom home yet?" He turns to check the other side of the bed, but his face tightens, as if a burst of pain radiated across his back.

"No, no." I guide him back onto his side. "It's still early."

He checks the alarm clock: 11:28 p.m. He smirks. "You

leaving me another note? Most teenagers just do the respectable thing and sneak out."

"I am totally sneaking out. We're just having a conversation first." I check the notepad I put by his bed. "It looks like you could take another pain pill. Do you want one? More water?"

"I'm fine. You have fun at that frat party now."

"Sure, Dad." I kiss him on the forehead. "Don't be surprised if I come home pregnant."

"Don't forget drunk and high!" He sticks his thumb up.

I close the door on his laugh.

Rushing back to my room, I grab my stick and backpack, and tap my Tar Heels poster for good luck before dashing down the stairs and out the front door.

When I slide into the big van's passenger seat, Ava smiles at me. "I'll bet you a giant plate of Tully's chicken tenders and mozzarella sticks that you left a note."

I refuse to look at her. "Shut up and drive, Cap'n."

"Aye, aye, Cap'n." She laughs. "I'll also take payment in anything cheesy . . . Doritos, nachos, pastelitos, Cheetos. What do Os have to do with cheese?"

We drive down sleepy streets, windows open, gathering our team of girls dressed in black who tumble out of their windows, forward roll down their front lawns, and pile into the back of the van, their sticks clanging against the metal floor, their laughs bouncing off the roof. The girls bump into one another when the van turns, limbs tangling.

We take Lakeview Road, with its small one-story houses packed tightly on one side and the expanse of lake on the other. The lake is big enough that you can't really see the other side, especially at night. A ways down, the road winds away from the lake, and the only people with access to the view are the ones who can pay for it. But here, it's open to all of us.

We pull into the empty lot of the beach. North of Syracuse, this is about as close as we get to a real beach. I pretend the lake with its dark water and dark beyond is the ocean, that I'm someplace better and warmer than here, and that I'm on the edge—the very edge of everything old and new and just beginning. I breathe in the air thick with water, lake weeds, and tumbled earth and let the warmth of it soak in.

Tonight it's nothing but us, sand, water, and moonlight.

We scramble out of the van, and the lake bounces our laughter back to us. Four girls plant goals with glow-in-the-dark flags, while others volley the glow-in-the-dark ball back and forth on the flat of their sticks. I slide face paint across Ava's cheeks, the neon-blue streaks bright against the night.

"Blue team here!" Ava shouts, and she paints her team as they come to her.

Liv marks me with my favorite color. "Green!" I call, and my group clumps together, marking one another's faces. Our individual features fade away, and we become darkened bodies with glowing stripes in school colors that crinkle when we laugh.

"What do you say, Cap? No rules?" Dylan wiggles her eyebrows, her peroxide-blond hair catching the moonlight.

I tilt my head at her. She's always pushing it. "Save it for parkour. Tonight's all about fockey."

Liv knocks her stick against Dylan's. "Besides. Your version of no rules might involve someone losing a leg."

Dylan smiles, twisting her stick in her hands. "I just think these sticks would look better with a little blood on 'em."

Liv laughs.

We knock sticks and run to position. "Sticks Chicks!" Our two centers tap the ground beside the ball and click sticks three times before each tries to strike it. Green wins the ball and takes off, and Blue swears as we whoop toward the goal.

Sticks beat shins, faces eat sand, and arms throb from whacking the sand dunes that rise and dip around us. Beach hockey makes for some mad conditioning. After months of training plus a summer of midnight games, our bodies are weapons-grade. And it doesn't matter what's happening at home or that school's starting soon because beaches and moonlight make everything better. When we break for water, we're panting, but smiling.

Last fall, we finished yet another sucktastic season of field hockey where we lost nearly every game. So in a radical move, Coach made me and Ava co-captains, seeing as we were the only players who'd ever tried anyway. For ten months, we handpicked and trained a new fockey team for the coming season. *This* fockey team.

"Not a bad group," Ava says.

I look at her. "*We* made this happen." We click sticks.

"Coach is going to shit herself when she sees a full-blown *team* show up on Monday."

"Ew." Liv crinkles her face at me. "I haven't met the woman yet. I definitely don't want to see her shit herself."

I smile, but I'm thinking of our team, of Coach's face. Because of us, we're powerful enough to get to States *and* bring the scouts. The sureness of it fills me up as big as the lake, until my feet can't stay still. I race across the sand, slamming it with my stick. "Fockey time!"

Blue takes it first, but Green steals it back, and the ball soars to me. I tap-tap it over the sandy divots, their edges hard in the moonlight, their dips like black holes. The goal flags wave at me from the other end: an invitation. I run against the wind, lifting my stick high to drive the ball over the dunes and between the flags.

Something blurs my vision.

An animal storms onto the sand. No, not an animal. A girl. My stick connects with the ball all wrong and it arcs through the air and splinters the flag post.

"Hey!" someone yells at her. "What's your problem?"

"Who runs out in the middle of a game?"

"I—I'm sorry." The girl's out of breath and twitchy. "I didn't . . ." She looks behind her and I follow her gaze, squinting toward the parking lot, to the houses I know squat beyond. But the night is too close, too dark, and I can't see anything. A car door slams in the distance and she jumps. "I—I have to go." She turns.

5

"Are you okay?" I reach out my hand, but she flinches before I even touch her.

"I have to go." She looks back into the blackness, then at us, then back again, pressing her hands down her shirt again and again like she's trying to press out the wrinkles. "I—I'm sorry about your game." And just like that she takes off down the road, the opposite way from where she came.

It isn't like running or jogging. It's more like crashing.

"They said 'venti coffee?' She said, 'twenty coffees.'"

"That's a walk of shame. Did you see her shirt?"

"I know! It was buttoned all wrong. Someone was gettin' busy."

"I think her name is Nikki. We had Health together last year."

"Nikki Cassavetti?"

Ava looks toward the goal. "Shit. Our flag broke. Nice going, Cap'n."

But all I can think of is the girl. Nikki. Of the way her eyes didn't seem to see anything at all. The way her white shirt blazed against the night. The way she shuddered and ran. And I wonder where she was running to—or what she was running from.

"No goal, no problem. Let's swim."

We strip down to our underwear and splash into the cool water, laughing, diving. Our shouts dance across the lake with the moonlight while our sweat and paint wash away in the dark water.

But every time I slip under and the voices dull above me, the cold dark closes in.

TWO

THE NEXT DAY, I PUT on my work shirt, and I remember Nikki's buttons, glaring and wrong, as I do up mine, shiny and right.

When I pull up to Big Bob's Scoop Dreams, Liv's there already, which is great. But so is Eileen, Uncle Bob's fourth wife, which isn't. Eileen's like one of those sweaters that looks fine but is super-itchy and tight once you put it on. I'm just waiting for Uncle Bob to figure that out and move on like he always does. Until then, I avoid her as much as possible. Right now, she's stacking flats of flowers, bags of soil, and goodness knows what else to "pretty things up." I wait until she's gone around the corner again before I park in the back and go inside.

This is what Eileen doesn't get: Scoop Dreams is exactly perfect. It's an ancient shack made of thin, splintered boards weathered a deep brown, with squeaky service windows that open onto a gravel lot. The only newish-looking thing is the lit-up logo of a cow asleep on a crescent moon that can be seen for blocks. Being run-down is part of its charm.

Also, it sells the best ice cream in town. Some say the state.

Dad's convinced it's the best in the world, not that he's biased. Big Bob, the owner, is his little brother. Well, nobody would call Uncle Bob *little*, but he is younger.

There are perks to having an uncle who owns an ice cream stand. Since Dad's construction accident a few years ago, we could practically bathe in the amount of free ice cream my uncle gives us. Even better, Uncle Bob had the good sense to hire me *and* Liv to work the stand. He also pays me more than he should, which means that—at least in the summer—I have enough money to go to the movies now and then.

Outside, Eileen stoops low and snatches a tuft of grass from the gravelly lot with a grunt. Like living takes an obscene amount of effort.

Uncle Bob has amazing taste when it comes to ice cream. Wives? Not so much.

Liv and I lean on the counter, shoulder to shoulder, enjoying sample spoons of Uncle Bob's latest s'mores recipe. We're watching the traffic collect and pass at the light like waves when I see the girl from last night—Nikki—waiting at the corner and I straighten. But then the girl turns. It's not her.

I move to the sink and run some water over the scoops.

"Anywhere in the World?" Liv asks. I don't remember when we started asking each other where we'd go if we could be anywhere else in the world, but over the years, the question's been whittled down to just four words and we've traveled the globe in our answers.

"Easy. Holding a house-size trophy at the State Championships."

Liv laughs. "Typical. But I said any*where*, not any *time*. We need to make the team first. Do you think we'll all make it through tryouts on Monday?"

I glance back at her. "Yeah, I do."

I want everyone to make the team. Because we have to be good this year. Really good. If we don't make it to States, the scout from UNC Chapel Hill won't come. And if she doesn't come, she won't realize she can't live without me. And if she doesn't realize she can't live without me, she won't hand me a full ride. And that's the only way I'll ever pay for college.

Liv grabs two spoonfuls of cookie dough ice cream and passes one to me. "Here's to a winning season, Captain Alamandar."

"We better win, or Coach Webb will never forgive me for stealing you from cross-country."

Liv tosses her empty spoon into the recycling. "I've got news for you, Zo. Coach Webb will never forgive you. Period."

Liv wants to be some international-humanitarian-diplomat-rock-star and she's applying to supercompetitive schools— Georgetown, Stanford, even the London School of Economics. And any school would want to see her long-term commitment to a sport—as well as the diamond-studded recommendation that Coach Webb could give.

But I love that I get to spend a season with my best friend. I've always loved fockey—the intensity, the rhythm, the skill. The only thing that was ever missing was a good team and my best friend. And now I have both. Besides, even Liv said her shift to fockey will show spontaneity, which is apparently lacking in the average applicant to the LSE. I can handle Coach Webb hating me. I can even handle—sometimes—the idea that we'll be at different colleges. But I will never forgive myself if I screw up Liv's chances as well as mine. It's just one more reason to make it to States.

I wish I hadn't eaten that last spoonful.

Just then, a green Triumph pulls into the lot.

I squeal and scrunch low. *The* 1978 green Triumph Spitfire. Convertible. I know nothing about cars. But this car. This one I know.

"What the—" Liv starts, then she looks out the window and smirks. "Oh."

"It's him, isn't it?"

"Uh-huh." She nods. "Mmmm mmm, that boy is looking goo-ood. If I wasn't already—"

"Shut. Up." My face feels hot. Grove Williams is *here*.

"I mean, break me off a piece of that—"

"Olivia Liu," I whisper-beg, pressing my face against the freezer to cool down. Some people are blessed with the ability to flirt with crushes. Then, there's me.

His car stops on the gravel. Staying crouched, I half crawl, half waddle around the machines so I can squeeze into the small space in the back of the shack.

Liv laughs harder. "You look like a penguin. A short, drunk penguin." His car door creaks and closes.

I pull my feet in close. I can't risk him spotting even my right toe. Not that he'd recognize my toe. Or any other part of me.

"Hey," he says. Oh. My.

It should be illegal to say the word *hey* like that. It's like his words come from a whole different biological place than for the rest of us. If I melt any more, I'll endanger the ice cream.

"Hey," Liv says, and I hear her trying not to laugh. "What can I get you?"

"Ummm . . ." He's probably reading the menu. I look up and see it through his eyes. It's old but pretty in a worn kind of way, with vines and flowers around the sides. He and I are looking at the same words. The same swirls. Right now. "How about a Shaken Cookie?"

"Chocolate chip or Oreo?"

"Chocolate chip, of course." I hear his smile. Oh, I hate Liv right now. I want to see his smile. Or make him smile.

"Of course," Liv repeats.

"Zoeeeeee?" Eileen calls in her high-pitched, squeaky voice. My name is ugly in her mouth. And two syllables too long. And she seriously needs to work on her timing.

"Um." Liv steps toward me to fix Grove's shake. "I think she's around back?" My legs cramp. This is what I get for playing beach hockey last night.

"She is *not* around back, Olivia," Eileen huffs. I can sense her hands on her hips. She is a hands-on-hips kind of woman.

Please let him leave. I twist the bottom buttons of my work shirt.

"Where *is* she?" Eileen sighs. "I wanted her help with the manure."

11

Liv kicks me but doesn't look down. "I'm sure Zo will be happy to help you with your, um, manure problem." She kicks me again. "You know, when she gets back."

Eileen's feet crunch away on the gravel. Liv looks down at me and widens her eyes.

"Manure, huh?" Grove says. I love the way I can hear his smile. Not everyone can smile with their voice.

Liv makes her way to the counter. "Sorry. Just try not to think 'manure' while you eat."

"I'll try." Grove laughs. "You're Jake Montag's girlfriend, right?"

"For about a year." As if she doesn't know exactly how long, down to the minute. She's probably fiddling with the tiny globe-pendant necklace that Jake bought her for her birthday.

"I think I saw you guys at some of our games last year." I hear the ding of the register, the clink of the coins, the scratch of paper money. I bet his hands are a calloused kind of soft. I hear something papery go into the tip jar.

"Oh wow," he says. "This is good." Something slaps the counter. His hand? I wish my ears could see. "All right, thanks a lot. Say hi to Jake for me."

"I will. Have a good day."

His door slams, the engine turns, the wheels crunch the gravel. Liv's feet appear in front of mine. She looks down at me. "You are six kinds of pathetic, do you know that?"

"Is he gone?" I whisper.

She peers out the window. "He's pulling out of the lot now.

It's the sexiest pause before merging with traffic I ever did see."

I stand and shake out my kinked-up legs. "Did I get ice cream on my butt?"

Liv raises her eyebrows. "Since you will never let Grove see your butt, I will not dignify that question with a response."

I twist and try to see it myself. I pat it. It's cold but dry. "I hate you."

She grins. "He said 'guys.'"

"What?"

"He said he'd noticed *us* at his games. He didn't say I saw *you*." She punches me. "He said 'I saw you *guys*.'"

"So?" I feel like hiding behind the cooler again.

"So, that's you, you idiot."

I shake out my hands. I can't think about that. "Tell me everything. Start from the beginning. Imitate his walk."

Liv shakes her head. "You are entering a seriously screwed-up dimension of the crushing universe. Someday you will have to let him see you."

I pick up a rag and rub the counter. Somehow it's always sticky.

"Seriously, Zo." She leans on the counter so I scrub around her. "Guys check you out all the time. And thanks to our fierce workouts, you've never looked hotter." She backs away when I push her elbow with the rag. "Why do you run away every time one comes close?"

"Not just any one," I mutter.

"It's not even like you really know him. It's just—"

I turn to face her. "Maybe I don't want talking to mess it up."

Liv busts out laughing. "Mess what up? This tantalizing game of hide-and-seek that only one of you is playing?"

"Well, now he associates my name with manure, so I've got that going for me."

"Yes. That and the invisibility thing will surely get you a date for prom."

I scrub the counter harder.

"Zoeeeee," Eileen screeches.

I roll my eyes before I turn back to the windows. "Yes, Eileen?"

"Where have you been?"

I gesture toward the back. "Restocking?"

"And you couldn't hear me?"

"You called?" I try to make my eyes as wide and innocent as possible. I can practically hear Liv itching to laugh behind me. "How can I help?" I smile.

"I'd love your help with the planting."

"Of course!" I bounce and turn. Liv stifles a laugh as I pull the door shut behind me.

"Button your shirt!" Eileen says when she sees me.

I look down. In my Grove-induced panic, I rebuttoned the bottom all wrong.

I think of Nikki last night, her hair wild, her shirt crooked. I button myself back together.

THREE

MONDAY MORNING, WE SCRUNCH TOGETHER on the low bleachers, mouthguards tucked in our bra straps, the hot metal sticking to our thighs. I press my half-frozen water bottle between my wrists.

"Can you believe how many people showed?" Ava whispers.

Liv leans in. "Tryouts aren't usually like this?"

I shake my head. There. Are. So. Many. People. And it is so hot. Too hot.

What if Liv doesn't make the team, and Coach Webb is so pissed he doesn't take her back on cross-country? What if Ava and I picked the wrong people? Oh, fock. What if *I* don't make it? I'll be the first captain in the history of captains to not make her own team. Why did Coach choose me and Ava last season anyway? What if I've turned into a total fockey flake? What if—

Ava says something, but I can't hear her above the noise in my own stupid head. "What?"

"Respect the grind, Cap'n." She knocks my knee with hers. "We worked for this. It'll show."

I exhale.

"Girls." Coach marches over, her neon-blue clipboard tucked under one very freckled, pink arm. "I'm Coach Parker. Welcome to Northridge field hockey tryouts. Over the next several days you will probably come to hate me. But, remember"—she scans our eyes—"pain is the touchstone of spiritual growth."

Well, at least Coach hasn't changed.

Some girls behind me shift at "spiritual." Coach is a fan of Alcoholics Anonymous. I'm not sure what about it is anonymous since Coach talks about it all the time. If there's an AA quote book, she's memorized it. She throws a few more quotes at us for good luck before waving us onto the field.

"She's kind of weird," Liv whispers as we scramble off the bleachers.

"She's perfect," Ava says.

An olive-skinned girl in baggy clothes runs onto the grass. She's missed the AA-laced pep talk. Her dark hair is pulled back and a small scar slices her right eyebrow. I recognize her.

"This is the only time I will allow you to be late," Coach says. "Ever. Understand?"

The girl nods.

"Pair up."

Any other day, I'd partner with Liv. But my feet walk me to the new girl. "Nikki, right? I guess you liked what you saw on the beach, huh?"

Nikki flushes red. I feel like a jerk, except I'm not sure why.

Coach claps her hands. "All right, girls. Warm-up time. Captain Cervantes?"

Ava runs to the center to lead us. Ava's fitness-goddess mom works at every gym in town, and I'm pretty sure baby Ava held a dumbbell instead of a bottle. Even though Ava says she wants to win States to attract colleges just like me, I'm pretty sure she'd love a few trophies of her own to slide next to her mom's on the mantel.

Afterward, the real fun begins: fitness tests. I glance at Nikki. I'm not sure if I want her to kick ass or just fall on it.

Liv settles next to us with Bella, one of the triplets. Ava and I recruited Bella first because she's savage on the basketball court. Triple bonus that her sisters, Sasha and Quinn, are just as fierce as their hair is red.

"One-minute push-ups. Partners! Count accurately. No cheating." Coach narrows her eyes. "Cheaters only cheat themselves."

"Does she always talk like that?" Liv whispers. "I feel like there should be a giant kitten hanging from a tree squealing 'Hang in there, girls!'"

"Or Albert Einstein telling us how often he failed," Bella says, tying her hair up.

"Einstein didn't fail," her sister Quinn says. "He just figured out a hundred ways not to make a light bulb."

Liv laughs. "That was Edison."

"Go!" Coach yells.

I'm a jack-in-the-box. When my arms sing, I imagine I'm in the water, weightless. When they scream, I'm a machine. I get thirty-eight, twice as many as last year.

As I count for Nikki, I scan the others. Some barely

17

try—their butts high or drooping low, bodies like hammocks. Not our recruits. Their arms pump hard. Jack-in-the-boxes.

Next the sit-ups. Then the forty-yard dash. Liv comes in first, of course, but so many of us bring in the numbers. It's just how this year will be. I can feel it.

The fitness tests wear on into the afternoon and bleed into the next day. Each hour separates further those who can from those who can't. The ones Ava and I trained—we sprint, push, drive faster, stronger, harder than the others. Than we ever have before.

On the third day, eight of the others don't bother to come back. Fine with me.

Some fly so loose with their sticks I can see their futures mapped out in bruises. JV can keep the flyaway girls. We'll keep the ones in control, the power girls.

Coach plays us in every position, on turf, on fields, on dirt. And then, on the fifth and final afternoon, when we're reddened with heat and blood and dirty from grass and mud, Coach makes her choices.

She talks about never giving up and staying off the sauce. Finally, she calls our names one by one. I make it. Ava makes it. So do Liv, Dylan, and the triplets. So do all the other girls we counted on—even the subs—except for one. Instead of Alana, she picks Nikki.

Nikki who didn't train with us all year. Who looks too skinny to be fierce. Who flinches when you look at her too hard. There's something off about her.

But that something is not in her game. All week she was on

fire. I have no idea where she learned to play, but she knows how to handle her stick, her feet, her ball. And, well, Ava and I aren't building a sorority. We're building a State Championship team.

So she's in.

I'm cleaning my stick when I get a text from Ava.

> AVA: Tonight? Or are u too busy cleaning ur stick?

I look at my stick. I hate how well she knows me.

> ME: Shut up. Ice cream?
> AVA: 🍨
> ME: No beach hockey before our first game. We'll be wiped.
> AVA: Not fockey. 🙂

Great. Parkour. I was all about it when Ava suggested spicing up our workouts last spring. I was sure learning parkour would make us even stronger—and I'd be running up the sides of buildings the same way I plow down the field. But that wasn't what happened at all.

> ME: U wanna break some bones before we've even had our first game??
> AVA: Nobody's broken anything.

19

ME: Yet.

AVA: We need em revved and confident. Nothing like parkour for that.

For everyone except me.

AVA: Come on Cap'n. Pllllllleeeeeease?
ME: Fine. Pick me up?
AVA: Absofockinglutely.

It's the kind of early-September evening with an edge, like it could dip into humid but chooses not to. When we arrive at the playground, everyone's gathered, a hodgepodge of tamed and wild hair, tank tops, and ripped shorts. And maybe it's seeing our teen-size bodies against this elementary school playground, but it makes me so aware of how on the cusp we are to this epic season. I grin at Ava. *We* brought all these different girls to this single team, this single moment.

As we get closer, I realize all the girls are looking up. At Dylan. She's perched at the top of the metal roof of the clubhouse, shrouded in the blue late-day light. Of course.

Dylan was Ava's pick. Even after nearly a year, I'm the least sure about this girl with her snake tattoo and ready fists. I *am* sure she'll win most carded player of the year. Still, there's no question she's a killer defender.

Dylan throws open her arms . . . and leaps.

She does a double flip and lands with a roll, her shoulder easing across the grass. Out here, she looks like she belongs in a ballet more than a boxing ring. All the girls whoop and cheer.

Kiara, Dylan's best friend, moves to the base of the slide, runs her fingers over her tight braids, and adjusts her sweats. She flips backward three times. Like it's nothing. She brushes off her shoulder like a brag, eyebrows arched.

"Fock yeah!" yells Dylan, making Kiara's brown cheeks glow.

Bella walks across the monkey bars on her hands, her red hair kissing the bars, while Liv floats between one thing and the next like her insides are all spun sugar and air. Even Michaela loves it. She takes a deep breath before adjusting her pastel headband that pops against her straightened black hair and dark skin. Then she smiles big as she tucks into her perfect roll. Michaela was *my* pick, and it took a bit to convince Ava that Michaela, who'd never lifted anything heavier than her AP textbooks, would be a good fit for the team. But Ava never saw her debate that dickhead science teacher, Mr. Pickney.

They all explode and jump, twist and spin. Like they're the smoke *and* the fire.

And then there's me. I might as well be another bench.

"Back-handspring time!" Liv runs up next to me and squeezes my hand. "Come on, Zo. It's just like gymnastics in the old days." She lines her toes up next to mine. "Go on three. One, two, three!" And then she's not there anymore. She's swung her hands up and back and her body followed, just like it's supposed to. But not mine.

The others fly like they're made of wings and stardust, not rocks and roots. Ava was right. Parkour is exactly the thing to get our team loose and confident. Everyone but me.

"Try a flip instead." Ava pats me on the back.

I am *not* the girl who gets the sympathy pat on the back.

I stand straight, release my jaw, close my eyes, and picture it. I bend my knees and push up, but my feet don't leave the ground.

I shake out my hands. Try again. This time, my feet do leave the ground. I'm up. But as I tuck into my knees, the ground rises and suddenly I'm flat on my back.

Everyone rushes over with their "are you okays." I smile and nod, but I'm clammy and shaky, trying to look like someone at the end of a medicine commercial where everything's back on track—when really I'm the mess at the beginning. Except there's no cure for me.

Because in that instant when the ground rushed up, I saw my dad—falling.

I wasn't there when it happened, but I've imagined it a thousand times. He used to walk along rooftops like he owned them, like I own the fockey field. His hammer would swing from his hip, and when the sun was at his back and his radio was blasting, his silhouette would dance, and I used to think he was made of different stuff than the rest of us.

And yet, he fell.

So while everyone else practices their flips and handsprings, while they twist and tuck, dart and dance, I return to the bench and keep one hand on it at all times, trying hard to shove down the memories. It doesn't help that every time I try to spring over the bench, I see the hospital room: the ugly whiteness, the tubes, the beeping machines always off rhythm, my dad's eyes dark and deep in their sockets. And that watch. That stupid watch.

When he fell, he smashed a watch that I'd bought him for his last birthday. The watch that he still wears. It wasn't even that great a watch. But he keeps it because I gave it to him. Because it reminds him of how fragile life is. Of how lucky he is. Of how he should appreciate every second.

But that's a lie. I think it reminds him of the moment that everything changed. The moment everything stopped working—not just him but all of us. At 10:17 a.m., time stopped. And here I am, stuck on this bench, watching my teammates flip like it's the easiest thing in the world for feet to wheel over hands.

For the hands of a clock to keep spinning.

FOUR

I TIPTOE AROUND THE KITCHEN in the morning half-light, putting on the coffee, emptying the dishwasher, and swiping the counters clean. I eat my first breakfast of cereal at the counter. I'll fit in another before I go. Apparently, field hockey and parkour—even the pathetic way I do it—require me to down calories like LeBron drops buckets.

The hum of the coffee maker and the crunch of the cereal sound too loud in the near dark and I miss the old mornings when the kitchen was bright and busy. When Dad sang and danced while he cooked. When he made a huge deal of the first day of school, taking the morning off to whip up a breakfast of thick, homemade waffles or pancakes.

Now he's lucky he can walk at all, and I'm eating cereal by myself in the dark.

Upstairs in my room, I yank my ponytail tight and smooth my white home jersey over my blue-and-green kilt. Since we have a home game on our first day of school, we all get to wear our uniforms. True, my knees are covered in bruises and various stages of turf burn, and my shins sport a ridiculous shin-guard tan, but I would happily wear this every single day. I turn to see my number 11 in the mirror, two straight lines rich and blue against the white. The whole team is probably doing the same thing right now. Except Cristina will pair her uniform with Louboutin heels and movie-star shades. And Dylan's probably trying to figure out how to attach her wallet chain to her kilt.

When I come back downstairs, Mom's peeling a hard-boiled egg at the sink.

I put some bread in the toaster. "Dad up yet?"

Mom shakes her head. "Last night was rough." She says it to the egg.

"What do you think is wrong?"

"Maybe we need to switch his meds? Try yet another physical therapist?" She leans on the sink and looks through the window to our backyard.

The toaster dings, so I can hide my eye roll as I slather some butter and jam on the bread. I'm not the nurse in the family. She is. And yet she has zero clue how to help Dad.

She leans in and kisses my cheek. "Let me look at my girl." She holds both my shoulders. Her eyes grow glassy. "I can't believe you're a junior. I've only got one more of these first days to go."

"Mom." I wriggle away, shove the toast in my mouth, and pour myself a half cup of coffee. "I forbid you to cry." I focus on smothering my coffee with milk.

She smiles and rubs at her cheeks. "Okay, baby."

I lean against the counter and sip some coffee. I hate the taste but love the jump. Maybe I'll get Ava to teach me how to make café con leche. But I don't think I'd ever sleep again.

25

"I do wish those skirts were a little longer." Mom looks at my thighs.

"Well, longer would mean I can't run fast, and if I can't run fast, I can't win games, and if I can't win games, I don't get a scholarship." I place the coffee cup behind her in the sink. "Also, I can't get a scholarship if I skip school. So . . ."

She kisses me. "Enjoy every minute."

I take the stairs two at a time.

"Dad?" I say into the dark bedroom as I make my way to his side.

"Zo?" His voice is quiet, but he tries to turn toward me. "I want you to have an incredible first day." He smiles even though he can barely move.

I nod. The cracked face of his watch stares back at me from his wrist.

"You play Sommersville after school?"

"Yeah."

"Good. Show 'em who they'll have to beat at sectionals." He takes a ragged breath as he shifts himself on the bed. "They're going to wish they'd trained harder after seeing you play."

"Do you want a pain med?" I grab the pad, ready to make a note of the time.

"No. I think I just need to stretch. But thanks, kid." He takes a sip of the water I hand him. "I hope you know how much I'd like to be there."

"I do." I lean forward, careful not to hurt him, and kiss him on the cheek.

26

"Get going." He pats my hand. "You don't want to keep Liv waiting."

I gently close his door, grab my stuff, and pause before the mirror. I smooth my ponytail before running out of the house and into Liv's waiting car.

She takes one look at me. "Your dad having a bad day?"

"So much for my game face."

"Your game face is perfect. I just . . ." She gives my hand a quick squeeze.

"Thanks, Livvy. You're the bestest."

"Distraction?"

I smile. "Fock yeah."

"First, it's game day. Second, this year we don't have to take the bus. And third—" She reaches behind her and hands me a bakery bag. I peek inside.

"A Geddes Bakery half-moon cookie?" She knows me so well.

She smiles and pops the clutch. And when I see the sad sacks at the bus stop, I smile too. With every turn, we put a little more distance between me and home. And each time she shifts gears feels a bit like a hiccup and a bit like freedom.

"I love you, Liv Liu," I scream into the open sunroof.

She laughs as the car jumps into third.

After we park, Liv and I act like each other's mirrors and smooth out our wrinkles. As we walk toward school, we pass a few guys leaning against the hood of a car.

They nod at us. "Damn," one of them says, stretching out the word like a snake.

"Why don't you sit on my face?" says another, and they all laugh.

We walk faster. I hike my bag higher on my shoulder, and the breeze circling my upper thighs makes me shiver. I cross my arms over my chest.

I look at Liv, arms crossed, jaw tight. When she catches my look, she rolls her eyes and loosens her arms. "Do you think," Liv says when we're out of earshot, "those guys actually think that sounds inviting?"

"Do you think," I say, "those stupid-ass racing stripes make their cars go faster?"

We push through the wide glass doors. Almost immediately, we collect the team like magnets. For the first time, we're all together wearing our uniforms and it's perfect. In our crisp shirts and bright skirts, it's like we're in color and everyone else is stuck in black and white.

We make our way to block one, peeling off to separate corners of the school. Liv, Michaela, Bella, and I all head to AP US History, which we get to take with Mr. Mac, our favorite teacher from last year. Best of all, when the bell rings, it'll be nine hours away from our first game. Nine hours until the best season of my life.

Mr. Mac stands outside his door, the fluorescent lights bouncing off his shiny white bald head. "Dobson! Liu! Salamander!" He calls to us like he's on the field, barking at his varsity soccer boys. The corner of his mouth creeps up. "Oh no, Morrison," he yells at Michaela, "you hang with these yahoos now?"

"These yahoos are my teammates, Mr. Mac."

"Well, well," he says as his eyebrows rise with something like interest. "You've assembled quite the team this year, Salamander." He's always called me Salamander and couldn't believe it didn't catch on—that no one else was as clever as he was.

"We might even beat your boys," Liv taunts, as she passes him into the class.

He crosses his arms. "Them's fighting words, Liu."

"I know," she sings.

He smiles and turns back toward the hall, calling out more names into the masses.

The rest of us push into the room. But I stop short and everyone bumps into me. And I blush for about a hundred different reasons.

Reasons one through ninety-nine lean on the wide window-sill looking out at the fields, just the way I probably would have if he weren't standing there. He's trimmed away his dark curls, but I know his silhouette, his stance, his arms.

Grove.

He starts to turn, so I pivot—and almost crash into Liv. She just shakes her head. Which only makes me blush more. Someone smart should invent a pill for Awkward Crush Syndrome. Clearly, I'm the poster child.

I slip into a desk next to Liv. In addition to panicking that Mr. Mac will call on me at random all semester—because talking in front of a whole class is like a pop quiz on steroids—I get to worry about Grove witnessing my tongue-tied stammering day after day. Perfect.

He tucks his books under his chair, and his T-shirt slides up his arm.

I let my eyes linger on the muscles that peek out. Hmm. We'll be here. Together. All. Year. Long.

Maybe this won't be so bad after all.

After the bell rings, the team comes together again. It's like we're all strands of yarn and gradually, as we walk the halls, we knit together and become something. Something bigger.

Ava nudges Dylan. "You know you're supposed to keep your stick in your locker, right?"

"Skipped homeroom. Never made it to my locker." She cocks her head at me. "Don't worry, Cap. I won't lose it."

I lean in to Ava. "That's not what worries me."

She laughs.

We're passing the science wing when we see Kups and a bunch of his friends clustered by the drinking fountain. Lance Kupperton is a football player who can pass for a sturdy appliance, but a "smart" appliance he is not. I have no clue how he made it to eleventh grade.

"Heeeeey." Kups leans back, taking us all in. I just keep walking, like always. We all do. "Gimme some fries with that shake, Cristina!"

I hold my books a little tighter. His originality stuns me.

Cristina slaps her own ass, spinning around to blow him a kiss. "You couldn't handle my shake, Kups."

"I could!" Robbie says, the people-pleaser of the football team.

"Dylan," sings Kups. Right there. The red do-not-touch switch. Not her. She'll just make it worse. "Ooooh, girl." He whistles. "You clean up niii-ce. Who knew those legs were hiding under those white-trash cargos?"

I risk a look behind me. Dylan exhales. Good. I speed up.

CRASH.

I whip around. Dylan has her stick thrust up under Kups's chin. What the hell. My adrenaline spikes like we're on the field, but this isn't a game with refs. This is a hallway in the middle of our school and Dylan decides to pick a fight on game day. On our *first* game day. With football players.

I'm so pissed I almost want Kups to take her down.

FIVE

KUPS PUSHES DYLAN AWAY—HARD—AND SHE falls into Robbie and Eric, who catch and hold her. Kups cracks his neck, first one way, then the other, and takes a step toward her.

"Let her go!" Ava rushes in, and we follow, filling the space between them.

Kups towers over Ava. If Ava gets hurt, I swear I will punch Dylan myself. I look around. If we all get suspended, we'll have to forfeit. But there's no teacher in sight.

"You mess with one of us, you get all of us." Ava's lip curls.

Kups looks down at her and laughs in her face. But he nods at Robbie and Eric, and they release Dylan. Kups smiles as we back away, his teeth slick.

"I get you all, huh?"

I turn away—we all do. Together, we're something bigger.

"That'd be one sweet orgy!" I see his reflection in the closed glass door at the end of the hall. He's pumping his pelvis back and forth and the guys around him laugh.

Ava spins around, cupping her hand to her mouth. "Go fuck yourself."

"Why?" Kups laughs. "When you girls are so ready and willing?"

We keep walking.

"Don't pretend you don't want to!" he calls. "I see you, Nikki Cassavetti, you slut. I heard about you and Jamison." He whistles again. I glance at Nikki, and her face turns gray. "That was sweeeeet. And if—"

I block out his words. I concentrate on the squeak of my sneakers, the hum of the water fountain. We just need to get through that door.

"Don't be such bitches," Eric yells. "I know our mascot's a dog, but you don't need to take it literally."

They high-five and howl as we turn the corner. We walk quickly. I search for a room—any room—until I finally see one without a teacher and we pile inside. Bella and Quinn stand by the door. Nikki slumps in a chair and Dylan paces.

Dylan's whole body is a storm waiting to burst. So is mine, but unlike Dylan, I know how to control myself. I dig my nails into my palms. She endangered our team. She endangered our game. Hell, she endangered my scholarship, because if I can't play, I can't get scouted. I look at Ava, but she's got her worried eyes on Dylan. Of course Ava's worried about her pick. The girl who skips class and treats in-school suspension like it's her living room. She may be fierce on the field, but if she wrecks my—

Liv puts her hand on my arm and just looks at me. I know what she's thinking: Dylan has a rough life. But you can't just beat people up no matter how rough your life is. You suck it up and walk on by. You don't throw someone—Kups of all people!—against a locker in a crowded hallway. And you definitely don't drag your teammates into a fight with a bunch of football players.

"Dylan." I try to make my voice quiet, calm. "We can't get into a fight with every guy who whistles at us in the halls. They all do that."

"You know"—she stops pacing—"I stopped being surprised at the things people did a long time ago." She points at me and her finger's shaking. "But there are levels. Whistling is whatever. But taking my stick and—"

"What? What did he do?"

"He lifted her skirt with her own stick," Kiara says. "It's—"

"He did more than that!" Dylan's hands clench into fists. "He stuck it"—her voice is low and shaky—"between my legs and pulled up." Her jaw tightens. "He tried to fuck me with my own damned stick. In the middle of the fucking hall." She looks at the ceiling. "What gives him the right? What gives any of them the right?" She kicks a desk over.

I sink into a chair. They've taken my stick and lifted my skirt. But they never did *that*. "I'm so sorry, Dyl."

"Why the fuck are *you* sorry?" She paces again. "They're the ones who should be sorry." She makes fists with her hands. "I tell you. They will be so sorry they ever messed with me."

A fight is the last thing we need. We're not even one game in and her temper's already jeopardizing our season. Kups was clearly in the wrong. We just need to tell someone what happened.

34

The door opens, and Bella and Quinn whip around. It's the dean. She's short, thin, and about as warm as a Syracuse blizzard.

"Dylan?" Her voice is a bored sort of bossy. "Come with me, please." She looks at the rest of us. "You should not be in an unsupervised room. Get to your next class."

Dylan shakes her head. "Tell me you talked to the assholes who started this."

"Dylan." The dean's lips tighten. "Now."

Dylan struts to the door, and even though she wears the same uniform as me, with her bleached hair and snake tattoo coiled around her arm, she looks more ready for a fight than the field. "Typical," she says. "I defend myself and—"

The dean puts a hand on her back.

"Don't. Touch. Me."

The dean puts her hands up, but her eyebrows go up too, like Dylan is just so ridiculous. Like this whole thing is just so ridiculous. And yeah, she shouldn't have picked a fight, but Kups was in the wrong first.

"Wait!" I say. The dean turns. Shit. I don't even know her name. I've never had any reason to speak to her. I can't believe I even opened my mouth. But Dylan just looks at me, and I wonder if anyone in her whole life has ever stuck up for her. "She was just defending herself. They—"

"We'll look into it." The dean nods. "You girls get going. It's pizza day. That's always a good day." She smiles at us like we're eight years old. Like it's nothing. Like what happened to Dylan doesn't mean a thing. The door clicks shut.

"Pizza day?" Cristina says. "Did that seriously come out of her mouth?"

"Dylan's screwed," Bella says.

We walk down the halls in a loud, buzzing kind of silence. The metal lockers slam and the fluorescent lights hum and so many, too many, people talk and push and shout. And even though school is always like this, it's different.

Dylan's words play in my ears: *What gives them the right?*

SIX

I'M IN ENGLISH, STEWING ABOUT Kups, Dylan, and the game against Sommersville tonight. Not paying attention to the grand introduction to Shakespeare's *Hamlet* Mrs. Hastings is trying to deliver. Thankfully, she talks to the ceiling instead of to us, so when my phone vibrates, I check it. It's a team text.

> AVA: Just walked by ISS. DYL INSIDE. WTF??
> KIARA: That is SO wrong. 😠
> LIV: Was Kups inside too?
> AVA: No
> QUINN: WTF???

I raise my hand to use the bathroom. Mrs. Hastings just waves her hand at me, not bothering to sign a pass. In the hall, a teacher smiles at me, not bothering to ask for my nonexistent pass, and it occurs to me that Dylan probably always gets pass-checked. I walk quickly toward ISS. Sure enough, Dylan slumps in the back, scraping her pen back and forth across the desk. Kups is nowhere in sight. My phone's still buzzing, but I ignore it and keep walking.

I've never been to the dean. Most of my classes don't even have the sort of kids who get called to the dean. It always seemed like the right kids got called out. But then again, I'd never paid much attention. Until now. I knock on the door right below her name: *Miss Eldrich.*

"Yes?" she calls from inside.

I open the door a crack.

A guy with shaggy hair and a band T-shirt is draped across a chair.

"Yes?" she says again, impatient.

"Excuse me. Sorry to interrupt, but"—I try not to look at the boy, though I feel his stare—"I just wanted to talk to you about, you know, what happened earlier."

"What happened earlier exactly?" She flicks her pencil against the desk a few times.

"Um"—I look at the boy—"before? In the hall?"

She sighs. "Miss . . ."

"Alamandar."

"Miss Alamandar, this is a large school and I'm a busy woman. Please get to the point."

I exhale. "I'm not sure I should talk about it in front of someone . . ."

The guy in the band T-shirt grunts. "Because I give a shit about—"

"*Mr. Anderson.*" He slumps farther. "In that case," she sighs again, "wait outside."

I nod and shut the door. There aren't any chairs, so I slide my back down the bank of lockers and sit on the floor. The tile is cold against my bare thighs. I rub them. I pull out my phone and open the team group chat.

ME: Outside deans. Going to tell whole story.

Texts light up my phone like fireworks on the Fourth of July, and they light me up too. We really are a team. I tighten my ponytail. Once I explain, everything will be fine.

I think of the Sommersville defense and the way those girls have always seemed twice my size. I wonder if that's how we'll look to them this year. Especially if Dyl plays sweeper. But I need to get her out of ISS for that to happen.

Footsteps squeak down the hall. I look up to see Ava, Liv, Bella, Quinn, and Kiara walking toward me. My smile feels bigger than my cheeks. "You came."

"Wouldn't miss it," Kiara says.

"Besides, missing Calculus isn't exactly a sacrifice," Quinn says.

We all just stare at her. "You're in Calculus?" Ava asks. "Aren't you a junior?"

"Shit, you're smart," Kiara says. "I'm barely squeaking through Pre-Calc."

Quinn shrugs. "I like to keep my nerds close."

I shake my head. "I kind of love you, Quinn."

"Thanks," she says with a wink. "I kind of love you too, Cap."

Miss Eldrich opens the door. Band-shirt boy shakes his

39

hair free from his face and pushes past us. She gestures into her office. "Ladies?"

We follow her inside. There are only two chairs, but I don't want to sit anyway. I guess none of us do, because we just line up against her back wall where she has a calendar of the Syracuse University basketball team. Behind her desk, there's a poster of a stick figure—literally a guy made of twigs—pushing a giant rock up a slope that reads: *Don't give up.*

"That's a great poster," Liv says, and I want to hit her for making me want to laugh.

Miss Eldrich brushes her blond bangs off her eyes and gives me a barely there smile. "Miss Alamandar, is it? I see you brought some friends." She pushes forward on her desk chair, and the wheels rumble against the floor. "Will the whole field hockey team be joining us?" She smiles like she made a joke.

We don't laugh.

"Miss Eldrich," I say, "I just thought you might want a little more information about what happened earlier between Dylan and Kups—I mean Lance Kupperton."

She looks at me and then at the others. "I know what happened."

Ava steps forward. "Then why is Dylan the one in ISS?"

"Shouldn't you ladies be in class instead of tracking the revolving door of in-school suspension?"

"Did Kups get ISS too?" Kiara gives her a stare-down.

"It's none of your business, and it's certainly not possible for me to discuss the discipline of other students with you." She neatens the papers on her desk. "Is that all?"

I try to swallow. "Miss Eldrich," I say slowly, "it's really important that you understand that Kups took Dylan's stick and lifted her kilt and—"

"Athletic equipment remains in lockers. That's school policy. And there's not much of that skirt to lift, is there?" She raises her eyebrows and looks at our thighs. I tug down my kilt.

"This is our uniform." Ava's face reddens.

"Miss Eldrich." Quinn's voice is even, like she's trying superhard to stay calm. "He shoved her stick up her—"

"We have video. It clearly shows Dylan Johnson slam Lance Kupperton up against a wall, using her stick to choke him. Thanks to the quick thinking of his friends, she was pulled off before she could do any real damage. If anything, she's lucky if ISS is all she gets. Lance's parents may want to press charges. Lance, meanwhile, is a solid student. He volunteers regularly at the Summer's End Retirement Community. He's—"

"What in the world does that—" Kiara starts.

"Girls," Miss Eldrich says, her hands braced on her desk, "watch your tone or you will end up in ISS right alongside your friend. And then you can forget today's game."

Silence.

I don't even know what just happened. I'm on that spinning ride at the state fair, plastered to the walls when the floor drops away.

Ava and the others storm out. But I'm stuck to the wall.

The dean's nails just click away at her keyboard. It's not just that she doesn't get it. She *refuses* to get it.

I search for words that will convince her, change her mind, but all the words have disappeared. I just don't get how she won't listen to us.

Finally, I take a step toward the door.

"Miss Alamandar?" she says, not looking up from the computer.

"Yes?" I squeak, and I'm grateful the others don't hear.

She leans toward her computer like she's reading something. "Zoe, right?"

I nod.

"Let me give you some advice." She turns to me, clasps her hands on her desk, and tilts her head. It's a wooden pose, like she ordered it out of an educational catalog along with her ridiculous posters. "You're a good girl. I can see that in your record." She nods at the screen. "That will take you far in life. You know what won't take you far?"

I shake my head.

"Hanging out with the wrong crowd." She leans forward. "Dylan Johnson is the wrong crowd. Trust me on this. You'll thank me one day."

"Dylan"—I clear my throat—"is a member of our team. A good member. She—"

She waves her hands at me. "I'm glad Dylan's found some extracurriculars this year that don't involve her fists. But in my experience, people don't change all that much."

She glances at the clock. "Better get a move on, Miss Alamandar."

SEVEN

AS USUAL, THE BLEACHERS ARE empty except for a handful of parents, Sommersville's varsity team, and us. On the field, our JV team is playing before us and they're getting their asses handed to them. I can't stand to watch. I walk around the side of the stadium and lean against the cinder blocks.

We need to be great out there. This is our first test and we have to pass. Even without Dylan. I want to go to UNC Chapel Hill. It's that simple. And that huge. Sure there are other good Division 1 schools, but UNC Chapel Hill is consistently number one and a top academic school. Besides, it's far away from here. But I need that scholarship. When Coach reached out to them, they said they couldn't come to Syracuse just to see me. But they did say they'd send a recruiter to States. So the whole team needs to be perfect.

Coach is talking, but my heart's loud in my ears and then we're cheering and charging the field.

The whistle blows, but we're too fast. A bump of the ball

on turf sends it flying and our bumps are slaps and our slaps are punches and our passes fly far and our shots coast wide.

I command upfield, while Ava directs near the goal, but it doesn't matter. Our reddened faces are everywhere and nowhere. My feet burn on the hot turf. The scoreboard ticks up for Sommersville, while we stay zeroed out.

"You want pillows, girls? You're sleeping out there!" Coach yells her voice hoarse from the sidelines, and I holler too, but the words don't matter because nobody's listening.

It's last year all over again.

I dive for the ball—hard—ripping my knee across the turf. It hurts like hell but I jump up because it wasn't enough. They got the ball.

The halftime buzzer rings, and we drag ourselves off the turf. Coach slaps her clipboard. "I could play better drunk at three a.m.—hell, my grandma could play better. What's going on out there?" Her gaze lands on my knee. "Ouch, Zo. Looks like the turf is beating you too."

Which is when I notice—and feel—the way the turf just sandpapered off my skin. To distract myself while Coach cleans my turf burn with saline, I glance up at the stands. At least there's not a ton of people to see us get yelled at. And I have no idea what I'm supposed to do. I'm not sure if I should yell right along with her or just nod like I have a clue. It was easier being captain before we played any real games.

Ava crouches down next to Coach while she finishes bandaging my knee. "It's not fair, Coach. Dylan should be here."

Maybe she's right. Maybe we'd win if Dyl were here.

Coach sighs as she stands. "Girls, I spoke with the dean, and with Coach Jeffers. There's—"

"Coach Jeffers the football coach? What does he have to do with anything?"

"Well, Lance Kupperton is one of his players and Dylan did attack—"

We erupt. Kiara stomps her cleat. "It wasn't her fault, Coach. Everybody's always blaming Dyl, but she was just standing up for herself."

I look at the stands again. Last thing I want is for people to think we're throwing a temper tantrum because we're losing. "Sure, Dylan's a hothead, Coach, but it was Kups's fault," I say.

"What's that supposed to mean?" Ava asks.

Kiara glares at me.

"I was just trying to say it wasn't her fault!" I look at Coach. "We did the right thing too. We went to the dean but she didn't listen. Which I still don't get. I—"

"This may be your first taste of injustice, Zoe, but it's not mine," Ava says, her voice low. "You don't know what it's like."

It hurts worse than the turf burn.

"Wait." Coach holds up her hands. "I'm missing something. What happened?"

"You know what guys say to us on game days?" Ava's voice is quiet.

Coach looks at each of us, then shakes her head. But her cheeks redden. She knows. She just doesn't *want* to know.

"When we walk down the halls in our kilts, it's like an invitation," Sasha says.

"They whistle, they hoot."

"I got, 'That skirt looks good on your legs but it'd look better on my floor.'"

"Gross."

Coach shakes her head. "I'm sorry. But that doesn't excuse Dylan's behavior. Fighting is not how you resolve things if you want to be on this team."

Which was exactly my point. But then again, the dean didn't listen when we tried to talk to her. I turn to look at Ava but she doesn't look back.

"So," Coach continues, "maybe we should stop wearing the uniform on game days?"

"No," Kiara says. "Because then they'd win."

"What we wear shouldn't give them permission to act like dicks," Ava says. "Besides, I'm proud to be on this team. Kiara's right. It'd be like hiding. They'd win."

Quinn pumps her stick in the air. *"Illegitimum non carborundum!"*

I just stare at her. "What?"

"It means 'Don't let the bastards grind you down.'"

Coach sighs at her.

"What? It's in the Harvard fight song. I mean, it's *Harvard*, Coach."

Then Coach looks over our shoulders. We turn and see Dylan. Still in her uniform.

"Hey, guys." She gives a weak wave. "I know I'm not allowed to play tonight, but—" She looks softer, quieter. "Well, it's better than just going home."

46

I walk over and grab her hand, pulling her into the huddle. "I'm glad you came." And right here, I feel like a real captain. Even if I'm still stinging from Ava's words.

Kiara throws her arm around Dylan and smooches her on the cheek until she laughs.

"What's the score?" Dylan asks.

"It's 0 to 2." Cristina pouts.

Dylan steps back. "Wait. We're not winning?"

I shake my head.

"They're that much better than us?"

"No," Coach says. "They're not."

"Well, fuck that!"

Coach throws her hands up.

"Sorry, Coach." Dylan laughs. "I mean, fock them!"

"Yes." Coach's eyes crinkle up like she's trying not to laugh. "That's so much better."

We do our cheer and race out to the field, but I can't stop thinking about Ava's words or the way Dylan's parked on our bench instead of running on the field.

We lose, 1 to 2.

And I'm further away from States and my scholarship than ever.

When I get home, I don't feel like cooking dinner or doing homework. So I head to Dad's room instead. He's watching *Sports Forum*. His legs are propped up, but he doesn't look great.

"Hey. You doing okay?"

"I'm fine, honey."

Liar. I cross my arms. "Where is it this time?"

"Upper back." He sits forward but his mouth tightens and he stops. "I can't seem to—"

"Want me to try the acupuncture cups again? That seemed to help last time."

He sighs. "You don't mind?"

"Nah," I say. "I live to torture you."

I help him sit so we can wrestle off his T-shirt and reposition him, facedown. I place the cups on his back and attach the tube to the vacuum gun. With every pull, his skin gets sucked up a little more into the cups. It's supposed to suck out all the toxins and increase blood flow. It's kind of gross but also kind of cool. I move them gently, up the suction, set the timer, and wait.

The sportscasters argue about which play was better and which team will win. They yell. They tease. And every other minute they dissolve into laughter. It makes me think of Ava. Everything was fine before we actually had school and games. Maybe any team can be great when there's no contest.

When the timer goes, I release the suction. His back is covered in perfect red circles, but it seems to help. A little. At least something I did today helped someone. Because talking to the dean sure didn't. Talking at the huddle sure didn't. I never liked speaking up before, but I felt like I was supposed to as captain.

Maybe I should just shut up for good.

EIGHT

THE NEXT DAY AT SCHOOL sucks. Practice sucks. Coach punishes us for the loss with planks and push-ups, sprints and squats. With each bend, the little scrapes on my knee break open again. And the whole time, I ignore Ava and she ignores me.

Great season, Cap'n.

Tonight's a Rebels night, which means my mom's best friends will arrive with a ton of food, so at least I don't have to make dinner. Upstairs in my room, I try to finish the mountain of homework Mr. Mac assigned, but I just keep thinking about Ava and Dylan and how unfair it is that Kups got away with everything and how, at this rate, we're never going to get to States. I put down my pen and knock on my parents' door.

"Come in!" sings Mom. She's changed out of her scrubs and put on jeans and an old sweater of Dad's. She adjusts it in front of the mirror. Dad's got his earbuds in while he watches *Sports Forum*. I crawl onto the bed and rest my cheek against Dad's chest, listening to the faint music from his earbuds, letting my head rise and fall with his breathing, while I half watch the show and half watch Mom.

"How do I look?" She twirls in front of the TV and grasps the bottom of the sweater like it's a dress and does a curtsy.

Dad laughs. "I had no idea my clothes could look that good."

She waves him off. "You haven't worn this in years. It's mine now."

The doorbell rings. Mom squeals and runs downstairs. More squeals. A lot of squeals. Dad and I look at each other, and he turns up the volume on the TV. It takes a lot to cover up the Rebels. I hang with Dad until I think it's safe to go down and grab some food. Because yes, they may be noisy. But they also know how to eat.

As soon as I round the last step, two bright blurs spin around the corner and squeal.

"Zozo!" Aunt Jacks throws her arms wide, bracelets rattling. She dribbles chardonnay on the tile and nearly decapitates Aunt Ruth behind her. Jacks is short for Jacqueline. Jacks has too much volume, too much spice, too much everything, for a name like Jacqueline.

Aunt Ruth shoves past her to get to me. "Oh baby girl, you look beautiful."

"Not that looks are everything!" Aunt Jacks sings.

"Not that looks are anything!" chorus my mom and Aunt Maya from the kitchen. The peals of laughter mix with the clatter of dishes. They must be at least a bottle deep in that wine.

Aunt Ruth pulls me in, and not for the first time, I think about how there's something to be said for big boobs. I have to duck since she's shorter, but Aunt Ruth gives the best hugs of anyone I know. She pulls back and presses her hands against

50

each side of my face, studying me with her brown eyes, and I squirm under her gaze. Aunt Ruth always knows what I'm thinking.

"Oh give it a rest, Ruth," Aunt Jacks says, "you're squeezing her head like it's a tit in a mammogram machine."

Nice. At least Aunt Ruth lets me go.

"Something's wrong," she declares, crossing her arms over her belly. Half of her seems worried and the other half victorious. "Ha!" She turns to Aunt Jacks. "I always know!"

Aunt Jacks drapes her arm around me, spilling more wine. I eye the glass, tilting against my shoulder. I grab for it with my other hand. "Now, now," she says, "no wine for you."

I shake my head, guiding her toward the kitchen. "Just looking out for you, Aunt Jacks. I wanna make sure more ends up in your mouth than on the floor."

She guffaws.

When we enter the kitchen, there's an Everest-size mountain of yum waiting for me: piles of grapes, wraps, cookies, brownies, chocolate-covered somethings, apple pie, and cheese. Which reminds me of Ava and her cheese obsession. Which pisses me off all over again. I still don't get how I became the bad guy.

"Help yourself, Zo," Mom calls as they head into the living room. "We've been grazing for a while now."

The four of them curl into their favorite spots—the same spots they probably chose twenty years ago when they started meeting once a month. None of them are related, but they've always been my aunts.

I carve a thick slice of apple pie and pop it into the

microwave. On Rebels nights, I always eat dessert first. The hum erases their voices, but I watch them like I have for years. The way they tuck their feet under themselves, lean in to one another, and break apart with a laugh.

The timer sounds, and I scoop some of Uncle Bob's vanilla ice cream beside the steaming pie.

"You went for my pie, didn't you?" Aunt Maya calls from the overstuffed chair.

"That's what she said!" Aunt Jacks howls while the others laugh and shake their heads.

Mom waves me over. "Come here." They all echo her.

I sink onto the rug next to the coffee table, careful not to bend my bandaged knee, and take a scoop. I close my eyes at the bite. "Oh wow, Aunt Maya. I would live in this pie if I could." I take another forkful.

Maya sits back and smiles, always a sucker for baking compliments. "Darnell and I went to the orchard and picked the apples ourselves."

"I wish I could eat like that," Jacks says, watching me like I'm an animal in the zoo. "When I eat that much ice cream, shit shoots out of my ass like a geyser. I—"

"Really?" I put down my fork and raise my eyebrows.

Aunt Maya swats Jacks.

Mom pats my shoulder. "Big Bob's ice cream has powers. Besides, she has to eat a lot to keep up with her training."

I didn't realize she'd noticed.

"Something's wrong with her," Ruth declares, still staring at me, "and it's not her ice cream."

The Rebels trip over one another to ask me what's wrong.

"Nothing," I mumble. I like the Rebels. But sometimes they're so attentive it's overwhelming. It's like being tumbled around in a washing machine of love.

"Boy trouble?" Ruth asks.

I think of Kups hurting Dylan yesterday and getting away with it. Yeah. Boy trouble.

"You can't say that," Aunt Jacks says. "You have to say romantic troubles." She leans forward. "Because if you want to discuss your sexuality with us, Zoe, you can."

"I'm not gay," I say to my apples and ice cream.

"That's fine, honey," Aunt Jacks says, "but have you tried it?"

Mom busts out laughing.

"What?!" Jacks cries. "Compulsory heterosexuality is bullshit."

Mom holds up her hands. "Agreed. But maybe don't tell my kid to have sex?"

Maya clicks her tongue. "Well, she's going to have sex whether you like it or not."

"And all I'm saying is, she should figure out who's the most satisfying." Jacks grins. "I mean, from personal experience—"

I put down my fork loudly. "Ohhhh kaaaay."

"They went too far, didn't they?" Aunt Ruth holds up her hands. "Zoe's sex life is off the table."

I blush.

"Nothing should be off the table." Jacks slaps the coffee table, bracelets jangling. "That's how they get you—by attaching shame to it. What's next? We can't talk about racism? Sexism?" She dunks a carrot into the hummus. "Status quo

53

exists on a foundation of assumptions. We must question the assumptions." She takes a bite before the hummus meets the carpet.

"I'm fine with questioning—as long as nobody dares question me." Aunt Maya laughs.

"Tyrant." Aunt Ruth coughs into her hand, then smiles.

"Wait," I say, surprising myself. "What does questioning assumptions mean? Like, I know what it means. But—"

"What does it look like?" Ruth asks.

I nod.

"I think"—she looks at the others—"it looks like not letting a wrong thing happen even if that wrong thing has been done for centuries."

I push the puddle of ice cream around my plate, and the Rebels are quiet.

"Tell us what happened, honey," Aunt Maya says, her voice soft.

So I do. I tell them about Kups and Dylan and the dean and how we did the right thing but Dylan was the one who got punished.

"Abuse of power." Jacks slams her fist on her knee. "Same shit. Different decade."

"Hang on." Ruth holds up her hands. "This girl did use force against the boy and—"

"He deserved it if you ask me," Maya says. "That said, if you react to everything some misogynistic man does, you'll be working twenty-four-seven." She waves her hand. "Most of the time, it's not worth the stress."

"It's almost like you have to decide not to hear it," Mom says. "I just try to let it roll off."

"But this wasn't just words, Laura. And besides, even if it were—what does that do for Zoe's generation? We let it roll off and now they're dealing with a landslide."

Ruth tilts her head at Jacks. "That's a bit of an exaggeration. I still say it takes two."

"Are you sure nothing happened to this Kups kid?"

I shrug. "I don't know. I just—" I drag my fork through the ice cream, making tracks. I put it down. "You know what it is? It's like what Aunt Jacks said. The dean made this assumption about Dylan. She said she was the 'wrong crowd.' Isn't that messed up?"

"Very," Mom says, putting her hand on my shoulder. "I think it says a lot about you that you're bothered by it. I'm so proud of you."

The aunts all mmm-mmm as I head back to my room but I don't feel proud of myself. I feel like I'm in an elevator and Mom thinks I'm going to the top floor but really I'm going to the basement. Because Ava didn't say anything that wasn't true. I don't know what it's like. I've never been called to the dean. I've never had someone take someone else's side over mine—at least not with big consequences.

Dylan Johnson is the wrong crowd. They're the dean's words, but they might as well have been mine. I made the same assumption based on rumors or clothes or her ISS rap sheet.

Maybe I'd pick fights too if people always assumed the worst of me.

NINE

I PULL OUT MY PHONE.

> ME: Sorry. I was wrong.
> AVA: Just screenshotted that.
> ME: Very funny.
> ME: U were right. I'm not used to injustice
> I guess.

The little dots appear and I fixate on them. I hope I didn't screw up again.

> AVA: Yeah . . . I think I was also defensive bc Dyl was
> my pick u know?
> ME: Yeah. But she's really good.
> AVA: Really good.
> ME: R we okay?
> AVA: Absofockinglutely
> ME: Sticks Chicks 4ever

AVA: 4ever. Unless we lose Castleton tmrw and then I'll never speak to u again.

ME: Fair

When I wake, I worry that our text apologies might not translate to the field. I worry that Kups will do something else and Dylan will fight back and then we'll be in the same place all over again. I worry that Ava thinks I'm some spoiled brat. I worry . . . that maybe I am. Or was. The whole day goes by without me seeing Ava, and my doubt festers.

I want to be done thinking about Kups. He will not mess up my season. This year is about winning. Winning isn't something I'm going to pull on and off like an outfit. It's in my muscles. My bones. But I need Ava.

When I reach the bus, Ava must already be on board, because I can't see her.

A car honks from behind. I turn.

Uncle Bob and Eileen. Great timing.

"Uncle Bob?" I lean in the driver's side. "Hi, Eileen. What are you guys doing here?"

Eileen points to the back. "Ice cream for the team. Your uncle thinks of everything."

"Wow. That's really generous, Uncle Bob."

He pats Eileen's knee. "I'm not the one you should be thanking. It was all Eileen."

Reluctantly, I turn to her. "Thanks, Eileen. That was nice of you."

"She used to be quite the field hockey player herself, you know."

I try to arrange my face to look more interested than surprised. "I had no idea."

Uncle Bob puts the car in drive. "I think you girls would have a lot to talk about if you took the time. Good luck today, kid." I wave as he drives off.

Great. Now I'm supposed to bond with Wife Four. The thing is, Uncle Bob falls fast and hard, and then poof. It's over. I'm not sure why I should bother to get close when they all just leave. Even if this one did play field hockey once upon a Facebook post.

I stomp up the bus steps.

"Captain, my captain!" yells Ava.

And just like that, I bust out laughing. We're okay.

In my seat, I put in my earbuds and turn up the music. I imagine us on the field. I see my stick slam the ball, and the ball slam the goal. Again and again, all the way to Castleton.

I wrap my turf burn, then take the bandage off. I'll be faster without it, and it's mostly healed anyway. I run in place. I shake out my hands. I stretch my neck, my legs, my wrists.

"Use it." Coach grips my shoulders. "It's your fuel, your fire, and it's going to propel you all over their field." She claps her hands. "Girls!" We gather. "Will Durant said: 'We are what we repeatedly do. Excellence, then, is not an act, but a habit.'

Let those words sink in. Excellence can be a habit." She looks at each of us. "In these last weeks, I've seen more potential and better *habits* from this team than I have in my entire coaching career. We can make it a habit to win. To persevere. To succeed. It's our choice." She looks at us. "Anyone have anything else to say?"

After every pregame talk, she invites us to speak. We never do. Today, I raise my hand.

If I've learned anything this week, it's that being a team is harder when real stuff is on the line, and yet being a team is the only way to get through it.

Coach nods, and I stand, gripping my stick. It's one thing to know I should speak up and another to actually do it.

I glance at Ava. "Sticks Chicks," she whispers, smiling at me.

"I don't feel right anymore without this stick in my hand. After this summer, I don't feel right when *all* of you aren't by my side." I look at Dylan, who flushes. "My stick, and you, have become an extension of me. Of who I am." I squeeze the stick tighter. "And I'm making the choice to win." I turn around to the whiteboard. Coach had written BEAT CASTLETON on the board above her drawing of our positions. I erase it and write: WIN STATES. As soon as I do, the girls—my team— thump their sticks against the hard concrete, a rattling, chaotic applause.

"Fock yeah!" Dylan shouts.

"Storm the castle!" Ava yells, and we roar out of the locker room, our cleats clattering against the floor, our sticks keeping time against the air.

Ava and I run to the center circle with the refs and call heads. The coin flips over itself in the air before landing on the ref's hand, heads up. We choose sides.

I love the national anthem: the loudness, the sureness. I don't really sing, but it shuts everything else out. I close my eyes, and I'm in the Olympics. Ready to win it all.

When we huddle, we ask Dylan to pick the cheer. She picks "Grind." So we crash our sticks in the air and scream it.

We do our superstitions: Ava crosses herself and hops twice as soon as she steps over the line into the goal. Cristina does a little spin when she gets to the wing. Bella touches the top of her stick to each shoulder.

Back when Dad came to games, he'd yell, "Chop your feet!" before the whistle. So I grip my stick, pretend I hear his voice, and run in place.

At the first clack of the stick, I know it. I can sense the ball's movement. Ava and I direct the action like a single conductor. Every time I pass, someone's there. Our sticks kiss the ball, and it flies. We jab, drive, push around the field in a strange ballet. We snatch the ball from Castleton so often I lose count. We weave around and between them like they're rocks and we're the river. We're fast. We're smooth. We're good. Hell, we're grace and strength in kilts.

We win. And we like it.

TEN

THERE IS SOMETHING UNIVERSALLY SEXY about boys in soccer shorts. It's a fact. I'm sure there are scientists studying why soccer boys are way cuter than the boys of just about any other sport.

Even watching them huddle before the game Tuesday afternoon is perfect. I can watch the way the 8 on Grove's jersey lies between his back muscles, and he's too focused on the game to notice.

Liv worked it out with her boyfriend, Jake, that our team will watch their game against Queens Falls if they watch our Queens Falls game too. I'm terrified about the second half of that deal, but for now, I'll watch Grove from the safety of the back bleachers tucked beside my teammates.

He looks up at us. Possibly at me. And smiles. Fockity fock.

I squeeze Liv's hand. Hard.

"Yes," she says, shaking out her hand. "I saw. Thanks to you I'll be lucky if I can hold my stick tomorrow." Turning back to the field, she screams, "Come on, Ridgebacks!"

"Down with the monarchy!" Our chants against Queens Falls beat out every other school.

Grove's feet speak a language that the other team can't translate.

He shoots, and his whole body is in the kick: The swing of his leg powers through his hips, and the ball slings into the back right corner of the net. First goal of the game, and it's Grove's. His teammates clap him on the back. And, oh my, he lifts his jersey to wipe his face.

"What was that?" Liv elbows me in the side, ready to laugh.

"What?"

She leans in. "You basically sex-sighed."

"I did not."

"You totally did. You sex-sighed."

I shake my head. I can't possibly sex-sigh when I've never even had sex. Or a boyfriend. I squeeze the edge of the bleachers.

To distract myself, I turn from Liv to Nikki, but she's looking pale. "Are you okay?"

She nods. I follow her gaze to number 12, Brett Jamison. I look back at her. Her elbows are locked, her knuckles white. I remember Kups saying something about Jamison.

"If you could be anywhere else in the world right now, where would you be?"

"Easy," says Liv, thinking I'm talking to her because this is our go-to game. "Maybe Myanmar or Russia. They've got enough political prisoners to tire out Mother Teresa."

"For real?" Cristina asks, eyebrows arched. "That's where you'd go? Out of anywhere?"

"Liv is destined to be a human rights superhero," I say. Liv elbows me.

"Shit," says Dyl. "I'll go to Florida and sit my ass on a hammock. You in, Ki?"

"Hells yes." Kiara leans for a beat against Dyl's shoulder. "Just us and the alligators."

I nudge Nikki. "How about you?"

A slow smile spreads. "Italy. Rome. For the art, the statues. I've always wanted to see a Bernini there of Apollo and Daphne. He's chasing her, hounding her, so she escapes by turning into a tree."

"That's messed up," Dylan says. "Does she change back?"

"No. But I like the contradiction—change caught in marble, that turning into a tree isn't an escape at all." She chews her cuticles, then tucks her hands under her thighs. "I don't know."

"I repeat," Dyl says. "I'd take the hammock by the water. You weirdos—"

We're interrupted by everyone screaming again. I turn to see Jamison steal the ball from Queens Falls. "Go Ridgebacks!" I scream.

When I turn back to Nikki, her face has gone white again. "Hey, you sure you're okay?"

She crosses her hands over her chest. "I thought I could—I think—" She looks at the field before pivoting back to me. "I think I'll go. I might be coming down with something."

"Go home and rest up," Ava says. "We want you all set for tomorrow's game."

Nikki forces a smile, nods at Ava, then picks her way down the bleachers.

I look back to the field, at Jamison elbowing his way past Queens Falls' defense.

I turn to Liv. "Did Brett Jamison and Nikki ever go out?"

She shrugs. "I didn't even know Nikki until this year."

"Same." I'd never even seen Nikki before she stumbled onto our beach that night.

Liv jumps to her feet screaming for Jake, who must've scored a goal. "Off with their heads! Down with the monarchy!" our side chants.

All the guys clap Jake on the back, including Grove. And when Jake looks up at Liv, Grove's eyes follow. For a second, I think he looks at me and I freeze, my hands in midair.

Ava slaps me on the back. "Okay, Cap'n?"

I nod. I'm sure I imagined it. I'm sure he wasn't looking right at me.

"Maybe we should do this more. You know, come to soccer games?"

Liv gives me a sly look while Ava nods and screams: "Go Ridgebacks! Off with their heads!"

The next day, the boys' soccer team shows. I'm pretty sure now will be the moment I completely forget how to play field hockey. Now I have to worry not only about States and my scholarship, but Grove too. I liked it better when I was invisible.

I need to think about something else. Anything else. I pan the stands. Ava's family whistles and cheers. Cristina's three little sisters bounce like Ping-Pong balls between their parents. And then I see Uncle Bob. Again. Uncle Bob never came to my games last year, and now he's two for three. Of course, Eileen is right there next to him waving with one hand, a video camera in the other. Great. Just what I need. Photographic evidence of my epic fail. In front of Grove.

I let the national anthem focus me. Forget the camera. Forget Grove. I'm here to win.

At the whistle, we move.

The crowd stomps their feet on the bleachers, and their energy channels into my thighs, pushing me down the field. They shout *Off with their heads!* every time we steal the ball, and their strength is in my arms as I drive the ball hard. I dodge the other team like they're cones, still and squat, my feet and stick moving in rhythm around them. I pass to Bella, and she scores. We run screaming back to center field.

I bend down, stick in position. The whistle sounds, and Quinn steals the ball. We pass it back and forth, skirting the feet and sticks of the Queens Falls players, and this time, I score, right in the back left corner. The goalie looks crushed. I almost feel sorry for her. Almost.

It's like that the whole game, against one of our biggest rivals. They can't get a shot on us. Ava and I rotate the ball to the right girl every time. And in the yelling from the stands, I hear my name now and then. Most of the time, I think it's the JV players or the other parents. Or Uncle Bob. But once, at least once, I'm almost positive it's Grove.

Here's a thing I know for sure: Every time I look up at the stands, he's watching. And not just the game, but me. And I don't hide, don't run, don't blush, don't cower. I just play like me.

The next week, we play Tuscaroga. Away games mean a sparse cheering section. Cristina's dad and Mrs. Dobson, the triplets' mom, for sure, with maybe a few others if they can escape work. But when I run out onto their field, Uncle Bob and Eileen are parked right in the middle of our near-empty section, complete with video camera and cooler. Right next to them: a handful of soccer boys.

Grove. Is. Here. This isn't next-door Queens Falls. This is forty-minutes-away Tuscaroga.

When we run out, and he sees me see him, he nods. At me.

I stop. Sasha runs into me.

"Sorry," I say. "I—I got distracted."

What does it mean that this is the second game in a row he's watched? What does it mean when half the team comes too? What does it mean if—

"Cap'n?" Ava knocks into my hip.

Fockity fock. Have I just been staring at him all this time? I should not be allowed in public.

"Are you okay?"

Clearly, I am not okay. Clearly, I am unhinged. "I'm fine!"

"Good," she says. "We need this. We need you."

I grip my stick so hard I feel it in my feet. I jog in place, lifting my stick into the air.

"What are you doing?" Ava looks at me, half worried and half amused.

"Getting focused?" I ask-answer. But it's working. If my body is busy, it shuts up my mind. And right now, my mind needs some serious shushing. So it doesn't matter—all that much—that I look like a freak. Besides, as long as he's all the way up there, I can play like me.

We run to the center for the coin toss. Ava calls heads, and we win. We play with the sunset at our backs. In half an hour when we switch sides, the sun will be completely down, and we'll play under the stadium's lights. I see the resignation in Tuscaroga's eyes. Like they already know they're going to lose. And it's all the invitation I need.

I crouch down, my back and knees bent, my stick inches from the ground. My shadow looks lean and long before me. At that first tap of the ball, I sprint.

Tuscaroga squints against the sunset, and I imagine they see our silhouettes tangled with our shadows—our bodies stretching impossibly tall, spanning the field. They can't stop us.

We win: 3 to1.

Our football team is a joke. But that doesn't stop our school from hosting a pep rally before the first football game of the year. We've already had four fockey games. This is their first. But *they* get a pep rally.

Liv, the team, and I crush into the gym, which I'm fairly sure cannot legally hold all of us. With every new addition to the bleachers, we squeeze closer.

"If one more person pushes into this row," Quinn says, her shoulders up by her ears, "I swear I'm going to pop like a zit."

Liv scrunches up her face. "Ew. I call foul. Unnecessary image."

"Sooooo," Bella begins, "I was thinking about asking Chloe Turner if she's going to be at Reilly's bonfire after the game tonight." She raises her eyebrows. "What do you think?"

"Eeek!" Cristina squeals and claps her hands, and Bella's tight smile relaxes.

"Chloe would be an idiot not to—"

"You'd be—"

"—the most adorable couple ever—"

"Okay, okay." Bella puts up her hands, smiling. "I'll ask her after the rally."

"I've never been to one of Dave Reilly's bonfires." Michaela smooths out her skirt.

"Well, he's pretty much an asshole," Ava says. "But the beach in back of his house is amazing. We should go as a team."

"Absofockinglutely." I nod.

After 2,700 kids squeeze into the gym, Coach Jeffers, loud and big, steps to the court's center, onto the painted snarl of Northridge's mascot, the Rhodesian Ridgeback.

"Are you rrrrrrrready?!" His deep voice thunders off the gym's walls.

We holler back. He's reciting straight from the *How to Run a Pep Rally Handbook*, but I don't care because I'm with my friends, laughing and screaming, and not in class.

"Okay," Liv says right in my ear. "I can't wait anymore."

I turn and raise my eyebrows.

"Grove asked Jake about you." Despite the swirling noise and pounding feet, I hear her.

There's less air. All 2,700 kids just inhaled, and there's not enough for me.

"Grove Williams asked Jake about *you*," she repeats. "And he wants to meet you at the bonfire tonight after the game."

ELEVEN

THE BONFIRE IS IN DAVE Reilly's backyard. He's on the football team and an ass, so it's a sure bet that Kups and other fridge-size assholes will be there. But it's been over two weeks since Dylan's run-in with Kups. Besides, there's a beach and a bonfire. And Grove.

At the bonfire, huge logs tilt toward one another in a flaming pyramid. The flames chase the breeze, while stray sparks dance like fireflies against the blackened sky.

Liv made me borrow an outfit and did my makeup, but what felt like a kind of armor in her room now makes me feel exposed. I tug at the skimpy shirt, but Liv swats my hand away. Someone taps me on the shoulder.

Grove.

"Hi."

"Hi." I turn to include Liv, but she's already disappeared.

He holds out a cup. "I got you this. I hope it's okay."

"That's really nice of you." I take a small sip. Truth is, I don't like beer, but carrying one around is better than people bugging you to drink.

His eyes go back to the fire, and I let mine follow. I spot Liv, Ava, and Quinn on the other side smiling. Quinn starts humping the air.

I quickly turn to Grove. "So you guys are doing really well this season," I say over the peals of laughter across the flames. Anything to distract him from the mime-porn.

He turns back to me. Our faces are closer than they've ever been, and my breath feels tight. His eyes are a warm kind of dark in the firelight. Oh fock, he's saying something. "What?" I manage.

He smiles. I try not to fall in.

"I liked seeing you guys play." He takes a sip. "You're pretty amazing." He pauses. "At field hockey, I mean." His cheeks redden. "Not that you're not amazing at other things."

I laugh and put my hand on his arm, and he looks down. I yank it back fast. Shit. My hand went rogue. I look at the fire. "You're really good at soccer."

"I'm glad you came." The raspiness in his voice makes me feel as though I'm hearing something deep.

A group of guys bump into us, screaming something about keg stands.

"You wanna walk down to the dock? With me? Where it's quiet?"

I like the way everything's a question. Like maybe I'll say no. Like I'm not a guarantee.

The shouts and laughs subside as we walk to the far side of the sand. A tall boathouse stands guard over a long dock stretching into the dark lake.

The metal dock sways a bit as I step on, and his hand closes around my wrist for a breath before he lets go. The breeze off the lake circles the space where his fingers were, and I shiver.

"Cold?" He pulls my arm. "Come on." We open the door to the boathouse. Different boats lap against the sides of the walls, while others hang from above. Along the walls are oars, rope, tools, and—sure enough—blankets. We steal two and walk to the end of the long dock. He throws his blanket down across the metal slats.

"Good call," I say as I crouch, glad the dock's metallic cold won't seep through my jeans.

He unfolds our other blanket and wraps it around my shoulders before sitting next to me. The warmth is immediate. He leans back on his hands, his strong legs stretched out.

"I like the lake best at night."

"Me too," I say. "When I was little, my dad and I used to go sunset kayaking."

"Sunset kayaking?" I hear his smile. I turn to him, but his face is in shadow, the bonfire blazing behind him.

"My mom's a nurse, so we'd explore when she worked nights. Honestly, he was probably just petrified of being trapped indoors. He's never been—well, he never was an indoors guy." I hug my knees. It feels forever ago.

"So it was an act of self-preservation. Kind of like this moment."

"What do you mean?" I ask.

"I hate parties. So I ingeniously escaped with you."

"I'm not a fan either." I lift my beer. "To self-preservation."

We clink cups and take small sips.

"You know what else I hate?" he asks.

"Dogs with sweaters? Children with leashes? Parrots?" For a minute it feels as easy as talking to Liv, and then I remember it's Grove. I flush.

He laughs. "All of the above. And—small talk."

"It's unseasonably warm for this time of year."

"Can you believe that rain we got last week?"

"We'll have to cover the azaleas before the frost comes."

"*We* have azaleas?" he asks. "What are azaleas?"

"Flowers." I imagine the two of us tending a garden. I send a thank-you to the darkness for masking my blush. "I hate small talk too." I wrap the blanket around me more tightly. "I wish everyone came with a fast-forward button. Like let's just fast-forward till we can talk about real—" And I remember how much I'm talking. And to whom.

"Me too." His voice is so soft and rumbly, it's like sliding into the black water. "Wanna go star kayaking?"

I smile. "What?"

"Well, it might not be as nice as sunset kayaking." He shrugs. "But when we went into the boathouse, there were, well, boats."

"Imagine that."

"Shocking."

"Let's grab one." I'm standing before I finish my sentence. We abandon our beers on the dock, grab the blankets, and walk toward the boathouse. On the way, we find a canoe tucked under the metal slats and pull it out. I climb in first.

When he climbs in, the whole boat rocks wildly, and we clutch each other until it steadies.

"Big boater, eh?" I laugh.

"Great," he says. "You've already saved my life, and we haven't even left the dock."

We settle ourselves—he's in front and I'm steering in back—and slip our paddles into the calm lake. Each stroke carves the water and we move away from the dock, from the party. I'm relieved that, for the moment, I don't have to arrange my face or my stomach or my words.

Before we reach the buoy, I pull my paddle from the water. I wish our canoe had lights so we could go farther. He slowly turns around to face me. And I'm struck by the weirdness of it all. I'm sitting in a canoe. In the middle of the lake. With Grove Williams. I shake my head.

"What?" he asks.

I shake my head again. "Nothing." I crane my neck and look at the sky. Way out here where the rich kids live, there are so many more stars. Maybe it's a good thing we don't have lights after all.

He pats the bottom of the boat. "It's dry," he says. "Want to lie down so we can see the stars better?"

I nod. We lay the blankets on the bottom of the canoe and edge down. We put our arms under our heads and knock elbows. "Sorry," we say at once, and drop our arms down by our sides. Thanks to the rounded sides, our hands touch again, but this time, neither one of us says sorry. Neither of us moves.

"I wish the night sky was always like this."

"Me too," he says.

"Isn't it weird that all these stars are always there, but we can't see them?" It reminds me of Dylan. Of how it can be hard to see the real her. "It's like people. Like there's all this stuff going on, but most people only let you see just a little bit, but every once in a while the sky clears and . . ." I think of us. I think of crushing on him for a year. Of never getting this close.

I feel his eyes on me. "That's a cool way to see it," he says. The water laps around the sides of the boat, and the small space between our fingers contains unseen fireflies, flapping their wings, sharing their heat.

I look down at the way his right knee angles ever so slightly toward my left.

Here beneath the lip of the canoe, the air is still, and yet I can tell we're moving by the shifting stars. I, who always know where I'm headed, have no idea which direction we face. It's a heady kind of freedom.

"I love that I don't know where we are."

"You're in a canoe." His fingers move, grazing mine. "With me."

I smile. "I mean, I like that we're down here." I wave my hand into the air. "We have no idea what's going on up there. Whether we're pointing away from shore—"

"—whether another boat's coming our way."

I sit up quickly, the boat rocking to his laughter.

"All clear?" he asks. I nod, and he pats my leg. "Then come back down."

I look at him and lie back, and even though I know we're too close to shore for another boat, I'm alert to every sound of the water. And to the space on my thigh where his hand was.

"I have no desire to get split in two by a Jet Ski," I say. I feel him smile, and I relax a little. "So how about this weather we're having? Quite a miracle, eh? Summer in September?"

He laughs. "You joke, but the Weather Channel is background music at my house."

"Easy listening not educational enough?"

"My mom is weirdly paranoid about the weather. She always needs to know what it is, hour by hour and for the next ten days. She says it helps her feel prepared."

"Yeah, except they're always wrong."

"I know!" He gestures broadly, and the boat rocks. "That's what I always say. It's pointless to make the weather your security blanket."

I laugh. "Security blankets should be more reliable . . . like seesaws—"

"—the stock market—"

"—cafeteria food—" We make gagging noises and laugh.

He turns his head to me. "What's a real security blanket for you?"

I turn. His face is right there. Right. There. His dark eyes under his thick eyebrows. His gray hoodie bunched around his shoulders and pulled tight across his chest. Wow. And now I have to come up with an answer.

"Field hockey. The team." I take a breath. "My dad."

"Do you live with both your parents?"

"Yeah," I say. "You?"

He shakes his head and looks back up at the stars. "My dad took off when I was two."

"That must be hard," I say.

He shrugs. "It's just the way it is. I know it sounds harsh, but I'm glad. You miss something more when you know what it's like to have it. I'm glad I don't know what it's like to have him around."

I think of all the missing I have with my dad. I wonder what things would be like if I never knew anything different. "You have a sister too, right?"

He turns and gives me a slight smile. "Yeah. How'd you know?"

I blush and hope the night hides it. "I think I've seen her at your soccer games."

"That's my younger sister. I have an older one too. She just left for college."

"Do you miss her?"

He nods. "Yeah I do. We're really close. She even named me."

"Named you? Like as in she . . . named you?"

"She's only two years older than me and was a big fan of *Sesame Street*."

"You're named after Grover? On *Sesame Street*?" I turn on my side to see him better. "I guess I always thought it was like a family name or something."

"Always?" He nudges me. "You've always thought?" My cheeks flame, but he continues. "Actually, I kind of think my name is the family curse."

"Why?"

He shrugs and looks up at the stars. "My mom wanted my sister to be all involved, but my dad thought it was stupid. My mom was too much of a free spirit for him or something."

"And yet he's the one who took off, and she's the one watching the Weather Channel?"

He turns to me, and his face is so open I think of the cloudless night sky. Vulnerable, visible. He smiles, and I bite my lip.

"You said you noticed my sister."

"What?"

"At *games*. Plural. As in you not only went to one game but many. And you noticed my family." He grins.

My skin prickles. I can feel every breeze off the water. "Yes, well, our whole team has been going to a lot of games this year."

He pushes against my arm. "And you noticed my sister."

"Shut up. I—"

He takes my hand, and I feel like I'm in the middle of a game, except there are no sticks, no refs, no team—and I'm right where I want to be.

"I didn't go to your games just to be a good sport." His thumb rubs a circle on the top of my hand. Every part of me stills.

"No?" My voice feels hoarse.

He shakes his head slightly. "I went to see you."

"Really?" I swear my voice is traveling from the bottom of the lake it's so far away and tangled in pondweed.

"Well, I had to check out the competition." He smiles wide. "Coach Mac said that we've got to beat your wins, you know—"

I hit his chest with my free hand, but he pulls my arm

against him until our bodies are side by side, our faces closer than ever, and everything feels faster and stranger than it ever has on the playing field.

He reaches out and strokes his thumb against my lips and somehow, with that one thumb, he's touching my whole body—the curve of my neck, the valley between my shoulders, the dip of my back, the hollows behind my knees, the tips of my toes. My whole body rests in my lips under his touch. My lips part, my lower lip wanting to stay with his finger as long as possible.

"Can I kiss you?"

"Yes," I whisper.

We close the space between us and I take his lips in mine for a second or a minute and his lips are so soft and sure and real and then he smiles and I smile and we laugh a breathy kind of laugh and I pull back and beneath his eyes are freckles I never knew were there and I breathe in the smell of him and the cool lake air rushes in but my head and heart and cheeks and stomach feel warm and swirled like hot chocolate with whipped cream.

I'm. Still. Smiling. This whole time. I didn't know you could kiss and smile.

His hand curls around my jaw and cheek back to my neck and tangles in my hair as he pulls me in, tighter now, lips crushing, and I'm breathing in all his air. My blood feels hot but my skin feels chilled and I push closer and the boat moves with me, the water moves with me, with us, and there we are, nestled in the bottom of a canoe, swaying beneath a ceiling of stars.

Kissing.

TWELVE

BY THE TIME WE PADDLE the canoe back to the dock, the great logs on the fire have collapsed into one another, and my friends are nowhere in sight. Unidentifiable couples kiss in the dark, while a loud group plays soccer on the beach. I pull my arms across my chest, missing the blanket and the boat. And Grove. And kissing.

Grove wraps one of the blankets around me and doesn't let go. "Cold?"

I smile. "Not anymore." Our faces are so close. Right there are those constellations of freckles, that yummy boy smell. His hands move to my cheeks, his shoulders pulled up as if he's wrapping himself around me. My lips open and we stay like that for a second, a minute, a year, just hovering in the breath in the anticipation until I can't take it anymore and my lips kiss his.

He smiles. "I win."

I laugh that smile-kiss-laugh and kiss him again. "Nope." I lean against his chest, and he wraps his arm around me, and we watch the soccer players pass the ball down the beach toward the makeshift goal.

He rubs my arm. "Wanna play?"

"Yeah." I smile. "Definitely. I'm just going to run inside real quick. Want anything?" I pass him the blanket.

He shakes his head, and as I turn away, he takes my hand and pulls me back toward him. His hand slides up my arm and lingers on my bare shoulder and we're kissing. Again. He pulls back and looks at me before releasing.

I turn and walk up the rocks leading away from the beach to the glass-and-stone house on the hill, where I hope there's a very empty bathroom so I can hurry back. I look over my shoulder, but he hasn't moved. He's still watching me. I smile and bite my lip.

Grove Williams is watching me. Me.

I practically skip up the hill to the house. Skip up the stone steps. Skip across the slate patio. Skip into the empty house, my steps echoing in the arched ceiling of the great room. Skip around the corner. Skip right into Dave Reilly.

"Hey there." He leers toward me.

I try to swallow my disgust. After all, I'm in *his* house. But he's footballer-big and drunk-wheezy, towering over me and breathing all the air. I smell the chips, dip, and beer all muddled together in his heavy breath.

He puts his arm out to steady himself against the wall, but I'm between him and the wall. I scoot down to get out of his way.

"Heeeeeyyyy, where you going, my slippery salamander?"

"Ha. Good one." I try to move around him, but his other arm blocks me. "Okay, Reilly. Let me go." I force a smile.

I don't want to sound bitchy. "I need to get back to my friends."

"Well, I have needs too, little salamander, and you are looking hooooot tonight." He presses his body closer and the wall at my back is unyielding and unforgiving. He snaps my bra strap against my shoulder.

"Stop." I look left, right, anywhere but in his face. There's nobody here in this dark hallway.

"Did you give him a blowjob?" His breath is hot on my neck.

"What?" I push him, but he just leans his weight against me, and he's so much bigger, so much heavier than me. A mountain. I push again. All that weight lifting all these months and I can't move him. "Get off me! Now!"

His hands press my shoulders hard against the wall but the wall is too hard and his hands are too hard and there's nowhere for them to go nowhere for me to go and he ducks his head into my neck and his breath is hot and sticky and he's kissing me and it's so wrong and wet like a dog. He yanks my shirt off my shoulder and I'm wriggling but his hands shove and push and I pull my knee up hard but he's too tall and I hit nothing and he shoves his hands up my shirt and mashes my breasts and I'm crying and trying to hit but I'm pinned like a butterfly and this can't be happening and his elbow is on my neck and I can't breathe and then I see his other hand pull down his basketball shorts no zippers no buttons down in seconds and he's ripping at my jeans and oh my God he's really going to and I want to leave my body just float away but I push and shove and lift my knees hoping they hit him somewhere but nothing—

"Reilly!" someone calls from the other room.

He lifts off me to look—and I run. I run so fast that I fall and slide but I run—

"Hey wait!" he calls after me, and then I hear him burp. A great echoing burp that reverberates off the white walls. Followed by a laugh.

I run out the front door, through the gate, down the drive, onto the road.

I run and run and run until a car swerves and slams its horn. I crash into the ditch on the side of the road. I dry heave again and again.

Nothing comes up.

I hear steps behind me and I shrink down.

"Zoe?!"

Liv. Oh thank God. Liv. I want to stand but I can't unbend.

"Zoe!" She wraps her arms around me, and for a second it's like she's holding me together. But it only lasts a second. "What happened?"

I turn to the side and try to throw up again.

She pats me on the back. "I'll get the car. Can you wait here? Are you okay?"

I'm so far from okay. I sink to the ground and hug my knees. I look down at the shirt Liv had me borrow. This shirt that she said revealed just the right amount of everything. I turn to heave again, but there's no getting rid of any of it.

Soon a car drives by slowly. "Zo?" Liv's voice.

I crawl out of the ditch. The car door is so heavy but somehow I get it open and sit down. Even though it's warm, I start to shake. The car pulls away. I grab a tissue out of the box on the floor and pull down the visor. I scrub at the makeup, but my skin just gets raw and red.

"I'm sorry about your shirt," I say.

"Screw my shirt. I'm worried about you," she says.

I shake my head. "I guess this is what I get for dressing like this."

"What? That's ridiculous." Liv pulls over and clicks on her hazards. "Zo, I have no idea what happened"—she puts her hand on my knee, and I flinch—"but you looked beautiful tonight. Did Grove—"

"No."

I've never felt less beautiful in my life. I think of Reilly's face pressed into mine. I open the door and lean out, only to dry heave again. I clutch my stomach, but it won't do what it's supposed to do.

I can't get rid of it.

THIRTEEN

I'M UP BEFORE THE SATURDAY sun. I'm not sure I ever fell asleep. I run where I always do—the trail toward the lake. I've always loved it because it's deserted in the mornings. But a few minutes in, my mind's still whirring, my skin's too sticky, my feet don't work, and I'm dry heaving in a ditch. Again. A crack of a branch in the woods, and I close my mouth against a scream. I run home so fast the tears on my cheeks don't have time to fall.

For the first time in my life, I skip practice. With Mom always working and Dad laid up, it's on me to do chores. But I skip those too. I silence my phone. I curl back into bed and pull my pillow tight over my head. I want to sleep through everything. But I can't.

Can't run. Can't sleep. Can't throw up.

I've been stripped raw and every little thing hurts. My dry eyes itch. My sheets scrape my skin. My heart's in my ears— thump thumping, closer and closer. I throw the covers off, begging the rush of cool air to change me, numb me.

I hear everything. Mom fixes coffee, goes to work. Dad

exercises in the living room, watching *Sports Today*. Outside my window, leaves push against one another. But it's all background music to the real show: his face, his breath, his hands, his shorts pulled down. I tug the covers back around myself and crawl farther into my bed.

My insides are shattered. Like all those months of training never amounted to muscles at all. All this time I thought I was made of rock, I was made of glass.

There's a light knock on my door.

"Yeah?" I ask from under the covers.

The door creaks open. "Mmmm." Even buried beneath my comforter, I recognize the sound of Dad eating Big Bob's ice cream.

I burrow farther beneath the covers.

"Best ice cream in the universe," he croons. The spoon clinks against the bowl as he scoops it up. "And I've brought tunes."

I pull the covers tighter.

"Tunes and ice cream are well known to possess mysterious healing powers," he sings.

I think of how I looked last night—that shirt, that makeup. At least he doesn't know that. A sob erupts, and I almost choke on it.

"Isn't any of this tempting?"

I gather the comforter in my fists and press it against my eyes, willing the tears to stay inside. I love him more than anything—but he is the last person I want to see right now.

I've never felt further away from him. I've never felt further away from myself.

Sighing, he sits on the bed. Everything feels tight and close, I can't breathe under the covers, and I don't know how much longer I can hold it in. I hear him set the bowl on my desk. "Well, I guess I'll leave you alone." He pats my arm through the comforter, and I tense. If I let go, the tears will drown us both.

He walks to the door. As he's pulling it shut behind him, he says, "Don't leave the ice cream too long, pumpkin. It's never as good when it melts."

When the door clicks closed behind him, I cry an all-over cry that rocks every part of me. It's a silent kind of wailing, but I'm thankful for the TV and Dad's less-than-perfect ears. When the tears finally stop, they stick me with a headache that presses down into my eyes. I look past the bowl of now-melted ice cream to the CD. I reach for it and flip it over to see Dad's lopsided writing: *Zo Tunes—not to be confused with Show Tunes. Haha.* I stand, legs unsteady, and cross to my dresser, placing the CD among the photos and medals. The face in the mirror draws me in—puffy, pale, weak. I slide my sleeve up to see dark red splotches eating at my skin. One, where my shoulder meets my chest, isn't as shapeless as the rest. A thumbprint.

I used to love to count the bruises on my legs, proof of fockey, of grinding. These are different. Like when it first snows how the whole world is papered in white and it's clean and fresh. But the second a truck drives across it, the snow spoils into slush. Because snow isn't much of anything really. It can't fight back either.

I take a picture. Pull down my sleeve. Put on a hoodie.

The doorbell rings. Grabbing the box of tissues, I climb back into bed, rewrapping myself in covers. Dad's footsteps are heavy and uneven. The front door opens to voices. Feet climb the stairs. I tunnel deeper.

The door creaks open, the covers get thrown back. All the girls are here—Liv, Ava, the triplets, Cristina, Kiara, Nikki, Dylan, and Michaela. They pile onto the bed.

"We decided you needed a care package of our love." Quinn flops herself across me.

They squeal and topple and hug until I can't breathe, until it's Reilly's arm against my throat, and I gasp. They pull back, laughing. I grab for the comforter.

"We missed you at practice," Liv says.

"What happened last night, Cap?" Bella asks.

I begin a thousand sentences in my mind, but none of them work. "I just got sick." Liv's face is so open I can't bear it. I look back at Bella. "How was your date?" I don't even know how I remembered. It's like someone else is talking, functioning.

"Swee-eet," she says. She holds up her phone. "She already texted me." She smiles. "Twice."

"My sister's got game," Quinn says. Everyone laughs. I can't take it.

"That's so great, Bels," says this other me.

"Let's let her sleep, you guys," Liv says, and I feel so grateful I want to cry. Again.

They say things I don't hear. Liv squeezes my hand, and I feel like everything might burst if she doesn't leave now. *Call me*, she mouths.

They close the door behind them. Finally. And I burst into tears.

"Hey." Nikki's voice is quiet as she steps back in and shuts the door.

I pull the covers tight, but the tears have already escaped.

"Listen." She sits on the edge of my bed and looks down at her hands. "I think something happened last night, to you, and I just want you to know that I'm here—if you need—if you want to talk."

I concentrate to untangle her words, to get them through the distance to me. The functional me needs to step in and tell her nothing's wrong, but then she looks at me.

I remember the way she looked when she crashed onto the beach that night, and how she looked at the soccer game, and the truth of it settles like the crushed glass inside me.

The words pile up on my tongue but nothing comes out.

She's quiet.

"It's stupid," I finally say. "It's not even that big a deal. Nothing happened." I try to laugh, but it doesn't come out right and sounds kind of strangled.

She stays quiet.

"What happened that night we met you on the beach? Was it Jamison?"

The muscles in her face tense. She nods.

I sink back against my pillows. "They're assholes." I shake my head at the ceiling. "I don't even know why I'm upset. Nothing happened."

"You said that already."

"Yeah." My fists bunch the comforter. "For a minute I couldn't breathe. For a minute I didn't think I'd get away."

"That doesn't sound like nothing." Her voice is soft.

I grab a tissue. "I don't even know why I'm crying."

"Who was it?"

"Dave Reilly," I say. "He shoved me up against this wall and—" All over again, his face closes in, his hands push, the wall's too hard against my back, and—I dig the heels of my hands into my eyes. It needs to stop.

She pulls my hands away gently. "I'm sorry," she says. "I'm so sorry."

"Ugh. I hate that I feel this way because of *him*."

"I know. Nobody should get to make someone else feel like this." She reddens. But not out of shame or embarrassment. It's anger. She rearranges a bracelet on her arm before looking back at me. "Jamison raped me. And I will never, ever, forgive him."

I take her hand, hold it for a minute, while her breath— our breath—steadies.

Something shifts in me. Like she walked right across all that jagged glass and opened a door I didn't know I had.

FOURTEEN

MONDAY MORNING, I WAKE TO a phone filled with unread texts—from Liv, the girls, Grove. I don't have words for any of them, so I say nothing. I wear long sleeves.

At least it's raining. Shitty weather for a shitty day.

In the summer, when I was a kid, the first thing we'd do after we came home from the beach was turn our bags inside out, shake the sand loose, and hose the bags off in the backyard before letting them bake in the sun. I want to turn myself inside out, let the rain scrub away that night, and dry for days.

But no matter how many times I've tried to throw up, no matter how inside out I feel, I can't get it out. I can't claw him out of there.

I text Liv I'll meet her at school and head to the bus stop for the first time since last year.

There are two girls and a few boys at the stop. I put my hood up to keep the rain off, praying nobody will talk to me. One girl holds a textbook over her head. This lifts her shirt, and two of the three boys at the bus stop stare.

She's just trying to stay dry while we wait for the stupid bus.

When I get to school, I notice more. The way guys look at girls as they walk by. The way they let their gaze land wherever they want. The way they don't even bother to hide it. The way they get away with it.

And I wonder *how many girls?*

In AP US History, Mac calls me Salamander. And his voice turns into Reilly's and I run out of the room to throw up. But I can't.

Later, I'm so distracted I take a different way to Math and at the end of the hall, he's there. Reilly. His laugh is so big it blows through the hall and I can't breathe all over again. I run back the way I came, but I'm sweating and shivering and can't catch my breath and nothing looks the same.

This doesn't even feel like my school anymore.

That night we play East Ridge. Grove sits in the stands next to Jake, even though it's raining, announcing a level of commitment that makes me want to scream. Liv elbows me when he looks at me, but I don't have the words to explain it. Grove's face moves from hopeful to hurt, and Liv's from confused to worried, and I just want out.

This time, they scream "Believe!" when we clash sticks. But I don't shout it with them. I don't know what I believe anymore.

The whistle blows, and I know straight off that it's not right.

That I'm not right. Ava's directing, but I can't see the game the way she can, and I can't find my voice in time. My legs are weak. My stick feels heavy and wrong. I'm all fumbles. My cleats catch in the turf twice. In the second half, I trip over my own stick. Like a seventh grader. Just like on Friday night, my own body is a traitor.

We lose: 1 to 3.

After the game, we trudge out together in silence. We splinter off toward our cars, and I'm left trailing Liv and her parents, my ride home.

Then there's Grove, expecting something.

I feel like I'm standing in the ocean, getting beaten by the surf. Everyone knows the only way through is to let go, to let the waves take you. But the last thing I want is to get taken.

I walk faster and step hard in the middle of a puddle. Perfect.

"Hey, Alamandar!" His voice snakes down my throat, finds the glass.

I hurry to put in my earbuds, hoping he gets the hint.

"Zoe?" He grabs my arm, the earbuds fall out.

Heat and pain rush to my arm. I yank it back, glaring at him. "What?"

His head snaps like I hit him. "Whoa." He holds his hands up. "I get that you had a bad game, but you don't need—"

"How would you know anything about what I need?" I dig my nails into my palms. My fists are right there. Ready.

Grove shakes his head like he's clearing it, like it's that easy to change things, to go back in time. "Look. I'm sorry if I

93

screwed up somehow. Last I knew, we were having a great night and then you just . . . disappeared."

And I'm right back in the Before. How amazing it felt to be kissing him beneath the stars on my favorite lake in the world. It was one of the best nights until—and Reilly's arm is at my throat. I cough. I can't stop coughing.

"Are you okay?" His arm reaches around my back.

I jerk my shoulders away. "Don't."

His eyebrows scrunch up. "I don't get you at all." His voice finds an edge. "You're acting crazy. I just—"

I step back, the tears pricking at my eyes. "Crazy." The word burns. "Well, you better save yourself and run along." I fumble to put my earbuds back in.

"Fine. But for what it's worth"—his voice rumbles low—"I liked the girl I hung out with on Friday. This girl"—he gestures toward me—"isn't her." And he walks away. Like it's the easiest thing in the world.

He keeps walking while the rain beats down. He doesn't look back. Somehow I still got battered by the surf.

I fantasize about sneaking up on Dave Reilly and punching him until he falls down, and I'll kick and kick and kick his stomach until he's curled into a ball of tears and blood.

But I say nothing. I do nothing. My bruises turn green at the edges, then purple like rotting fruit. I press my thumb into his thumbprint to see just how small I am. I press my thumb into my thigh, but I can never make a print like his.

In the halls, I turn. Run. Hide.

Grove stops trying to catch my eye. Sometimes I catch myself glancing his way during AP US History, out of habit. Liv asks me a dozen times what happened between us, but even she gives up. And I don't answer.

I can't answer. Because I'm not even sure myself.

My night with him got tangled up with what happened with Reilly, and I can't look at Grove without seeing Reilly's face, feeling his hands. I feel so pathetic and small it hurts.

I find myself watching Nikki. Wondering how she gets up in the morning. How she gets dressed. How she looks in the mirror. How she talks to anyone. Because if I feel like this and Reilly didn't even do anything, I can't imagine how she must feel. I have a raging hatred for Jamison. My fists clench when I pass him. I imagine slamming him against the locker, jamming my stick against his neck until he chokes.

But I don't do anything.

I just walk on, my head down, my hood up, my fists clenched, my nails marking my palms like scales on a snake.

A week ago we played Tuscaroga on their turf and won. I didn't allow myself to get distracted by the fight between Kups and Dylan, the epic fail with the dean, or even my dad and the fact that he can't seem to get better no matter how hard he tries. I pushed all of it out of my mind to win. But that was a week ago.

It only takes a week for the world to turn upside down.

Coach pulls me and Ava aside. "Sometimes when you lose a game, it's hard to remember the wins. And that's when you can slip into a losing streak. It's your job as captains to rally everyone and keep them focused. In AA, we say, 'Think of the solution, not the problem.' The solution is clear: We win. Got it?"

I glance at Ava. She nods like she means it. I say, "I'll try, Coach."

"Good," she says. "I'm counting on you."

When we walk beneath the purple-and-gold banners, I try to pretend they're our blue-and-green ones. I try to see the ball hitting the back of the goal again and again. In my head, I skate and push and drive and tap the ball the way I always do. I try—I try so hard to see my body working. But I'm faking it, and I'm pretty sure everyone knows it.

I run onto the field, and Eileen and Uncle Bob sit in the stands with their stupid camera.

It's wild how the world can stay exactly the same just when you've changed the most. Everything else is frozen like my dad's busted watch, stuck on 10:17, while I'm spinning so hot and fast I can't land on a time.

The whistle blows, and all I see is purple and gold where I want to see blue and green. I've got too much energy in all the wrong places, a fockey flake, a flyaway girl who can't commit to the ball. The other girls hesitate and pull back, like they've forgotten how to attack. Coach kicks over the sideline bench.

We lose. Again.

FIFTEEN

AVA SENDS YET ANOTHER TEXT about parkour. One more reminder of how I suck at everything.

Like this Pre-Calc. Before, I would've just texted Quinn. She'd tell me a story of fockey-playing koala bears and somehow she'd make this stupid equation melt into something that makes sense.

But nothing makes sense anymore.

Mom knocks on my door. "How was the game?"

I don't bother to look up from my Pre-Calc. "Sucked."

I feel her footsteps, feel her hand reach out before it settles on my shoulder, but I still flinch when it lands. She doesn't take it away. "You getting worried about the scholarship?"

It takes everything in me not to scream. Because that's just one more thing to add to the long list of things I can't do and won't have: math, friends, field hockey, and now college. I've let Coach down. I've let the team down. I've let my parents down. I'll start bottling them all up deep inside—the screams and the dreams.

"I really have to focus on this, Mom."

I count the seconds until she finally walks away.

Coach kills us in practice. We run and run until I can't feel my feet. Too bad she can't numb everything else too. But I feel it all, including the burn of her disappointment. She thought I'd be a better captain than I am. She thought this year would be different.

Me too, Coach.

Friday, another game. The sky is gray and flat, like nothing exists beyond the windows. In Mac's class, Grove glares at me, takes in my button-down blouse, and I want to hide. I wish we didn't have to dress up for away games. I wish I could walk around in my comforter all day long every day and have no eyes on me ever.

"Good luck on your game," Grove says, and I can't tell if he's being sarcastic, and it occurs to me that I *am* walking around in a comforter, muffling everything and everyone, including me. I draw my invisible comforter closer and walk past him, past everyone, through the day, through the motions.

During last period, the sky darkens, and the wind twists the trees. We leave school as soon as the other buses clear the parking lot, right as the rain cuts open the sky and pounds the roof of our bus.

There's nothing peaceful about hard rain on a bus roof. It's all anger. All force. We drive south in the onslaught, to the Sparta Free Academy Tournament.

We're playing two games—one tonight against Endsburg,

and another on Saturday. The whole thing is supposed to raise money for cancer and be fun, but it does count toward our league record, which, thanks to me, is going to shit.

I hate playing in the rain. I hate driving home all wet.

But not tonight. I'll throw off my comforter for this.

The second we run onto the field, the rain soaks us. It washes us clean, focuses us or something. I only know, even as my socks squelch in my cleats, that we've got this.

Except we don't.

For every pass we make, they steal it. For every goal we get, they match it. And here's the thing: We do everything right.

But it's just not enough. Endsburg wins: 2 to 3.

On Saturday, the sun burns the trees gold and red on the long drive to Sparta. Last night, while Endsburg beat us, Sparta won their game 4 to 0. And now we have to play them, on their turf.

We all have our earbuds in, listening to our own versions of war music. I listen to Motown. Before Dad's accident, we had Motown Mondays, where we danced all out while Mom cooked dinner. Dad spun me in the air, and I remember that lag of my stomach trying to catch up to the spin, the weightlessness as my feet left the ground. Motown is like this warm jumble of home and a wild-safe freedom.

But even Motown can't cut it today. I song surf until, finally, I just turn it off and listen to the whir of the wheels, the hum of the road.

In the locker room, Coach rallies us. "Yesterday you did so

much right. But games aren't won on technicalities. They're won with heart."

If that's true, I'm screwed. Because I'm not sure where my heart went, or if I even want it back.

On the field, Sasha gets me the ball. But within seconds, Sparta swarms in, their red socks and kilts blocking the green of the field. I need to whack the ball but there's no room to drive, no space to push, no air to breathe. My stick swerves back and forth, but they dig into my moves. My shins feel battered even beneath the shin guards. Finally, they steal the ball.

I race after them.

Kiara rushes in and sticks slam against one another, and the ref should call hacking but she doesn't, and the ball barely moves. Then somehow it's free, rolling toward our goal, and Nikki lunges to push it away.

But it doesn't travel far. Sparta is there. Again.

They hammer our goal while Ava collapses to her knees over and over. We try everything, but the game is played in Ava's lap and while she saves many, two get through. At halftime, it's 2 to 0 and we trudge back to the locker room, my legs and arms beaten.

It's a fact: They're just better than us. And they drive, push, and score this fact into the next half. We lose: 4 to 0.

We do the right things, and it never matters.

After the game, Coach pulls me aside while everyone's boarding the bus. She's probably going to tell me no captain has ever been worse than me. She'd be right.

"How's your dad doing these days?"

100

It's so unexpected, I shrug.

"I thought so." She sighs. "Zoe, you shoulder a lot. Probably more than what's fair. So many of you do." She looks at the girls boarding the bus and so do I. She's right. Dylan's foster home sucks. Ava barely survived her parents' messy divorce. Nikki's forced to see her rapist every day. Nothing about any of it is fair.

Coach sighs. "I wish everything were as fair as field hockey."

"That's pretty much my main complaint with life."

She smiles. "Me too."

"Wouldn't it be great if referees were just everywhere?"

"Yes! I always say that." She leans in. "But only the good ones. Nothing worse than a bad ref." She smiles at me. "But just because field hockey doesn't push into the rest of your life the way you'd like doesn't mean you have to let the rest of your life push into it."

I look at her. "You mean, focus on the game."

"I mean," she says, nodding back to the field, "out there is the one place you don't have to worry about school or your dad. You get to just play fockey. So draw some boundaries. Enjoy it. You know, one player doesn't make a team, but one player can have a tremendous impact. And you do. When you're down, everyone's down."

"I'm sorr—"

She shakes her head. "Don't misunderstand. I'm not blaming you. Look. I think I might have put too much on you and Ava. School is hard. Life is hard. If anyone gets life spinning out of control, it's me. I'm just saying you have power here.

101

You have power on that field. You have power with this team. Don't be afraid to use it."

On the bus, everyone's quiet, wrapped in their sad playlists, while I replay Coach's words. I don't know if it's that easy to just wipe it all clean when I hit the field. I don't know how to find my way back.

Ava sends out a team text.

AVA: Team adventure. Attendance mandatory. Surprise destination. Text ur rides. I'll bring u home when I'm done with u.

I tuck my phone into my pocket while it buzzes away, the team talking without me. I close my eyes. I'm too tired to even come up with an excuse. Whatever. I can handle Tully's.

Please be Tully's.

SIXTEEN

IT'S BEEN A LONG TIME since we were all together, rolling into one another in Ava's van. At least, it's been a long time for me. This time, I'm in the back, not riding shotgun. This time, though we're still a tangle of legs and feet, I can tell us apart.

I've never felt so apart.

Liv rolls into me. "I've missed you, Zozo."

"I've missed you too," I say. Automatic.

"So why've you been avoiding us, Cap?" Quinn leans into me from the other side.

"I haven't." I force a smile. A laugh.

"You are totally avoiding us," Ava calls from the driver's seat.

"No, I'm not," I say.

"Yes. You are." Liv's voice is quiet and when I look at her, her face is a tumble of hurt and sad and confused, and I've never seen her look at me this way.

"I was sick and then I had all this work and I—" I don't mean to lie. But these are the words coming out of my mouth.

Quinn throws her arm around me, pulling me toward her, and for a second I feel like I'm choking, and my arms flex, ready to break free, but then her arm relaxes and she rests her head on my shoulder. Her soft braid falls against my neck, her fruity shampoo fills my nose. The rumble of the van hums beneath me. "Whatever's wrong, we handle it better together, okay?"

I want to believe that. Liv squeezes my hand and Kiara knocks my foot with hers from across the van. Maybe Coach was right and I can draw boundaries. Maybe for one day, I can pretend we're back in the Before. Maybe, for today, I can pretend that this bunch of girls can rewind time and I can exist as the old me. Just for today.

Even from the back of the van, I can tell when Ava exits the highway, the Syracuse buildings thick and tall against the gray sky. Here, late September hasn't touched the trees. There's just gray—gray cinder blocks, gray concrete, gray clouds, gray sky. No city does gray better than Syracuse.

Being in Syracuse means we're definitely not playing fockey. We're not going bowling. We're not going to the mall. And we're definitely not ordering a plate of Tully's chicken tenders. Which I guess is good for my bank account because goodness knows I fell off the scholarship-bound truck about three miles back, but I really wish it was something other than this. Because it looks like Ava's graduating our parkour from playgrounds to the city. Here, it's easy to find shells of buildings, empty warehouses, abandoned alleys. I'm sure she's imagining us leaping over rooftops and scaling walls like they do online—like I did, before I actually tried parkour and couldn't get my feet off the ground. By the end of the day, the rest of the team will be flying while I'm stuck on the concrete.

Under the elevated highway, we pull into a parking lot, its blacktop pocked with holes and webbed with cracks. Standing over it is a warehouse: hollow, forgotten. This is definitely not the playground back home.

"Come on!" Quinn says, tugging open the van's door.

"Um." Michaela flattens the bottom of her bright pink Black Girl Magic T-shirt. "Are we sure about this place?"

No. There's no way to be sure about a place without a roof.

"Yes," Ava calls, no hesitation.

I'm the last out. I look up into the building and can see through the windows of the second and third stories—some with glass, some just holes—straight through to the sky beyond. An arrow of birds flies above.

Ava walks up to the door and rams her shoulder into it, shoving it open.

"What if there are people living inside?" Sasha whispers.

Ava shrugs. "I scouted it two days ago. It looked okay." She walks inside.

Sasha turns to me. "I don't like this."

"Me neither."

But everyone troops inside anyway. A late-afternoon breeze kicks a paper cup around the lot, and the little hairs on my arm wake up.

"Come on," Ava calls. "We don't have that many hours of daylight."

I sigh. And follow. As soon as I step inside, my foot slips on a pile of boards and I nearly fall. Once I steady myself and look around, I see it's just four brick walls straight up to a few lone rafters and the sky beyond. There's no roof, no stories, no inside walls. There's not even glass in most of the windows. The floor is littered with the remnants of its past—broken shingles, broken rafters, broken doors. It's just a placeholder of a building.

Ava hefts a door off the floor and leans it against a wall. A bit of red dust crumbles out of the brick. She sets up some small obstacles and exercises. We cycle through. Kiara does them one-handed, Quinn skips through them, and Cristina sings through her turn. Thankfully, none involve leaving the ground. So I'm fine. I go through the motions. I'm getting good at that.

Ava clears a patch on the ground. Then she has us leap off a crate into a parkour roll. My feet follow everyone else's, up the small crates, onto the big one. My feet walk to the edge.

Leap.

My legs give out from under me and crumple when I land. I hurt. The others move on to something else. I leap again. And again. Collapsing every time. Hurting. I collect scrapes and pain and it feels like getting all the answers right on a test.

Nikki pulls me aside so we're facing the crumbling wall. I can hear the girls behind me, laughing as they leap, getting better at making less noise when they land. "Stop it."

"What?"

"Hurting yourself on purpose."

"I'm not."

She levels her eyes at me. "You don't have to pretend with me, remember? You're stronger than this."

There's nothing strong about me. I'm not sure there ever was.

She leans in. "You built this team. The way Ava tells it, you were the one who had the idea to go out and recruit and train everyone."

I turn to look at Ava. She runs up a wall and backflips to the ground.

Our recruiting talks were a century ago. I look back at Nikki. "We were stupid not to pick you."

She bows. "I'm happy to be your dark horse." Her face gets serious again. "Come on, Zo. You push us hard because you know we can do it. So I'm going to do the same for you." Her words float between us, not landing. She sighs. "You're the voice in my head, you know."

I stare at her. *I'm* the voice in *her* head?

She looks away. "When I think I can't do something, I think of you."

A loud burst of laughter erupts from me. "That's nuts."

She shrugs. "It's true."

"I keep thinking that I don't know how *you* do it."

"One foot in front of the other and all that." She leans back against the brick. "Clearly, we're both focked."

I lean next to her. "Clearly."

We watch the others for a bit, leaping and jumping and rolling, and they look so strong, free. My eyes start to fill and I squeeze them shut for a second. Nikki bumps her shoulder into mine and I look up. Her hands push deep into her pockets. "You know there's nothing you did or didn't do to deserve this, right?"

I think of Liv's shirt and all the skin I bared. I think of the girl at the bus stop lifting her book above her head just to stay dry.

Maybe. Maybe she just handed me a broom for all that broken glass inside me.

I link my arm through Nikki's. We watch Ava and the others drag stuff to set up a strange kind of obstacle course: boards stretch across cinder blocks like balance beams, planks crisscross the corner supported by open windows, and a series of steps of blocks and crates and barrels end at another open window.

"I bet you'd like it if you gave it a chance," Nikki says.

"Parkour?"

"Yeah. It's ..." She takes a second like she's picking her words. "It honors the possibilities of a thing."

"What do you mean?"

"Like the guy who invented the staircase did it to get from one level to the next, right? But when you do parkour, you realize that there are a hundred ways to get from one level to the next. And a hundred more ways to use that staircase. It's ... freeing. Like art. It makes me see things differently, fresh."

"I could do with seeing things fresh right now."

"Exactly."

"Okay." I nod to the obstacles. "I'll try."

Quinn goes first. She smooths her strawberry braid and flicks her bangs. She takes it at a run, skipping over the blocks and planks, and does an aerial between two beams.

"She looks like Spider-Man," I whisper to Liv.

"Spider-*Woman*," Liv corrects.

We applaud when she finishes, and she does a few aerials to rejoin us.

"My turn." Ava grins. She takes off right away, making it a whole new course. Instead of leaping up the crossed planks, she uses her arms to swing herself up. When she reaches the top of one of the crates, she backs up, runs at the edge, kicks her leg out, and twist-flips down to the crate below. We cheer and holler. Cristina cartwheels across the boards and then tries to take the wall of the crate at a run but she only makes it half-way, so Ava reaches out and grabs her hand and pulls her up.

After they hop down, smiles wide, Bella goes. Instead of starting with the beams, she uses the wall and crates to climb to the second-story window. She's not elegant, exactly, but she's fast. She slips and falls to the crate below and struggles to heave herself up, all elbows and knees. Finally, she reaches the open window, and even though she's standing silhouetted against the late-afternoon sky, I can tell she's grinning. She lets out a howl and front flips onto the top crate, flipping from the higher to the lower blocks until she gets to the ground. We cheer and scream, and when she's finally standing, she's still smiling.

"Try to go fast," she says. "Don't think too much."

Liv goes next, fast and sure, leaping from one board to the next like she's a pebble skipping across the lake. Then Dylan. She's upside down when I expect her to be right-side up, she's flying when I expect her to climb. At school, she always seems so weighed down—her wallet chain low and thick against her thigh, but here she's different. She skips across the beams and lands light and quick on the planks. And she's laughing. Even when she falls. Even when she gets a long scrape on her shin. She's laughing the whole damned time.

And it hits me—the thing I've hated about parkour all this time. It's the opposite of field hockey with its rules, lines, and whistle-ready refs. Fockey is a firefly in a jar. The containment is what makes it so bright. But parkour. Parkour is setting the firefly free. It's conjuring a field of fireflies out of air. It's making magic in a hollowed, broken nothing of a building.

Dylan and Liv are laughing together, chugging water, their bodies coated in a film of grime and red dust from the bricks they scaled.

I look down at this body that's run miles, lifted weights, beat defenders, won games.

I jump to the first plank, wobble, sway, and fall.

"You got this, Capitán!" Cristina shouts.

"Be fierce!" Liv calls.

I hop back up and look ahead, forcing myself to trust my feet. I cartwheel onto the next beam. They cheer. I stand, looking at my feet, my solid, strong feet that have run thousands of miles, and wonder if maybe they want a break, a taste of air and weightlessness. I close my eyes for a breath and remember what it felt like to be little, when twisting and flipping in gymnastics class was as regular as running. When swinging in Dad's arms was just how we danced. I bend my knees, swing my arms down, and whoosh.

Backflip.

I land on both feet with a scream and a laugh and look back at Liv, whose hands are on her cheeks. She's screaming herself hoarse.

I flew.

I spin back to the beam and I flip over it again, and again. Because I can. And then I remember there's a whole playground of planks and crates and I sprint hard at the corner, using my hands and feet to bounce off the wall and I am flying I am flying I am flying.

I bound up the boxes to the windowsill and look out over this worn shell of a building and I think that it's never seen so much life and beauty as it has today.

Nikki was right. The architect who designed it and the poor guys who slogged here had no vision of all the possibilities waiting to be discovered between these walls.

Coach said it's about drawing boundaries. But maybe it's about erasing them.

I'm coated in dust, my knuckles are raw, the smell of dirt and metal's in my nose, and my cheeks hurt from smiling. I howl up at the sky, the setting sun warm on my back, the cars screaming past the roofless hole. And I think there's nothing better than howling at their wheels and the sky and this broken city from this broken building.

I feel like a secret. Strong. Invincible.

The whole world is infinite, open—ours.

SEVENTEEN

LATER THAT NIGHT, WE COME back together for a sleepover in the triplets' furnished basement—complete with seventies wallpaper, a wooden bar, cheesy nautical accents, and a giant wraparound blue velour couch. I arrive with two gallons of Big Bob's ice cream. Ava brings a ton of soda thanks to her employee discount at Jake's Beverages. Nikki hooks us up with pies from her uncle's place, Pecora's Pizza. Cristina brings Doritos and Cheetos Puffs, mostly for Ava. Michaela tries to health us up with carrots, but they stay as untouched as Sasha's vegan cheeseless pizza. And the triplets' mom makes Rice Krispies Treats the size of my head.

"I'm glad you're back." Ava throws her arm around me while she's putting the sodas in the fridge and I'm loading the ice cream into the freezer.

"Thanks for knowing what I needed today."

She nods at me. "I need *you*." Ava's eyes hold mine. "I can't captain out there by myself."

"Sorry, I—"

She shakes her head. "It's okay. Whatever it was, I'm just glad you're back."

I've missed her. I've missed this. "Absofockinglutely, Cap'n."

She grins. "Aye, aye, Cap'n."

When we get downstairs, there's a cheesy movie on TV and the others are talking about our game on Monday against Lymesburg. Liv scooches over on the big couch and I squeeze between her and Nikki.

"I say we don't focus on the last few games," Ava says. "Instead, let's—"

"—focus on States," I say, the words lifting my chin.

"Yaaaaas," and "Absofockinglutely," and "Sticks Chicks," they chorus.

"Can we still qualify?" Sasha asks, her face a nervous question. "I mean, given—"

"We can take one more loss. That's it." Ava is 100 percent business. And I feel the weight of all she's been carrying on her own since . . . Before.

"Okay, then." Kiara claps. "Then we win. Because my dad made it to States for basketball—but he didn't win. We're gonna win."

"Fock yeah." Dylan throws her arm across Kiara's shoulders. "I want to see your dad's face when we take it."

"He's still bitter about it too." Kiara shakes her head, smiling. "As if he would have been a better baller than a lawyer."

"What kind of lawyer is he?" Michaela asks.

"Social justice stuff mainly."

"He's saving the world," Dylan says, a proud note in her voice, "one case at a time."

"Yeah yeah," Kiara says. "But did he win States?"

"Nope!" we chorus.

"My dad—I don't even know." Michaela shakes her head. "The powers of speech might just leave him completely. But I'm not doing it for him." Her voice is quiet, sure.

"Why then? For college?"

"No," Michaela says.

Kiara grins. "That's because Harvard goes to sleep with her picture on their bedroom wall."

We laugh, and Michaela swats Kiara.

"Noooo. I want to prove to myself that I can win here too, outside of school. Plus"—she wiggles her eyebrows—"it would be so cool to be valedictorian *and* state champ."

We whistle and clap. Michaela's smile widens.

"At least you'll have another shot next year, but not us. Right, Nikki?" Cristina slaps Nikki's knee.

"Screw that," Ava says. "We *all* have to bring it this year. Cap'n and I have scholarships riding on this."

"Yeah." Bella sighs. "Let's put it this way: Scholarships would make college hella better for our parents."

"Triplets," Liv whispers. "That's like—"

"Don't do the math," Quinn says. "It ain't pretty." She preens. "But I am!"

Bella and Sasha yell, "We're prettier!"

They do this goofy dance to "Three Is a Magic Number."

It's so choreographed you know they've done it a thousand times, and we holler as they fall onto the couch.

When I finally slip into bed that night, I know that even though I'll be sore, we'll win Monday against Lymesburg.

And we do.

I ride the high of it all—the warehouse, the sleepover, the win. Of how it feels to have life grow beyond one awful night.

The rush fires my muscles at practice. I want it to push us to another victory on Friday.

The last time we played East Ridge, we lost. Their cleats kicked our three wins in a row to the ground. So the night before, I do everything right: I work out without overdoing it; I eat my pasta; I go to bed early. We can't afford another loss if we're going to make it to sectionals.

But in the first half, their orange socks are everywhere and my stick can't escape theirs. They intercept every pass. They're at every turn. They snatch the ball mid-dribble.

It's 1 to 0 at the half. We cannot let them take this from us.

At the start of the second, the sweat pools in my goggles, the stick slips in my hands. I grip it tighter. Quinn takes the ball. She passes to Sasha, but number 14 steals it. Number 14 runs past me, and I snap my stick out and grab the ball. I drive it down, but they intercept again. Kiara takes it back, passes to Bella, but they steal it. Again. It's back and forth, back and forth, no goal.

Finally, we tie it up: 1 to 1.

Neither side gives up, neither side gains. In the final minute, we get a corner shot. I look at Quinn. I crouch, my knees graze the turf. I nod at Sasha and she passes the ball right to me. I stop it fast and nudge it just as Quinn flies in from my left. She drives the ball hard into the corner—just out of reach of the goalie.

I've never screamed so loud in my life. The ref has to blow her whistle twice to get us back to the center.

We hold it for a few seconds before the final buzzer sounds. We win.

It's Friday and we slammed two teams into the ground and we won we won we won finally. So I say yes when the team asks me to go to the party at Declan's farm. We'll stick together, and I won't drink. What really sways me, though, is that I hear Reilly is in NYC for the weekend.

Bonfire smoke rises against the cold October night sky, and the smells from the farm are as sharp as the breeze. Our boots crunch across the hay and hardened mud as we make our way toward the groups gathered around the fire.

I'm maybe there thirty seconds before I spot Grove. He leans in to hear something Hannah Scarlotta says. Then he pulls back and laughs, and I imagine I hear the sound of it and see the dimple in his cheek and then I feel the choke of Reilly's arm against my throat and—

"Are you okay, Zo?" Liv's voice is soft, but it pulls me out. She rubs my back. "Come on."

I follow her away from the fire to the side of a barn. I focus on the ground, on my boots avoiding the divots. I wonder how many tractors they have. I wonder what Hannah said to make him laugh. We round the corner of the barn and I start to cry.

"Oh, Zo." She overturns some crates leaning against the side of the barn so we can sit next to each other. "What's going on?"

And the words tumble out because I can't keep them in anymore. I tell the whole thing from lying in the bottom of the canoe when the whole world was just stars and fireflies to being trapped against the wall by Reilly.

Then words that were caught beneath the broken glass get free, and I know why I waited so long to tell her. Why I didn't want to. But I push through and say them anyway.

"I was so weak, Liv. I can't tell you how—"

"Nothing"—she squeezes my hands—"nothing about you is weak."

The tears come fast, but she holds me. I don't know why I didn't tell her before.

"Is that why you ignored Grove?" Her voice is soft.

I nod.

"Oh, Zo. I get it, I really do. But you know he had nothing to do with it, right?"

"He was kind of an asshole after."

She shrugs gently, trying to catch my eye. "He probably thought *you* were an asshole."

I cry even more. "I'm fucked up, Liv. I think I'm really fucked up. I just can't look at him without thinking about what Reilly did."

She wraps her arm around my shoulders and squeezes me toward her. "You aren't fucked up, Zo. The world is, but not you."

"I can't even imagine how messed up I'd be if Reilly actually—" And I think of Nikki just walking through her days, doing trigonometry and French and push-ups with the rest of us. Though she's never been to a party with us. Not once. "It's just that . . . for a moment, there was this future, and in it I was raped."

"Oh, Zo. That's so scary."

"But he didn't."

"Just because he didn't finish the job doesn't mean he didn't start it, or that he didn't hurt you." The cold cuts right through my jacket, my sweater, my skin, finds my bones. She squeezes my hand. "I'm really glad that future didn't happen. I'm so glad you got away."

"Me too." I feel calmer, but tears still run hot tracks down my cold cheeks. I lean my head against the rough wood of the barn. "See? This is why I shall return to hiding from boys. It's much safer. All around."

"You are amazing, Zoe Alamandar. A goddess. And Reilly is . . ." She shakes her head, searching for the words. "Well, lumps of shit. Like he doesn't even have the decency to pull himself together into one lump." She weighs her hands in the air like a balance. "Lumps of shit." She lowers one hand. "Goddess." She lifts her other hand high in the air. "I know you don't feel goddess-like just now. But she's in you." She leans her head on my shoulder.

I tilt my head against hers and we stay there for a moment. The breeze whips against the barn but I feel sheltered there, with Liv. "Anywhere in the World?"

I feel her smile against my shoulder. "Right here, sister. You?"

"What's the exact opposite of here? Southern Hemisphere, city, on maybe a girls-only island. As long as you're with me."

She laughs. "Absofockinglutely."

Across the dirt drive, two figures stumble toward another barn, gripping each other and laughing. Liv follows my gaze. "Ah." She sighs. "Drunk love. The stuff of dreams."

I elbow her. "Speaking of . . . where's Jake tonight?"

She cocks her head back at the party. "Over there somewhere." She smiles at me. "You're more important."

I rest my head against her shoulder. "Thanks, Livvy. Thanks for knowing I'm all kinds of fucked but loving me anyway."

"I do love you anyway."

"I love you anyway too."

We pick our way across the field back to the party. I don't see Grove, though I see Hannah talking to Cynthia Wilson. I'm not proud of the relief I feel, but it's there all the same.

We link up with the girls. "See?" Ava throws her arm around my shoulder. "I knew we'd get our season back." She leans her head against mine. "Sticks Chicks forever."

I smile. "Sticks Chicks forever."

"Fock yeah," Dylan says, and Kiara winks at me.

I clap my hands. "Okay. I've been out of it. Give me some gossip."

"Yes." Liv tightens her arm around me. "She needs some serious distracting."

"Dyl's debating whether to hook up with Callie Bircham." Kiara shoulder bumps her.

"Thanks, Ki," Dylan says sarcastically. "I like her but she always wants to talk."

Kiara laughs. "That's called a relationship, Dyl."

"Ugh," Dylan says. "Who wants that?"

We laugh.

"This isn't *The Dylan Gossip Hour*," Dylan says. "Pick a new target."

Cristina leans in. "I did see Breanna Culbert slink off with Jeremy Halker."

"Ew. Jeremy Halker?" Bella says. "Bre can do way better than him."

"Well, she was wasted," Cristina says. "Those beer goggles might be thick."

And right there. There's this sinking inside me, where somehow my throat and stomach and feet all tangle together.

"Do you think," I start, "it would be weird to check on them? To make sure—"

Cristina makes a face. "Awkward much?"

"I'd rather be embarrassed than raped," Liv says. And we all just look at one another. Because it's true.

We go where Liv and I saw the drunk couple earlier. As we move away from the party, we hear new noises. Noises that sound an awful lot like sex. Or almost sex.

Half of me wants to run back to the party. It's going to be mad awful if they're getting into it and we stumble in.

We hesitate at the edge of the barn, maybe to come up with some plan, or excuse, or to put off what we might see inside. But Dylan throws the doors open, laughing big, as though we're in the middle of some loud joke, and then puts her hands on her mouth when she sees them in the hay. "Oh!" Dylan acts all surprised.

I half smile at her, but then look at them. Jeremy's belt is unbuckled, and Bre's beneath him. She's super out of it. Her long hair's a mess, knotted with hay. Her arms cross her chest. Her jeans are still done up.

"Were you"—my voice shakes—"what were—"

"Rape," says Dylan. "You were trying to rape her, you piece of shit." She steps forward.

"What?!" His hands move fast to buckle his belt. "That's twisted. She wanted to."

Kiara nods at Bre. "It doesn't look like she wants anything right now."

"Except maybe a cup of coffee," Quinn says.

"I'm pretty damned sure she doesn't want your dick." Ava steps toward him. "I mean really, Jeremy. You have to get a girl wasted to have sex? I can't imagine the sex is very good like that. Unless"—she cocks her head—"you can't do it any other way?"

He snatches his jacket off the ground. "You're a bunch of fucking dykes."

"Because we don't want you?" Ava asks.

He backs away, head jerking with rage. "All you girls do is tease and then—"

"Wait." Kiara puts her finger to her chin. "I'm confused. Am I a dyke or a tease?"

He punches the door. "Fuck you." He runs off, stumbling in the uneven mud, and we laugh. So he runs faster. And we laugh harder.

He was scared of *us*.

"*That* felt good. Really good." Ava smiles.

"Homophobic dick. It would've been better if we'd kicked his ass."

"I don't know, Dylan," Cristina says. "He was drunk too."

"Honestly, I don't care." Liv looks right at me.

I crouch down next to Bre. "Are you okay?" I brush some hair off her forehead.

Her eyes are foggy, but she says something. I lean close. She lurches to her side. I jump away just in time to miss her vomit.

"Now *that* was worth sneaking out for." Dylan grins.

We lean down to lift Bre to her feet. She's going to be okay. She'll wake up tomorrow with a killer hangover and a bad hair day. But she won't have any bruises. There won't be a Before and an After.

We did that.

EIGHTEEN

SATURDAY, I WAKE UP FEELING like I'm back in that hollowed-out building, standing on the sill of the broken window, a breeze at my back. I wake up like the end of a fockey game when the ball smacks the wood at the back of the goal, like I can splinter anything with the right hit.

I skip downstairs as Mom's pulling out of the driveway on her way to work. I put on the pot of coffee, grab the cleaning bucket, and run back up to get started. I've got it down to a science: A basic clean every Saturday and I cycle through the nonessential stuff. Today's extras are the fridge and ceiling fans. I do every room top to bottom but Dad's, where he's still sleeping. Then I tackle the fridge, taking everything out, soaping it all top to bottom, and putting it all back. I make a shopping list for the week's dinners while sipping my coffee. By the time I'm done, I expect Dad to be awake. But he isn't.

I try to relax at the kitchen table, cradling my mug like I'm someone on a coffee commercial. But instead, I'm thinking about Dad up in his room.

This is the thing about Dad being sick that people don't

get: the worries. *Sick* isn't even the right word, but they haven't invented the right word. Right now, he's up there. Where I can't see him. Where anything could be happening. He might want something but not want to bother me. He might not be able to get out of bed. He might want distraction. Then again, he might just need sleep.

Or he might have fallen and knocked himself uncon-scious.

I try not to creak the stairs, and open his door softly.

"Zo?"

"Morning, Dad. Just checking you're okay." The room is dark. I open the shades.

He squints at me in the new light. "I could do with your help, honey."

I walk fast to his side. "Of course. What do you need?"

"I think today's a walker day."

"Got it." I turn to fetch it from the basement.

"Wait. Help me to the bathroom first? I have to pee like a—"

"Ew. Stop talking." I come back to the bed. Like always, I make my legs solid, engage my core, and lean over him. The workouts help with this too. "Put your arms around my neck." He does and I reach under his back to pull him to sit-ting. His breath is quick and shallow.

"My legs," he says. "Quick." I tug his ankles out from the covers and ease them to the ground while he puts a steadying hand on my shoulder. He takes a few long breaths.

"Okay?"

He nods. "Okay." I reach my hand under his shoulders around his back again but he shakes his head. "Give me a second." So I pull the chair by his bed around so the back faces him. He puts his hands on it. Takes a few more breaths.

Maybe he'll never get better. Maybe it'll only get worse.

He pushes into his hands and I help him stand, tucking myself under his arm so he can lean on me as we walk to the bathroom. I feel his muscles trying to work under his thin T-shirt.

Thanks to Mom's nurse know-how and Dad's construction friends, the bathroom is fully accessible with a walk-in shower and bars along the walls. But I don't leave until his breathing steadies and he tells me to go. Then I run down to the basement and bring up the walker, careful not to scuff the walls with the wheels.

When I get to his room, I do a quick swipe of the ceiling fan because I'm supposed to and can't focus on anything else until he calls for me.

When he does, I wheel the walker toward him.

He grabs on and walks slowly back to the bed. "Bob said you killed it this week. Lymesburg and East Ridge didn't have a prayer."

"I don't know about that." But I smile anyway. Because he needs distracting and so do I. So I arrange his pillows, tuck him back into bed, and pull up the chair.

"How are your 3D skills coming?" he asks.

"Oh Dad. You should've seen a lift I pulled. I faked left and lifted right and it was so quick the other player went sprawling in the other direction."

He laughs. "What about your jabs? You been practicing those?"

"I kind of forgot about that move for a while but I used it in the East Ridge game and it totally derailed their offense."

He smiles, crossing his arms over his belly. "That's my girl. I miss watching you play," he says.

"I miss that too."

"After your season, maybe we'll buy some turf for a corner in the basement. I'm sure I can get it at cost. I'll set up my chair down there and watch you play."

"I'd love that."

He wiggles his eyebrows. "You won't love it when I tell you everything you're doing wrong."

I laugh. "Truth." Except he's wrong. I'd love it. We find a USA versus Canada field hockey game and watch it together. We pause it to talk about spacing and speed, and I run and get my stick and practice a combination move one of the players does.

And everything is perfect. Except for Dad's pain and the fact that we're in his room instead of our backyard.

When it's time for another muscle relaxant and he dozes off, I leave quietly.

I text Ava.

ME: I need me some parkour. Stat.
AVA: 😆
AVA: It was only a matter of time.

The playground's draped in that dusk-blue light and even though everyone's wearing different clothes, we all look like we belong to the same team.

Ava passes around a Tupperware filled with puff pastries.

"What are they?" Dylan asks.

Ava clicks her tongue. "These, my deprived friend, are quesitos. Naturally, they are stuffed with cheese. Like everything should be."

Ava drags me onto the spinning merry-go-round while Dylan, Nikki, and Kiara sprint around us, laughs tumbling out of our sugarcoated lips. We're turning, turning, turning, our faces and limbs blurring together into a whirl of us. Cristina takes a spinning panoramic photo that will undoubtedly end up on the school's wall the way her photography always does. And I'll see it and remember we were here.

Then we play.

We stand on swings and march atop bars. We skip over railings and flip beneath bridges. We jump and leap and fly and use everything exactly the opposite of the way it was intended. With every leap, I erase a line drawn by the designers and thousands of unimaginative feet that followed the paths laid out for them.

Nikki's perched on the back of a bench, drinking water. I sit beside her.

Every muscle feels sore. But it's an alive kind of sore.

We sit, watching our team fly across the structures, their features blurred, their bodies fierce. And I want us to stay like this. Exactly like this.

I turn to Nikki. "You know how we told you about Declan's party last night? About that dick Jeremy Halker?"

She nods.

"What if"—I look back at the girls cheering as they leap— "what if we did more of that?"

"What do you mean?"

"What if we went around"—I take a breath—"saving girls?"

She tilts her head at me. "What, like superheroes?"

I shrug. "Kind of?" She raises an eyebrow, but I meet her gaze. "I hate what they did to you. To me."

"Me too."

"All the guys who think we're there for the grabbing. Who feel entitled to us."

"It's not all guys," she says quietly.

"No, I know. There are good ones. My dad. My uncle."

"Grove?"

I look at her. "Maybe?" I lean forward. "But there are a lot of assholes too."

"So what, between classes we'll just go all vigilante? Like, excuse me while I get my textbook from my locker and bash you with it?"

"Noooo." I look at the team, how the darkening sky cloaks us in a different kind of uniform. "Maybe we wear black. Do it at night. It'd be safer."

"So you want to play dress up?" She smirks. "Cristina and Quinn will love that."

"It's not about dressing up." I watch the girls flying and

falling and laughing and jumping, and it just feels bigger, or more important, than that. Or, like it could be important. "I want to not feel so powerless, to fight back."

"Oh." She picks a bit of nothing off her leggings. "That."

"What if we could do something about it? Like help other girls?"

"I went online, you know, after . . ."

"Yeah?"

"Yeah. It happens to a lot of girls."

"That's what I'm talking about."

She's quiet for a minute. "Okay."

"Okay," I say.

Liv and Ava join us, panting for air. "Are you two plotting something?"

I look at Nikki. She nods.

I turn back to Ava. "Yeah," I say. "Gather the team. I've got an idea."

NINETEEN

WE MEET, SHELTERED BY THE rope bridges and monkey bars, our hoodies wrapped tight against the October air. The merry-go-round squeaks in the breeze, a cat calls in the distance, a tree creaks in the woods. I stand on the end of the slide.

My mouth dries up, but I talk anyway. "I love the feeling we get when we play fockey or do parkour."

"Invincible."

"Powerful."

I sit on the edge of the slide. "What if it doesn't have to end?"

Ava sits up, the spinning circle squeaking to a stop. "What do you mean?"

When Ava and I first began to build the team, we started slowly—first by talking about our killer workouts. Then, bit by bit, we unfurled the idea. But this feels bigger than hockey.

"I've been noticing things," I start. "At school. Like how guys just feel like they have a right to us. To girls in general," I add quickly.

"What do you mean 'they have a right to us'?" Sasha says.

I don't know, I almost say. But I do know. I take a breath. "The way they're always talking to our boobs. The way their eyes just roam all over us like we're for sale or something."

Silence.

I rush on. "Yesterday I saw this guy just reach out and squeeze this girl's butt. Like it was his to grab."

"Gross."

Dylan stretches for one of the monkey bars. "She means they're the ones with all the power."

"Exactly," I say.

"What are you suggesting?" Michaela asks.

I feel like if I say it out loud, Michaela might say no and then everyone might say no. I shake out my hands. "I just know they shouldn't have power over us."

A motorcycle revs a few streets away. A small animal rustles in the brush nearby. The night sounds collect in the silence. Maybe I never should've said anything. Maybe we can pretend I never did.

"One night," Kiara says, "I was babysitting, and the dad drove me home." She pauses and a small shudder crosses her shoulders. "He put his hand on my thigh. And we were driving fast—too fast for me to jump out of the car—and his hand just kept traveling up and—" She shakes her head, her lips tight. Dylan crosses to sit beside her. Kiara is always sure, always fierce, but right now, she's more open than I've ever seen her. She looks up. "I was scared. Really scared." Dylan wraps her arm around her shoulder.

And that's all it takes. Like a trickle that widens into a

stream, one by one, the stories release. A forced kiss. A pro-
longed touch. A blowjob she didn't want to give. A string of
pressuring texts. Small moments that snowball into an everyday
fear—the onslaught of comments and calls, stares and gropes,
day after day after day. Unwanted, uninvited, unwelcome.

The cold air fills with the sounds of our stories.

That's how we're all crouched outside Billy Jackson's house an
hour later. Our hair is braided and tucked beneath our hoods.
Across our faces, we've tied pieces of cloth ripped free from
an old black T-shirt Sasha had in her car.

Billy lives at the edge of a development, fields stretching
beyond his house, waiting to be turned into cul-de-sacs and
trim lawns. Nearby sit the beginnings of a house. There are no
walls, just rows of wooden studs, and we can see from one side
of the house to the other.

Smoke curls against the bruised sky. Forty people or so are
clustered around a small firepit back in the field. They're far
enough away from the houses to escape the cop call.

"Are we ready?" Cristina asks in a loud whisper.

"Nice stage whisper." Liv shakes her head. "Do you want
them to hear you?"

Cristina shuffles closer to us. "My voice doesn't come with
volume control. Much like my beauty."

We muffle our laughter.

Ava leans toward me. "What do you think? Want to try to
get to the house?"

We run quickly, our bodies low—just like we're playing fockey, our feet fast while our sticks kiss the ground. It's like all along we were training for this.

Once inside the skeleton house, there are no walls to shelter us, and our shoes are loud on the floor, but nobody from the party seems to notice. I creep toward the unfinished stairs and climb to the second floor. Above, the rafters slice the sky, and my arms itch to swing from them. Instead, we cluster near the opening to what will likely be a two-story living room below. We can still see the party outside, people gathered in the firelight.

I sit between Nikki and Liv.

We stay still for a long time, listening to noises from the party. My butt starts to feel sore. The whole thing feels seriously anticlimactic. A few hours ago, we were parkour gods leaping free. Now we're huddled in a half house, still, silent, and bored as hell.

"At what point," Michaela asks, "is this called stalking instead of saving?"

We all look at one another. It does feel like a bit of a bust.

"I don't know. It's not like I *want* something to happen," I whisper.

"We need a bat signal," Quinn says.

Dylan shakes her head. "I'm sure wherever we go there will be dicks being dicks. It's not like there's a shortage of assholes at our school."

We laugh a quiet kind of laugh. Because of course that's how we all ended up here in the first place. But maybe this is the one party without a dick quotient.

That's when I hear the giggle. I hear a deeper voice, and Nikki goes rigid next to me. I look at her. *Brett*, she mouths at me. Sure enough, as I peer down, I see Brett Jamison leading some giggling girl up into the house. She's got to be a freshman.

We're frozen. Their steps are loud on the flooring below. She's laughing and he's clomping. She twirls into the open space below us. He puts his arms on either side of her as they lean against an almost-wall, but then she laughs and slips through the studs to the other side. He catches her again, and this time she slips beneath his arms. On the third time, they kiss.

This is an awkward I didn't anticipate. I definitely do not want to be sitting up here spying on sex. If Liv and I were playing Anywhere in the World, I would literally say: *anywhere else*. Liv and I widen our eyebrows at each other and I know she's thinking exactly the same thing: We're trapped.

I'm going to have to sit here, afraid to move on this loud floor, listening to sappy sexy times between a giddy freshman and shithead Brett Jamison.

That's when I remember Nikki.

TWENTY

I PUT MY ARM ON Nikki's shoulder, and she starts shaking. I pull her closer, as though I can hold her together. But it's a lie. I can barely hold myself together, let alone someone else, and it's my fault that we're here, and she's having to see this and—

"Brett!" The girl's voice isn't playful like before. "Please," she says. "Please." There's rustling. He's saying things, but I can't hear him and I can't see him. And then loudly the girl says, "No."

I look at the others.

We hang off the edge and use the ceiling joists to flip down to the first story. We race toward the other side of the stairs, toward Jamison, toward the girl.

We don't say a word, but the house announces us.

"What the—" Jamison spins around, his pants falling to his ankles.

The girl looks at us for a second, clutching her shirt across her chest. She snatches her sweater off the ground and runs.

We surround him. Here, we're shielded from the party. Here, it's just him against all of us. Eyes wild, he crouches to pull up his pants, and Nikki springs, planting her foot in his bent back. He tumbles beneath the open staircase.

I jump up, grab on to one of the staircase treads, and swing into him. He stumbles. Dylan body checks him from the other side and he crumples to the ground.

Jamison groans and rolls onto his back. Nikki moves to kick him, but Ava grabs her arm. The girl is safe. We're done. Soundlessly, we leap from the house, our feet pounding on the pavement, our breath ragged against the cold night.

On Monday, I'm full of secrets like Clark Kent, but so much more badass. He was so tortured by his secret. But it's not a torment. It's a gift. I float from class to class.

Two girls that walk these halls are better off because of us, because of me.

I look at other girls in the halls, wondering how they spent their weekends. I wish I could give all of them this same feeling. This firecrackers-lit-filled-to-burst-don't-mess-with-me feeling.

I tell Nikki I wish Reilly had been in the half house too. All of us raining terror on *him*.

She smiles a not-all-the-way-there smile. "It was great—to help that girl, I mean. But . . ."

"But what?"

She shakes her head. "I don't know. It's just big I guess."

I nod. Exactly.

Tuesday, I'm running late to third period. Usually I walk with Liv to the science wing but I've missed her because my stupid locker was jammed, and the way I usually take is blocked off because someone spilled chocolate milk all over the hall. I detour through the English halls, walking fast because Mr. Ross likes to lock you out if you don't get there before the bell. I round the corner to run down the stairs.

And I can't.

Can't run. Can't turn. Can't move.

Right there, taking his time like he owns it, walking up the steps like he owns them, walking toward me like he—is Reilly. He's turned to someone behind him, laughing his big, wheezy laugh.

Everything warps. Like walking into a house that was mine, to rearranged furniture, too-bright lights, and doors leading to wrong places.

Someone bumps me from behind on my shoulder.

Grove. He gives me this ugly look, like I shouldn't be standing breathing living here.

And I run. I run back down past the English classrooms, down the stairs to the first floor and into the girls' bathroom just as the bell rings.

I put my hands on the cold tile wall. Press my feet into the floor. Lean against the door.

I am not Superman. I am not Clark Kent. I am not anyone.

At practice, I drive myself hard. We've got a game against Danver Springs tomorrow and I plan to kill it. With every smack of the ball, I picture Reilly's face. By the time Liv drops me off at home, I'm exhausted.

"Hello?" I let myself in the front door. Marvin Gaye answers *"How sweet it is"* from the kitchen, while Dad's voice reaches for the high notes. Yes. Motown is exactly what I need.

". . . I wanna stop and thank you, baby . . ."

I sing down the hall toward him, *"How sweet it—"*

But the song dries up in my mouth the second I enter the kitchen. Mess covers the counters: bowls, spices, stirring spoons, bits of chopped vegetables. But it's not the mess that stops me. It's Dad. He must have been prepping this for a long time, which means at least an hour on his feet, which will not end well.

But he's smiling as he spins toward me, his apron splattered with goodness knows what. He pulls me toward him, dancing and singing.

It's obvious how much it's hurting him.

". . . I wanna stop . . ."

I shuffle him over to the kitchen chair. "'Stop' is right, Dad. You need to chill."

He smiles as he sinks into the chair, a little breathless. "Nobody's chiller than Marvin."

I smile, turning Marvin down. "Truth. But the last thing you need is a relapse." I eye his busted watch. The last thing any of us needs is to go backward.

I see the realization of it cross his face.

"You due for some meds?"

"Nah. I'll wait until dinner. Better with food anyway."

Which, of course, I know. But I want to remind him how long he has to wait. "Speaking of food . . ." I nod to the mess. "What's the plan?"

"I just wanted to make dinner. Mom's been working so hard—"

That's when I see the flowers on the table. The wine. "Wait. You went shopping too?"

"Well, yeah. Mom's working late. I had to—"

"Dad! I would've done this for you. I was coming home to cook for you guys."

He waves his hand. "I knew practice was late tonight, so I figured you might grab something with Liv."

"I'd never—I wouldn't—"

He laughs. "Oh, honey. I just wanted to do something nice is all. And this time, doing something nice for Mom also got you off the hook for cooking. So win-win, right?"

"Win-win." But none of us will win if Dad relapses.

I make my way to the stove and finish sautéing the vegetables while Dad drums the table and hums, the meat loaf already in the oven.

After I finish the dishes, I see a missed FaceTime from Nikki. I head up to my room and call back. She answers right away, her hair splayed against a pile of ocean-blue pillows.

"You going to sleep? We can talk tomorrow." I shut my bedroom door behind me.

She shakes her head. She bites her bottom lip and I take in her blotchy face, her red-rimmed eyes.

"What's wrong?"

She shakes her head. I wait.

"I just get so sick of it, you know?"

"Of what?" I whisper.

She sighs big and looks up at her ceiling, sinking farther into her pillows. She pulls a blanket up to her shoulders. "Of seeing Jamison. Zo, I see him everywhere. Everywhere. I go to lunch, there he is. I go to my locker, there he is. I go to Math. There. He. Is."

"Nik, I'm so sorry." I spiraled when I saw Reilly. But we're not in the same classes, the same grade. I can't imagine being forced to sit through a whole period with him right there.

She shakes her head. "Usually I can move through it but today . . ."

"What happened?"

Her face crinkles up and tears pool in her eyes. She blinks and a few escape down her cheeks. "Today he was in the art wing. That's *my* space. Mine. It's like the one place in that whole damned school that I can count on being him-free, you know?"

"Oh, Nik. That's so unfair. That whole place should be yours." I wish I could reach through the phone and hug her. "It's so wrong that this is your life."

She half laughs. "I know, right? Like why isn't this *his* life? Why isn't *he* afraid of *me*?"

"He was pretty afraid of you at Billy Jackson's when your feet sent him flying."

140

She sniffs. Then smiles. "That did feel pretty good. But he's still around, you know?" She wriggles down deeper into her bed. "My portfolio teacher could tell I was in a mood, and painting wasn't going to cut it. She let me try working with wood today. Using a chisel and hammer felt pretty good too."

"You're doing wood carving now?"

She nods. "Yeah. Although I'm not sure I can call what I did today carving exactly. It was more hacking the shit out of a block of wood until it was a mess of splinters."

I laugh. "I think that'll make an excellent title. You'll probably sell it for a million dollars one day."

"Ahhh," she says. "The artist's ultimate revenge."

"You sound like my Aunt Jacks. She does wood carving too, actually."

I tell her about Aunt Jacks and the cool workshop she has behind her house. I'm glad that Nikki has a teacher who lets her switch things up when she needs it. And I'm glad she got to take her anger out on a hunk of wood. But none of that makes any of this okay.

Because Jamison should be scared of Nikki. *He* should be the one crying in the bathroom and running the other way. *He* should be the one scared to go to school. *He* should be the one hiding in the art room. They all should.

But instead, they strut the halls like they own them, while we cry into our pillows. It's not like the dean would ever take our side over theirs. She made that perfectly clear.

Maybe, though, after we're through with them, they'll be the ones crying into their pillows.

TWENTY-ONE

WEDNESDAY, WE PLAY DANVER SPRINGS. They've got a seventh grader playing varsity who's supposed to be some phenom. But their school is about half the size of ours. So I'm hoping their definition of *phenom* is wildly different from mine.

On the way there, Nikki teaches us a new cheer she wrote:

We're not cute.
We don't purr.
We shoot and score so hear us roar!
Say we're small?
Say we're weak?
We're made of mean and we ain't sweet.

We clap and scream "Love it!" and "Yaaaassss!" We chant it on the bus and chant it running out to the field.

Coach pulls me aside. "Zoe, your intensity has been incredible—in the last couple of games and during practices. Those jabs have been spot-on, and that V-drag you pulled last practice was pure elegance."

"Thanks, Coach." It's hard not to beam like an idiot when Coach compliments me. I'm glad everyone else is too busy getting ready to notice.

"That drawing-boundaries stuff worked, huh?"

She looks too happy for me and too pleased with herself for me to correct her. *No, Coach,* I want to say. *It turns out playing nighttime superhero and treating the world like my playground was the cure.* But instead, I say, "You were right. Thanks, Coach."

"That's my girl." She pats me on the back. "Now go show Danver Springs who we are."

"Yes, Coach."

We take our places. Ava crosses herself and hops twice when she enters the goal. I chop my feet. Liv closes her eyes and has her "meditative moment." We're ready.

They win the toss, so they get to start. Their seventh grader's small and quick.

But one girl doesn't make a team.

She's got moves and sometimes she spins around us like she's on wheels. But nobody else on her team can receive a pass. They ignore what's happening in the back. They hide. They give up the ball the second we near. Their whole game plan is her. I gotta give her credit. She's trying. So hard. She's calling and pointing and sprinting and pushing and driving and dribbling. She's controlling so much but not enough or maybe too much. She's good. But we've got eleven greats to their one.

We take it.

My celebration ends as soon as I get home.

Sure enough, Dad is laid up. Also predictable: Mom's working.

I wish being right felt better.

I'm furious at him for being so stupid last night. It's bad enough to see the pain in his face, but the worst part is I never know how long these relapses will last. An hour? A day? A week? A month? Even singing to Marvin isn't worth this.

Thursday, I come home straight after practice to check on Dad. But he must have had another rough day, because he's sleeping the deep sleep brought on by pain meds. When Mom comes home, carrying a bunch of groceries, I think at least she's going to cook dinner and help him. But when three wine bottles come out, I know I'm staring at a Rebels night.

Living with Mom is like the ref making the wrong call. Every time.

"We're celebrating. Jacks has her art opening this weekend. Remember?"

"Right," I say. I'm playing Sommersville Saturday, or I'd go too. "Good for her," I say because it's true. I love Aunt Jacks. But I don't wait around to hug her. I go upstairs, escaping the Rebels' entrance just in time. I creep into Dad's room to see if he needs anything. I don't understand how Mom can be downstairs getting drunk with her friends while Dad's suffering upstairs. I stand silent in the doorway, in the dark, waiting.

I don't want to get too close because I don't want to wake him, but I just need to make sure—and then he takes a big snore of a breath. And I can breathe better too.

I head back to my room and take out my homework. Like I'm supposed to. Like I do every night. But AP US History is filled with a bunch of old white guys and Hamlet's being a whiny emo brat who won't just hurry up and do what he's supposed to, and it's really hard to concentrate while Dad's sleeping away his pain and Mom's partying it up.

A couple of hours later, when I've finished all my homework, I head downstairs to see if there's pie. When I turn into the kitchen, I see the aunts in the living room, draping a blanket over Mom. She's passed out on the couch. Aunt Maya tucks the blanket in around her.

Aunt Ruth picks up a stack of plates and walks into the kitchen. "Hi, Zo," she says. She nods back toward the couch. "Your mom's had it, I'm afraid. She works so hard."

Yeah. So do I. As I look at the stack of plates, a scream rises inside me.

But then Maya gives me a kiss on my forehead and looks in my eyes. "We've got this, little one."

"I—" But Maya's already rolling up the sleeves of her blouse and Jacks is piling the food into containers and Ruth is walking me toward the stairs.

She hugs me. "Your mom's lucky she has you, Zoe." She releases me. "Don't forget you're lucky to have her too."

It's Friday night, and I'm so glad because I get to escape for a bit of parkour. Friday nights used to be us shivering on the stands, as spectators. We're not spectators anymore. Tomorrow we face Sommersville. But I know that after a night with the girls, we'll be ready. I'll be ready. We paint our cheeks with glow-in-the-dark stripes, blue on one side, green on the other. Tonight, we're all the same team.

But Dylan's missing.

At first, we think it's just Dylan being Dylan, always late. But when she doesn't show after an hour, we get worried.

"I hate her foster parents," Kiara says.

"You've met them?" Liv asks.

Kiara shakes her head. "No. Dylan always insists on meeting me somewhere else. I think she doesn't want them to know anything about her."

I can't imagine.

"There have to be so many good people who are foster parents. It's such shit luck that Dylan got them," Quinn says.

"That's sort of Dylan's life story," Kiara says.

Finally, Dylan arrives. "Hey," she says to Kiara, "can I crash at your house again?"

"Of course. You know my parents love you." Kiara tries to meet Dylan's eyes, but Dylan keeps them locked on the pavement. "They being assholes again?"

Dylan just shrugs. And I know that she needs parkour even more than I do.

We leap and swing, flip and climb. We rush and run, tumble and twist. It feels delicious, the night air against our skin, letting our bodies move where they want, how they want. The paint on our cheeks erases our features and we're strange black clouds rolling above the playground, making our own kind of thunder and rain.

When we've had enough, when our skin is bruised and our muscles are tired, we go. We walk together, heads high, as close and silent and fierce as a pack of wild wolves.

I get permission from Uncle Bob and bring everyone to Scoop Dreams. In all the time I've worked for him, I've never brought a bunch of friends after hours. We squeeze into the shack and Liv and I scoop—strawberry, s'mores, brownie, fudge swirl, and, of course, cookie dough.

"They should invent a cheese ice cream," Ava says, taking her cone from me.

I laugh. "The dairy is already covered by, you know, the ice cream. Usually the idea is to add something that isn't dairy."

Liv ducks under the counter and searches in the back of the cabinet. Finally, she pulls out a bag of Cool Ranch Doritos and hands it to Ava.

"Focking goddess!" Ava shouts.

"Where did that come from?" I ask.

"I put it there last time I worked. I forgot about it till just now."

"You are so weird," I say.

"You are so brilliant," Ava says. She rips open the bag and dips a chip in her cookie dough ice cream. "Ohhhhhhh. This is—" She takes another bite. "I just—ohhhhh."

We laugh. "Nice cheese-gasm."

She moans. "You do not know what you're missing."

I steal a Dorito and try it. It's kind of incredible. "Uncle Bob totally needs to invent a Doritos ice cream."

"Absofockinglutely!"

We eat and laugh and talk and gossip and it's fun. But somehow it's not enough anymore. I think of last weekend and feel . . . restless, itchy.

When we're finished with our cones, Quinn elbows Sasha. "You want to show them what you made?"

"Oh right! I forgot I put it in the trunk." Sasha runs outside.

"What is it?"

Bella grins. "Just wait."

Sasha hauls a giant shopping bag into the shack.

"I made us something. And"—Sasha looks at Dylan—"you're not allowed to make fun of it."

Dylan holds up her hands. But honestly, nobody can really make fun of Sasha. She's probably made of unicorns and stardust.

Sasha tosses black bits of fabric at us. I unfold mine and see that it's a kind of hood: light and airy. We all put ours on; they're cut and sewn so that the hood is loose and long in the back to cover our hair but fitted in the front so only our eyes peek out, like a better version of a ski mask. And since the fabric is thin, we can breathe just fine.

"You're a genius," Kiara says. Sasha blushes.

Thanks to Sasha, we have the perfect disguise for our midnight missions.

148

I feel so grateful for these girls and this thing we're doing—whatever it is.

"Well," Nikki says. "Are we just going to sit around and play dress up or are we going to put these things to the test?"

We all look at one another, and the inside of this ice cream shack has never felt so alive.

"There are always people in the Old Cemetery," Cristina says.

TWENTY-TWO

THE CEMETERY IS DRAPED IN shadows and we hush our voices as we near. The lights from the street don't reach far beyond the gates, but splashes of moonlight filter through the scattered trees to the graves below.

Quinn vaults onto a gravestone and stands on her hands. She turns around twice before bringing her feet down and backflips off the stone. Michaela hurdles a bench, followed by Ava, who balances on its back and then dives into a parkour roll. We roll, jump, leap, vault our way toward the back graves, the ones that dip down into the valley.

Buried beneath us are the old ways, but we fly free above them all.

Slowly, the sounds of a party overtake the sounds of the night. There are only fifteen or twenty people gathered among the overgrown graves. Two of us shinny up a tree. A few perch on a pedestal at the feet of a stone angel. I climb another tree, Liv at my heels. Even though she's masked, I'd know my best friend anywhere. Since our talk at Declan's party, we've never been closer. Twin strands in a tightly woven rope.

We find a crook in the branches, two hunt-ready hawks. We wait, like all good hunters do.

"So," whispers Liv, "I'm thinking about having sex with Jake."

I'm so shocked I almost fall out of the tree. I grip the bark, its edges pressing into my palms. "And you choose this moment to discuss it?"

She shrugs. "I was just thinking about it."

I force myself to go light. "You're thinking about sex with your boyfriend while we're in a cemetery? Liv, you've been seriously holding out on me."

She muffles her laugh with her hand. "No. I guess I've been thinking about it all the time. I just finally opened my mouth."

She's been thinking about it all the time but she's only just now telling me. Maybe we're not twin strands in a tightly woven rope. "Well," I say, "if you've been thinking about it so much, you're probably ready, right?" I look back at the party. "I mean, knowing you, if you say you're ready, then you are. Do you think you're ready?"

There's a pause, and I don't know what she's thinking beneath her mask. In the pause, I realize I don't want her to have sex. It feels like it'll put her on the road away from me. The road where she studies in Europe, not North Carolina, the road where she travels the world for real. Without me.

"I remember Cristina saying that she wanted it to be about everything else as long as possible before she and Mateo did it. That once you have sex, then it's all about sex. But I'm not sure it has to be like that."

151

I try to push down thoughts of Liv across an ocean and concentrate. Liv always knows what she wants, so the fact that she's debating it says a lot. And she's talking to me, which is a best-friend thing to do, even though I am the last person in the world she should be talking to about this. Just thinking about sex makes my stomach hurt.

I bury that too.

"I think it can be however you want," I say, because I want that to be true—and maybe it is true . . . for Liv.

"That's just not how everyone talks about it though, is it? That it's however we want?"

Light bits of laughter and deep voices drift to us from the party.

"I mean," she continues, "it always seems like a seesaw. Like one person's pushing harder than the other, one person's floundering in the air."

I remember us, me and Liv, opposite each other on the seesaw at Tyson Road Elementary. "But isn't flying the fun part?"

Liv turns to me, and while I can't see her face in the dark beneath her mask, I can feel her gaze. "You're different," she says.

The breeze picks up and I grip the branch tighter.

"I mean, yeah. We used to love that seesaw when we were little. Then, after . . ."

"After my dad's accident," I finish.

"Yeah."

"I got all rigid and anal and—"

"No, I wouldn't say that," she says.

We're quiet, the shadows gathering and moving over the graves and drinkers like ghosts.

"Well, Liv Liu," I say finally. "You are the most amazing person I know. I seriously won the best-friend lottery. And, as far as I can tell, Jake is one of the better guys. So, if anybody can rewrite the script, it's you guys."

I hear her exhale a deep breath. "Thanks, Zo."

I said it because it was the right thing to say. And Liv deserves all the right things. But I can't help but feel that I just opened a door that reads *Abandon Zoe This Way*, and she walked on through.

Liv gives a small laugh. "I'll take notes. You know, for when it's your turn."

"Um—"

Dark shadows dart below. A few of our teammates are racing across the grass, leaping over gravestones. The partygoers scatter.

The hunt has begun.

Liv and I swing down and fly after them. Two guys are standing around a girl, her wet white shirt clinging to her body. She's shaking, crying.

"They poured their beer on her?" Liv whispers. "Disgusting."

Two of my teammates slam into one of the guys. The girl runs away. But the other guy grabs for my teammates. I run at him like he's just another gravestone and pounce onto his back. He buckles, and I flip off him before he hits the ground. Another lunges for one of us—maybe Dylan. But she ducks out from under him and shoves, toppling him off-balance. Liv looks at me and, even with the mask, I can tell she's smiling. They didn't have a chance against us.

We leave our prey moaning on the ground, the gravestones etching long shadows across their faces. We sprint back through the graves, the cold, dark night keeping our secrets.

Girl number 3 saved. Us, 3. Them, 0.

Nobody expects us to win today. Northridge has never beaten Sommersville. They won our first game of the season. They're undefeated. And they *always* go to sectionals.

But our first game was a long time ago, in another lifetime. I was a different girl. Our team was a different team. We lost that game because of Kups. Now we're more than just a field hockey team. We're a team of parkour–flying, ass-kicking, girl champions. And when I think about *that* team going out to face Sommersville, well, I almost feel sorry for them.

Almost.

On the way, we make up new cheers.

We are the team.
We are the chicks.
We have the skills, can't beat our sticks.
You are the lost.
You are the beat.
You are the mud beneath our cleats.

When they run onto the field, the cockiness rolls off them like stink off the dump. But it doesn't ruffle me the way it did six weeks ago. Instead, I give them an eyes-narrowed, all-knowing kind of smile. They might as well be splashing in the backyard kiddie pool while we're flipping high dives at the Olympics. I look across the field at my teammates. They feel it too.

We hold more power than anyone told us we could.

When the whistle blows, we explode.

It's a dance, but Sommersville doesn't know the steps. Every time we steal the ball or pass it out of their reach, their swagger slips. We chisel bits of pride and grit off them, and by the half, the field is littered with shavings of their former selves. They yell at each other. They storm off the field. They may know what it is to win, but they have no idea what it is to be a team.

They may have been undefeated, but we're unbeatable.

We win: 4 to 1.

And I'm hungry for more.

We're in the locker room changing after the game and I cannot be looking at this empty Saturday.

I put my hands together and make puppy eyes, "Pretty please? Pretty please with sugar on top? Pretty please with Doritos and quesitos and Big Bob's ice cream and Rice Krispies Treats on top?"

They laugh.

Sasha shakes her head. "I am so beat, you guys. I just want to veg out and watch stupid rom-coms."

"Yesssss," Michaela says. "Between our weekends and my AP classes I haven't had just a night to relax, you know?"

"But it's a nice Saturday, and there's sure to be a party somewhere." I tie my sneakers. "Besides. Don't you guys feel good about what we're doing? We're *saving* girls."

Liv nods. "It does feel pretty great."

"There's one under the bridge." Cristina releases her hair from her ponytail.

"Oooh," Dylan says.

"See?" I say. "The bridge! It would be so fun!" After summer rains, people always bridge jump. Well, daring people do.

Cristina finger combs her curls. "I love that bridge. It's the best for taking photos—those curved iron arches, the rust-covered tracks. Just imagine doing parkour there."

"It *would* be sweet to fly across those arches," Bella says.

"I don't know." Michaela adjusts her headband. "We'd be really exposed. It wouldn't be the same as the other places."

"So?" Kiara says. "Let assholes see they can't get away with being assholes." She swats her with a sweatshirt. "Come on."

"Do you think we could get hurt though?" Ava asks. "Falling off an arch would break some bones."

"No way," I say. "Those arches are fat. There's plenty of room for us. All fun. No broken bones."

Liv gives me a funny look.

Michaela raises an eyebrow. "It *would* be fun."

Ava looks at me, a slow smile spreading. "You're really in this, huh Cap'n?"

I grin back. "Absofockinglutely."

The bridge is an arched iron cage, big enough to host a herd of wild animals. We creep along the abandoned railway tracks, and the music grows louder, bouncing between the bottom of the bridge and the river.

Tiki torches line the edge of the river, creating halos of light every few feet along the rocky riverbank, marking the line between the rocks and the river for the fifty or so people clustered beneath the bridge. I spot some yellow-and-blue varsity jackets—Queens Falls kids. Silver kegs catch the light.

The river rushes by black and wild.

We stroll down the tracks, the overgrown weeds brushing our legs as we aim our feet for the railroad ties. The music echoes off the bridge's underbelly, wrapping the partiers in a sound cloud, us above it all.

I take one of the steel arches at a run, my sneakers clinging to the bumpy iron. We swing across and between the diagonals and curves. The bridge keeps our secret. After all, the bridge was built to hold trains. A few girls don't make it creak. We're silent assassins. We perch in the joints, a gathering of crows.

No, a murder of crows. A group of crows is called a murder. Something powerful snakes through me.

We hear the guy's laughter first. A couple clambers up the embankment. The guy wears a Queens Falls jacket, and I don't recognize the girl.

"Just wait," he says. "You'll love it."

Wordless sounds from the girl.

"Come on." He tugs at her arm but she holds firm. "Babe, I swear."

If a guy ever calls me "Babe" in that whiny, entitled voice, I will punch his face.

"It'll be so fun," he says.

They step out onto the tracks. We hold our breath, waiting.

"Lie down," he says.

She shakes her head. "Jay, I'm telling you this freaks me out." She tugs at his arm. "Come on. Let's just go back to the party."

"Don't be such a wimp." He sits down right in the center of the track. "Trains don't even run here anymore."

She edges over and sits next to him.

"I promise you it's even better lying down." He lies down, his head in her lap, his body long between the rails of the track. He doesn't seem to notice us in the darkening night.

"Jay, I really—"

"Leah." He gets up on all fours. "Come on. It'll be hot."

He crawls over her so that she's lying down and he's on top of her. He kisses her neck.

"Jay. I don't like it here. Really."

"Come on. Just a little longer." He stops and then gives a holler. "Oh man, can you feel it, baby?"

She shakes her head. "Feel what?"

"The train!" he shouts. "The train's coming. This is going to be so hot."

She punches him in the chest. "Get up! Get up!"

He laughs and rolls out of the way, and she leaps to her feet.

"I was just messing with you, babe. You're so gullible."

They're both standing now.

He grabs her arms. "Come on." He's kissing her neck, saying things I can't hear.

"No!"

He steps back but he still grips her wrists. "Look what you did." He nods his head down to the tent in his sweats. "You can't expect me to go back to the party like this. Just take care of it for me."

He says please as he shoves her head down, down, down.

I look at the others.

We are bullets bursting on a bonfire.

TWENTY-THREE

WE SWING-JUMP-SOAR. WE RAIN HELL.

"What the—" He pushes Leah off him, and she races down the track.

I run straight at him, planting my foot right on his knee.

But he grabs my leg fast and slams me on the tracks. My knee twists and the back of my arm hits the rail. White-hot pain blooms in the center of my triceps.

Shit.

I'm flat on the ground, arm throbbing. He stomps toward me, his feet deliberate between the tracks.

He looms, tall and strong.

I refuse to let him win. Not tonight. Not ever.

I struggle against the pain to push up, to get clear.

Two of the others run up from behind, swinging a third into him, and he falls. I roll out of the way just in time.

He howls and stands up slowly, blood pouring from his nose. "Oh." He wipes his hand across his face and looks at it. "You guys picked the wrong guy to screw." He jabs at one of us, but she ducks fast and rams her shoulder into his stomach.

He throws a punch at my head, but I grab his arm and use it to push him toward the edge. The water rushes below, alight from the fire of the Tiki torches.

I hesitate for a second.

Then I let go of his arm just in time to ram my foot into his back.

He yells as he falls off the bridge and crashes into the water below.

We lean over to see him gasping to the surface and bellowing the second his head clears the water. "Those assholes jumped me!" he shouts. "Did you see that? They tried to kill me!"

We race across the bridge, leaping from one railroad tie to another, fast, strong, and deadly as a train.

Girl number 4 saved. Us, 4. Them, 0.

At school Monday, everyone's talking about the bridge party. A gang of guys came out of nowhere. They shoved Jason Stimple off the bridge. They were from Queens Falls/East Ridge/the City.

Jason Stimple, a kid I never even knew before Saturday night, becomes like a fucking god Monday morning.

There's even talk of calling the police.

We never hear Leah's side of the story.

Ava leans up against my locker after fourth period and I can see the irritation on her face.

"Can you believe this shit?" I say. "People are talking like we're the bad guys. Like we're the ones who need to be policed."

"Maybe we are." She says it to her shoes, and her voice is low and the halls are loud and I'm pretty sure I heard her wrong.

I must have heard her wrong.

"What?"

She turns to me. "He could've gotten hurt, Zo. Real hurt. Like hospital hurt."

I cannot believe these words are coming out of her mouth. "So?"

Her eyes widen. "So?" She shakes her head. "We're supposed to be helping people, not hurting them."

"I *was* helping. His girlfriend is fine because of us. Because of me. Besides. People jump off that bridge all the time in the summer."

"After big rains. When the water level is high."

Her words storm in and start rearranging everything inside my brain. I'm trying hard to put it all back where it belongs but it's like the shelves changed size or something. "Whatever. He was fine."

"Thank God."

I roll my eyes. "I think *we're* the ones who should be getting thanked. *We're* the ones protecting people."

"Are we?"

I stare at her. "What the hell does that mean?"

Ava bites her lip like there are words tumbling around inside her mouth that she's biting back. I'm not sure I want to hear them.

162

"Look." She exhales. "There's a difference between being a team and a cult. We're not a cult."

I laugh. "Well, yeah. Obviously."

She nods slowly. "Just so we're clear. We're not going to follow you off a bridge."

"Way to be dramatic, Av." I smile and she smiles a weak one back. "Nobody's going off a bridge but the bad guys."

She walks off.

Any fockey player knows that when you play hard, you get turf burn. That's all this is.

My right arm's still bruised from smashing against the train rail. It's not broken, but it definitely hurts to grip the stick. My knee feels out of whack too. So I'm not great at Monday's practice. And, I'm not sure if I'm imagining it, but everyone's treating me weird. Like I'm a thing that could break or explode. I don't think I'm imagining it.

Monday night, I massage arnica into my muscles, alternating heat and ice when I can. I need it to hurry up and heal. In time to beat Queens Falls tomorrow.

We play on their turf. Even though they're our rival school, our section is sparse. But a few parents—and Uncle Bob, Eileen, and their stupid video camera—are there and they yell, "Off with their heads! Down with the monarchy!" against the beating feet of the home side.

Their taunts against us can't be screamed. In whispers, they hiss, "Whores bitches Northridges." We hear their rhymes on the mid–October breeze. We've heard them before. We'll hear them again.

I shake it off. We're heroes. We're saviors. We can win this.

I try to start up one of the cheers. "Say we're small?"

But the others don't join in.

"Let's just do a simple word, okay?" Ava says. She doesn't ask it like I have a say.

"Sure," I say.

"Sasha?" Ava asks.

Sasha looks between us. She shrugs. "Teamwork?"

You've got to be kidding. Everyone shouts it. I fake it. Because teamwork doesn't look like boxing your captain out.

When we crash onto the field, I try to focus. The enemy is in yellow and blue, not green and blue. But right now, the colors feel a little too close for comfort.

I race into position. I can beat Queens Falls with my eyes closed.

Bella takes the ball from the start. She passes it to Sasha, who knocks it to Quinn. But Queens Falls steals it. They drive it hard, and it flies over my stick, landing in front of Kiara, who knocks it back.

Our girls are playing scared.

The ball shoots back and forth between their sticks and ours. Nobody's gaining. It's like a grandfather clock going ticktock with every tap-tap across the field. I'd be hypnotized by it if I weren't so pissed.

We're sweaty and tired at the half, my arm is killing me,

and something is up. I run to Ava in the goal. "What's going on out there?"

"I don't know." She takes off her helmet but avoids looking at me.

"First you pull that power crap before the game. Then—"

"*I* pulled power crap?"

"Yeah. You. Did you talk to the other girls about me? Did you—"

She holds her hand up. "I didn't have to."

"What's that supposed to mean?"

She sighs and starts walking toward Coach. "You freaked everyone out on the bridge, Zoe. We just need time."

"What, I'm like on probation now?"

She walks faster, even with all her pads. "Maybe?"

"I need to trust that you guys have my back out there. I can't win this by myself." I'm talking to her back.

"No shit, Cap'n." She turns and glares at me. "And *we* need to trust *you*. Think about that."

"Girls!" Coach says. "You beat them before, you can do it again. But you've got to keep those passes tight, Zoe." She gives me the stare. "Your pass to Liv was like a lazy turd. If you lay a turd on that field, you better race yourselves in to flush it down the toilet. Ava, you're holding strong, but Dylan! You've got to keep the ball out of her lap. She needs help out there. Nikki, you've got long legs but this isn't a runway. Let those bad boys loose. Like we say, it's easy to talk the talk, but you've got to walk the walk. Do you want to win this or what?"

They scream their way out onto the field, while I try to forget the screams in my arm, my knee, my head.

Straightaway, we plow through them. The triplets are a pinball machine, tap-tapping the ball between them. But Queens Falls's sweeper slings it back and they get the ball. I steal it away and drive it toward Nikki. She stops it and passes it on to Liv, who takes it to Sasha, who runs it right down the field. But we get whistled. I flick the ball over an opponent's stick and get whistled. Every time we get momentum, we get called. It's like the ref is so old she needs to slow us down so she can catch up. We get third-party obstruction and raised ball and dangerous use of stick and stick interference, all of which means dangerous play, and she threatens us with a yellow card. The call always goes their way. Coach turns herself purple trying not to tell the geriatric ref where to stick it.

They win: 0 to 1. It was close. It was so close. And we made them fight for it. But we still lost.

And now, if we don't win our next game, we can't go to sectionals. We get just one more shot.

TWENTY-FOUR

AFTER THE GAME, I DRIVE home with Liv. We talk about homework and how she's applying for a job at the mall after the season's over and other nothings that don't add up to somethings. I don't even know if she's had sex with Jake yet. I don't want to know.

I feel itchy again, like I need to run, like I need to be the girl who dresses in black and hurdles gravestones and swings from rafters. And yeah, like I need to be the girl who pushes dickheads off bridges. Because I don't really see that it was all that bad. He was fine. And so what if he wasn't? He deserves a broken leg. Or more.

Right when we turn onto my street, she says, "Are you okay?"

Which pisses me off because she knows I'm not.

"Because," she goes on, "I'm worried about you."

Oh, thank goodness she's on my side. "Thanks, I—"

"I mean," she continues, "since when did *you* become the person jumping off things, tossing people off bridges? Think of your dad. You—"

"Yeah," I say. I cannot believe she brought up Dad. As if I'm ever *not* thinking about him. "Ava already schooled me."

She nods and pulls into my driveway. "Okay then. I—"

But before she can finish I'm out the door, hurrying up the driveway. She always waits until I get inside. It's the nice thing to do. It's a best-friend thing to do. But so is sticking by your best friend, no matter what.

When I get to the door, I hear the music. If Mom is having a second Rebels night in two weeks, I'll lose my shit.

I open the door. Down the hall, I see Dad. Dancing. I walk closer. He's baking cookies. Mom's sitting on a stool at the counter.

I can't even.

Does nobody remember what happened the last time he tried this?

Of course, Dad slept through the aftermath on pain meds while Mom passed out on the couch with the Rebels. So yeah. I'm probably the only one who remembers.

"Welcome home, champ!" He pulls me in for a bear hug. "I've been watching some video of you, and man, you are having a season to beat."

"What are you talking about?"

"Eileen put together this little highlights movie for me. She just sent it over today. Zo, I thought I was watching a *Sports Forum* feature." He wraps his arm around my shoulder. "You are a phenom."

"Thanks, Dad." But it feels like a lie. Because I didn't play well today. Anybody can look good in a highlights reel. It takes a star to play a highlight *season*.

Dad dances his way over to a bowl and starts to stir.

"Wasn't that nice of Aunt Eileen?" Mom asks.

Nice? It would be *nice* if Mom were the one cooking instead of Dad, since she's actually home for once. But instead I say: "Really nice. I had no idea she was doing that."

Dad laughs. "You didn't notice Eileen filming you? Man, we've got to work on your observation skills. You—"

"No. Trust me, it's impossible to miss her. I was just trying to pretend that flaming ball of embarrassment didn't belong to me."

"Don't be mean, Zo," Mom says.

I try not to eye roll out loud. I open the fridge to hide it. It looks like they chose to make cookies over dinner. But I am so not cooking tonight. I grab a bowl and fill it with cereal.

"Actually"—Dad scrapes the sides of his mixing bowl with a spatula—"you might like Eileen more than you think. After all, she was quite the field hockey player."

I'm sure she was an epic benchwarmer.

"That's right!" Mom says. "She played for SU, I think."

"Huh." Syracuse is a top D1 school. I didn't know she was *that* good.

Dad waves the chip-covered spatula at me. "You just never know, Zo. You never—"

He drops the spatula onto the floor and grips the counter. Mom comes around the counter to his side.

I close my eyes for a moment.

What I don't say: *Great choice, Dad. Too little too late, Mom.* What I do: grab the spatula and clean up the mess. I sneak glances at Dad. He looks exhausted. He's probably trying to do something nice for us again and instead of helping, Mom just sat there.

"Dad was in bed most of the day, but he got up about an hour ago," Mom says, like she's making excuses.

I can't even look at her. "Are you okay, Dad?"

He breathes deeply for a minute before smiling. He spoons batter onto the tray.

I pull up a stool. To cheer him, I dip a spoon in the bowl of batter. "Mmm."

"No batter dipping on my watch." Dad smiles, steals my spoon, and drops it into the sink.

Mom starts the dishes. For once.

Dad dances over to the fridge, and I sigh. "Do you think you should be dancing around?"

His shoulders rise like he's taking a deep breath.

"Mom? Don't you think he should take it easy? In your medical opinion or whatever?" If she can't act like a nurse, then she should at least act like she gives a shit.

Mom drops the sponge, turns off the water, and just stares at me. She wipes her hands on her apron and walks away from the rest of the dishes in the sink. Typical.

Dad smiles tight and catches Mom before she leaves the kitchen, pulling her into his dance, singing along to the music, until she's smiling.

I walk to the sink to pick up where Mom left off. I take a

deep breath and try to chill. I close my eyes and focus on the suds, the sponge, the music. "This is a cool song. Is it new?"

I hear him stop dancing. I turn.

"What?" I ask.

"I put it on *ZoTunes*. The CD? The one I made for you?" He shakes his head. "You never listened to it, did you." It's not a question.

I drop the sponge and turn all the way around. "Oh, Dad. I'm so sorry. I—"

He shrugs. "It's okay. It was for you. You could listen or not. It's up to you."

"No, you don't understand. I—" And I can't tell him why. I can't tell him what happened, how every time I saw the CD on my dresser I was reminded of what happened, and how I felt that morning. How I tucked the CD away so I wouldn't have to keep facing it. I can't even tell him all that I've been doing since to make it all better, to change things not just for me but for everyone. And Mom's looking all judgey-eyed at me, and I just feel like yelling because nobody's getting what I'm doing here. I swallow my scream. "I'll listen to it tonight, Dad."

Mom takes his hand and spins herself in for a kiss. "Well, at least she likes this song. Oh! I know," she says into his shoulder, "you can make a playlist for the next Rebels night."

I wish I could punch something, or someone, right now. I turn back to the sink.

"What's wrong with you?" she asks me.

"Nothing." I keep my back to her and just scrub away at the stupid bowl.

She shakes her head. "You know, you've been really self-centered lately. Maybe if you spent a little less time moping around, you'd notice things like that gift from your father. Maybe—"

"*I'm* self-centered? *I* should notice more about Dad?" I shake out my hands and dry them on my jeans. "I notice plenty. Trust me. I'm not the one who needs to—"

"Okay, okay." Dad pats the air with his hands. "Let's just calm down."

I shrug. "Oh, I'm fine, Dad. No problem here. I don't have to do the dishes. I've got plenty of homework anyway."

"Good," Mom says.

Unfuckingbelievable.

Sure enough, next day, Dad's laid up. Again. I pour my screams and *I told you sos* and *How could yous* into tiny little bottles and screw the caps on tight. I tuck them away on the back shelves inside me but those shelves are getting crowded.

Life would be a lot easier if everyone just listened to me.

My friends avoid me. I want to wait for them after their classes, but if I get off schedule, I might run into Reilly and that can never, ever happen again.

Every day, we walk through the same halls. At any minute, he could be on a different route and bump into me. Every time I turn a corner, I think this might be it. And when I'm safe, sitting in class, while the teacher talks about nothing important, I think I was right.

I was right to push that kid off the bridge. Because nobody else did. Nobody else would.

I look toward the Greenville game. I'll prove myself to the team. Win them back.

Saturday, we count cows on the way to Greenville. Once we're beyond the curving streets with short driveways and clipped lawns, beyond the trailer park hidden off the thruway, beyond the columned mini-mansions by the lake, it's like falling back in time. Cows lounge against hillsides, the afternoon sun lighting them against the browning grass.

I can't imagine growing up here—the closest house miles away, the chores that come from living on a farm, the food coming from your land instead of the supermarket.

We pull into the school, but I don't let myself look at the girls. I don't let myself wonder whether they're stronger from lifting hay bales. If we win this one, we're off to the sectional semifinals. That's further than our team has ever gone. We'll be back on track.

We take our laps. We run our small drills in our small groups.

In the locker room, Coach talks, but her voice buzzes around my ears. I only hear the slamming of the ball against the backboards. Again and again.

Finally, we race out of the locker room, the sound of our cleats matching the beat of my heart.

We shake hands with Greenville, and I train my eyes on their hands instead of their faces. They're calloused and tanned.

I call tails. The coin flips and lands on heads.

I don't let it rattle me. Nothing will get between us and this win. It belongs to me, to us. Like our uniforms, our sticks.

I sink into the national anthem, letting it drum through me as it builds to the finish.

Right away, Quinn steals the ball. She passes it to Bella, who drives it long to Sasha. Sasha leans low, her whole body pushing it toward the goal. It slips between the goalie's legs.

The triplets hug and run while the rest of us cheer. I run up and knock sticks with Sasha. She smiles. Maybe this is us getting back to normal.

After that, Greenville wakes up. No more cakewalks to the goal. They score on us: 1 to 1. Their sweeper is big and fast—she drives the ball hard anytime it comes near.

We get another goal. Then, so do they: 2 to 2.

We hold it steady to the half.

Coach is jittery on the sideline. It's all she can do to contain herself. "I've heard some people in AA say 'You can eat an entire elephant one bite at a time.'"

Liv nudges me with her foot.

Quinn drops her braid to raise her hand. "I don't want to eat an elephant, Coach."

Coach flaps her hands like little wings. "Oh, shut up, Dobson. You know what I mean. Just take it one pass, one push, one drive at a time and you'll make one goal at a time right to the finish."

She's right. We just need one goal for the win. Ava and Dyl can hold them off, and we can put one in. It's that simple. And that hard.

I run in place. Stretch. A boxer readying for a fight.

The whistle blows, and green and gold take it. But I plow in, my stick a scalpel, carving a new path for the ball. I knock it to Liv. She sends it up to Sasha. But it gets blocked.

I try to do the same thing in the next play, but they're ready and dodge me, their sticks sending the ball toward Ava. She barely knocks it clear.

The score holds tight, neither side gaining, minutes ticking. We're a few minutes from the end, and I refuse to go into overtime. This game is ours.

At the next whistle, something unleashes in me. A heat. A fire. A lunging sort of power. I roar toward the ball, shouldering the others out of my way, my stick a magnet for the ball.

We've got less than a minute. I don't hear anything, everyone and everything are just background, and I drive toward the goal through a tunnel. I shoot and score.

Yes! We're going to sectionals. For the first time in Northridge's history, *we* are going to sectionals. I turn and whoop.

But my team isn't rushing at me with hugs and screams.

On the other side of the field, there's a clump. A mess of kilts, sticks, and cleats. I see two cleats. Toes up.

Someone's hurt.

I barrel across the field to my team. With each step, I see more—ankles, knees, blue-and-green jersey. I run faster.

It's one of ours.

TWENTY-FIVE

SASHA.

Her head rests at a funny angle with her eyes closed. A Greenville trainer rushes up, kneels down, and holds her head in between his hands. Mrs. Dobson runs onto the field and sinks to her knees.

She lets out a hiccup-cry. Bella and Quinn cling to each other.

Sasha opens her eyes, and we breathe again. But she closes them fast against the trainer's questions.

Someone says, "The middie's stick." That's what got her.

Nikki mutters something. I step closer. "She just collapsed. Like she didn't have any bones." I move away when she starts to repeat it.

The ambulance should be here by now.

Tears streak Kiara's cheeks as she squeezes Dylan's hand.

The middie sobs into the arms of her coach.

Bella and Quinn look lopsided. Like they shouldn't be able to stand without Sasha. Singing and dancing to "Three Is a Magic Number" just doesn't work without Sasha.

It takes forever for the ambulance to come, and the whole

time I'm thinking of all the stupid farms in between where we are and wherever they are.

The ref rules my goal counts. We won. I can't believe we're going to sectionals. I can't believe we're going, and I feel this awful.

Finally, the ambulance arrives. They ease Sasha onto a stretcher, keeping her back straight. They talk about CAT scans and MRIs, and her mom clutches a tissue and runs beside the paramedics. The doors slam behind Sasha and Mrs. Dobson, and the siren wails. We're left behind, as out of place as the ruts dug into the field from the ambulance's tires.

Our bus drives us to the hospital, and we pile out. Our grass-stained knees and mud-caked cleats track through the shiny halls in search of Sasha. Everything is wrong.

"It's a concussion." Red strands of hair stick to the sides of Mrs. Dobson's puffy face. "Concussions are nothing to mess around with," she says. "No, no."

I'm not even sure she's talking to us anymore.

In the darkened room, I rest my hand near Sasha's shoulder. "Are you okay?" I whisper.

"Hurts." Her eyes stay closed.

A nurse brings in some dark glasses and places them on her face. Even though her eyes remain closed, the wrinkles ease across her forehead.

None of us wants to say it out loud, but we're all thinking the same thing.

"How long until she can play again?" Ava finally asks.

"Too soon to tell," the nurse says. "Two weeks if we're lucky."

Ava and I look at each other from across the room.

In one week, we play Sommersville in the sectional semi-finals. Somehow we have to get through it without Sasha. Because I refuse to let our season end here.

I look at Mrs. Dobson, clutching the shoulders of Quinn and Bella as they look at Sasha, and I feel guilty for thinking of sectionals at all. I don't know Sasha like I know Quinn and Bella.

I don't know Sasha's favorite color. I don't know her favorite teacher. I don't know if she takes photography like Cristina or studio art like Nikki. I don't know where she wants to go to college. I don't even know if she has a crush. She's not out there like Quinn or grounded like Bella. She's just . . . Sasha. She knows all the words to every Disney movie and can down a thousand roasted chickpeas in one sitting. She's quiet, but her laugh is always ready. She's the right forward to Quinn's center. She traps smooth, jabs strong, and drags just right. She loves flipping upside down on the playground because, she says, it gives her a new perspective.

And seeing her this way gives me a new perspective too. I grab Ava's hand and pull her out into the hall.

"I'm sorry. About the bridge."

Ava looks at me for a second, then nods. "I know." She looks back into Sasha's room. "Do you think she's going to be okay?"

I look at Sasha in the bed. It's weird how still she is. "I don't know. I feel like most people are back on their feet after two weeks. But then you hear about others . . ."

"Yeah."

We're quiet for a minute, just watching through the window like it's on *Grey's Anatomy*. Except it isn't.

"It's not just that you went too far," Ava says, and it takes me a second to understand what she's talking about. "It's not even just that I'm worried about you—because I am."

I wait.

"It's that you forgot that what you do affects the rest of us, on and off the field. And I don't think we can win States without you, you know? I need that scholarship to SU just as much as you need yours."

Coach's words from forever ago come back to me: *You have power with this team. When you're down, everyone's down.* I just wish Ava would understand I wasn't trying to pull everyone down. I was trying to fly us up.

"Besides," Ava says, "I don't *want* to win it without you."

I don't want to play without her either. Even if Jason deserves to be tossed off a thousand bridges, I'd never choose him over Ava, or the team.

"And now," she continues, "Sasha's hurt and I have no idea how we'll win without her either."

I squeeze her hand. "We'll do it."

She looks at me. "Don't flame out on me again, okay?"

I nod. "Okay."

On Monday, everything's messed up. Practice just doesn't work without Sasha. Bella and Quinn's rhythm doesn't work with just two. Our forward line is off beat. Anna, her sub, tries hard to pick up the slack, but she can't. Nobody's where they need to be. The ball ducks under sticks and between cleats. Usually, our moves and bodies interlace into a tight web that the ball can't escape. But today, we're all holes.

After practice, I brace myself for one of Coach's angry rants or a fifty-mile run. She has every right to school us. There's no way we're going to make it to the sectional finals playing like this.

Instead, Coach pulls us together in a circle. She places herself between Quinn and Bella. "Hold hands."

Ava widens her eyes at me across the circle, but I have no idea what's coming either.

"Girls, it's painful when someone you care about gets hurt. I want to teach you something that we say in AA. You've probably heard of it," she says. "It's called the Serenity Prayer: God, grant me the serenity to accept the things I cannot change, the courage to change the things I can, and the wisdom to know the difference."

I can feel the heat in my palms from the girls around the circle.

"There's nothing we can do about the fact Sasha got hurt. So we accept it. But that doesn't mean we stop." She releases Quinn's and Bella's hands and wraps her arms around their shoulders instead. She squeezes them until their shirts wrinkle, and they fall into her. "You can decide that this team is simply a group of girls playing field hockey. Or you can decide that this team is bigger than any one of you, bigger than all of us together. You worked so hard this year to get to this point. What will honor Sasha most? Losing because she isn't here, or winning to honor all the hard work that she—and all of you—did to get us here?"

We're quiet. Coach lets the silence sit, lets the breeze move the trees, lets the sounds from the football practice drift toward us.

"We should play. To win." Quinn's voice is quiet but sure.

Bella nods.

I nod too. "Then we need to figure out how to win without her."

"Agreed," Coach says.

"What if we shuffle the positions?" I say. "Maybe if everyone is in a different spot, we'll all play differently, all stretch more to cover the loss. You know?"

"Great idea, Captain," Coach says.

It's hard to walk through the halls without Sasha. We're quieter, tighter. Somehow I'm less aware. I trip three times. Liv steers me away from a swinging locker door.

In Mac's class, Liv kicks my leg, and I realize I've just been staring at Grove for who knows how long. Even weirder, he's staring right back. I redden as I try to refocus on Mac. Liv gives me this confused look like I've forgotten to fill her in, but honestly, I have no idea why I was staring at him.

Except that . . . it's like there's been a seismic shift without me noticing, a line separating my time with Grove from what happened with Reilly. Our time on the boat comes back and Reilly's there, waiting, but it isn't poisoning the memory with Grove like it did before. Instead, the memory of us—me and

Grove, kissing, on the starlit lake—frees itself and floats to the surface. Which, of course, makes me stare—and redden—again. Then Liv answers something Mac asks, and she's probably being all smart like always, and I have zero clue because all my smarts left the building weeks ago.

After class, we meet up with the others, though we don't talk much. Without Sasha, I crave our team even more now.

Then we see Kups. Everything about him takes up too much space—the way he leans, the way he talks, the way he stares, the way he laughs. I wish I could shove *him* off a bridge.

I keep my eyes down. For once, it'd be great if he just didn't notice us. Goodness knows he doesn't notice most things that matter.

"Hey," he calls to Bella, "I heard about your sister. Too bad. You think she could use some cheering up? She's been a vegetarian so long she doesn't know what she's missing." He laughs. "Hey, you're like a vegetarian too. All bush, no sausage."

"Disgusting," Liv mumbles.

My nails dig so hard into my palms I think they might bleed. I look down at them. Snake scales. I wonder what would happen if I really was a snake. If I could just shed this skin, slither over, and finish Kups for good. Finish all of them.

We turn the corner, their ugly laughs at our backs.

"One of these days," Quinn says, "we're going to have to get him back."

"Yeah." Dylan's voice is hard. "What good are we if we can't even get Kups to shut the hell up?"

I catch Nikki's eye. Exactly.

TWENTY-SIX

I WOULD LOVE NOTHING MORE than to toss Kups from a bridge, but there are no bridges nearby and Kups is too much of a beast to toss. Instead, I decide I need time with Nikki. And Nikki needs time with Aunt Jacks.

So after a few texts, and a stop at the vending machine for Twizzlers and Rolos, we're all set to drive to Syracuse after practice. Even though Nikki's driving, and we're in her car, she only knows we're headed to the Westcott area, near SU's campus.

"You're such a control freak."

"As my Aunt Maya says, there's no such thing as a control freak as long as the right person is in control. And in case you were wondering, that right person is obviously me."

Nikki laughs. "What's up with you and your five million aunts again?"

"They're just my mom's best friends."

"That's cool," Nikki says. "My mom doesn't really have close friends like that."

She's quiet while she merges onto 690. I've never really

thought about the fact that other people's lack of aunts is about their mom's lack of friendships. "You want to get off at Teall Avenue."

"Yeah. I come to Westcott sometimes."

We exit the ramp and have to sit at the light. She looks over at me. "Can we talk about how much we hate Kups and how we want to toss him off a bridge?"

I look at her.

The light changes and she turns right. "I gave you space because I thought you needed it. But the team was being ridiculous." She puts on her left turn signal.

"Just keep going straight."

"Nah," she says. "Imma teach you a shortcut, Miss Control Freak."

I smile.

She takes us past a concrete factory. The dust from the concrete and gravel lifts around our windows. Then, just like that, we're past the factory and headed up a hill.

"Anyway," she says, "you pulled an action-hero move and because of you, that girl got away."

I sink back into the seat. It's amazing to hear her say that. We cross East Genesee onto Westcott and I know where I am again. Every other tree along the street has a hot-pink flyer stapled to it. Probably for some university band's gig. I give her directions.

"And if you ask me," she goes on, "we should absolutely go after Kups. And Jamison. And Reilly. And any other predatory prick who walks those halls."

"That's exactly what I want too." I point. "It's up here on the left. The yellow bungalow. Park on the street."

She parks and we both get out. It's a cool evening and I grab a hoodie out of my bag.

"Here's the thing, though," I say as we cross the street. "I don't want to jeopardize the team. I've got scholarships to worry about. Ava has scholarships. The tripl—"

I can finally read what's on all the bright pink flyers flapping in the breeze.

> Speak Out Against Sexual Assault
> Saturday, November 1
> Schine Student Center, 8 p.m.
> Stand Up. Speak Up. Be Heard.
> Heal.

We just stand there staring while the pink paper ripples angrily in the wind. Like it's shouting. All down the street, all these pink pages, flapping in people's faces.

"What is that?" I finally ask.

Nikki shakes her head. "No idea. I guess a thing where people . . . speak out?"

"Like people who've been attacked?" I can't imagine saying what happened to me in front of anyone. I could barely tell Liv. I pull my hoodie close.

"Wow," Nikki finally says. "That would be . . ."

"Awful? Terrifying?"

She hesitates. "I don't know. It must not be if people want to do it, right?"

I shake my head. "The fact that there are enough people for them to make an entire event . . ." I turn away from the flyer.

We follow the stone path behind Aunt Jacks's small house to the large shed in back. The high-pitched whir of the saw masks our steps.

"You're not going to saw me up into little pieces, are you?" Nikki asks.

"Nah. I thought I'd save that for our second date."

She laughs. We follow the path until Aunt Jacks's studio opens before us.

Nikki stands still. "Wow."

I grin. "I know."

I cross the threshold. The saw clicks to a stop and Aunt Jacks removes her earmuffs. She gives me a wide smile and walks over in her splattered, dusty overalls. "Hi, Zozo," she says, giving me a big hug. "Jen's bummed she had to work. You know how much she loves to shower you in baked goods. She hasn't gotten to see you since the season started."

Jen is Jacks's wife. She owns a coffee shop and bakery downtown. "Give her a huge hug and tell her I will eat *all* the baked goods when I see her again."

Jacks smiles and turns to Nikki. "You must be Zo's wood-carving friend, Nikki."

Nikki nods.

"Well, don't just stand there catching flies," Aunt Jacks says, waving Nikki in.

Nikki steps inside like she's walking into church. Line drawings paper the walls, and wood curls crunch beneath our feet. The air is thick with the smell of paint thinners and wood. Shelves hold a collection of wood planers. A long beat-up table holds chisels and clamps, blades and mallets, and a hundred tools I don't have names for.

Aunt Jacks smiles at Nikki. "Want a tour?"

"More than anything," Nikki says, and I laugh.

While Nikki gets the grand tour, I wander free.

I've always loved Aunt Jacks's studio, though I haven't been here in months. Several pieces in various stages of completion are scattered around. On one table, there's a big, round, lumpy bit of wood. Next to it, a printed picture of a tree with a large lump stuck to the base of its trunk. I realize the hunk of wood on the table is the same one as in the picture. I study the photo. It's like the roots grew up into the trunk of the tree but got caught.

Like words trapped in a throat.

I think of the angry pink flyers stapled to the trees outside.

I gently put my hands on the wood and imagine all the words that might be stuck inside, unable to get free.

"Ah," says Aunt Jacks, coming over to me. "I see you discovered my treasure."

"What is it?"

"This is one of my favorite signs of nature's twisted sense

of justice." She runs her fingers over the bumps and lumps along with me, and Nikki joins in. "It's called a burl."

"It's a mess," says Nikki. But she doesn't say it like it's a bad thing. She says it like a mess is the most beautiful thing in the world.

My fingers rise and fall so much on the bumps I could be playing the piano.

"What causes it?" Nikki asks.

"Technically," Aunt Jacks says, leaning back to study the thing, "it's caused by some kind of bacteria or virus."

"So basically, it's a giant snot ball?"

Aunt Jacks laughs. "Kind of. They think that when the tree is attacked, it sends all this help to that one spot and the growing goes haywire. Burls don't seem to hurt the tree." She pats it. "But this tree had to come down anyway. I just got lucky."

"Lucky?" I ask.

Aunt Jacks raises her eyebrows and smiles. She goes to the back of the workshop and lifts a wooden bowl off a shelf. "This is a bowl I made out of a burl—a much smaller one. I couldn't bear to part with it even though it's worth a lot more than my other bowls."

She's left the sides of the bowl uneven. Inside, the grains don't run in parallel lines like they usually do. Instead, they're a jumble, a tangle. The color is uneven too—slashes of dark twist into bits of light.

"It's the most beautiful mess I've ever seen," I say.

"I know," Aunt Jacks whispers.

Nikki rubs her hand over the uncut one on the table. "Will this look the same?"

Aunt Jacks shakes her head, her hair spilling out of its tie. "Nope. It's a secret waiting to be released." She loops her long hair up in another messy bun. "I have to let it talk to me a while longer so I can figure out what it wants to be."

Nikki smiles. "I like that."

"Why'd you say it was 'nature's twisted sense of justice'?" I ask.

Aunt Jacks winks. "You know me, Zo. I just like it when anything rebels." She places her hand on top of the burl. "A deadly bacteria came along and tried to take this tree. And the tree said, 'Nope. Not only are you not going to take me down. But you've just made me more valuable than ever.'"

TWENTY-SEVEN

SATURDAY MORNING, SASHA AND HER mom come to the parking lot to see us off. She's healing well, the doctors say. But even beneath the baseball hat and sunglasses, she's squinting.

"You look like a movie star," Cristina says.

"Darkness is my friend." Sasha's voice is quiet. "Sorry I can't come."

We fold her in hugs. I think of her healing and us winning, and I wrap it all in the hug.

"We're going to beat them for you." Bella squeezes her sister. "And then you are going to finish this season with us."

Ava walks up to Bella and writes Sasha's number 19 on her cheek in face paint. "To remind us why we're winning today." We all mark our faces with blue-and-green 19s.

Coach steps off the bus and walks over. "Nice artwork, girls, but you've got nothing on me." She opens her jacket to reveal a neon-green T-shirt with *Sticks Chicks* written on it in bright blue puffy paint. When I look closer, I realize she's scrawled *all* our numbers around the words. It's perfect.

The bus ride to Rome feels long. The sectional semifinals

are on neutral turf, so at least we won't play Sommersville on their field. Motown singing in my ears, I lean my head back against the cool seat. The bus fills with the quiet sounds of fingers tapping, heels bouncing against the floor, wheels rolling fast against the asphalt. The windows rattle, and the bus driver hums softly to the radio. All these quiet nothings rumble together into an expectant kind of something.

When we jog out onto the field, I hear my name and search the stands. Uncle Bob and Eileen are there, but so is Mom. They're standing, holding their hands high, a giant banner blazing *#11* between them. And beneath the banner sits Dad. I can't believe he came. I can see the grimace of pain beneath his smile, but he's smiling all the same. I blow him a kiss and wave big. And then I notice the boys' soccer team.

And Grove.

I stare at him for a moment, and he lifts his hand a touch off his knee in a small wave. I give him one back and run to the center for the coin toss.

We've gone further than any Northridge field hockey team ever has. But it's more personal than that. All these people drove all this way for us.

For me.

Quinn takes right forward, Sasha's favorite position. And she's the best for it. Bella moves to Quinn's center. I play left center. Ava jumps up to center middie, and Dylan suits up for goalie. Coach reshuffled the deck and dealt a perfect hand.

I dip low to the ground. My stick's strong in my hands. This body has flown up buildings, somersaulted over gravestones,

191

leaped across a bridge—if I can do that, I can do this. I slap my stick against the turf. This is our field now.

The whistle blows.

A gust of wind cuts across the turf and slices through my leggings, but it just drives me faster. Bella takes the ball off the top and passes it to Quinn, who races downfield. Sommersville pushes it back, but Kiara stops it, passing it to me. I spin around one of theirs and flick it to Bella, who barrels down the center.

For the whole first half, we keep the ball down at their goal, but we can't land it. Nikki and the others cheer us from behind, but no matter what we do, we can't break their defense.

By the time the half hits, we're out of breath and tired. But I still feel triumphant. It's 0 to 0, but we're close. We're closer than they are.

At the top of the second half, they get it away from us, but Nikki lifts it, and the ball arcs through the air. Liv stops it mid-air, controls the drop, and curves it my way. Nobody's open, so I plow forward, gliding around their girls like I'm on skates. Finally, I slide it toward the goal. The goalie dives for it. It slips between her arm and the ground, rolling to a stop against the back of the goal.

Liv screams so loud as she races toward me I feel like she's jumped into my ear. Bella punches my shoulder so hard I'm sure it'll welt up later. But I don't care. We scream all the way back to position.

Now we're winning. All we have to do is hold it.

Sometimes it's hard to hold steady. Sometimes being the one on top makes you an easy target. But, today, we hold it.

The game ends: 1 to 0.

Liv, Nikki, Cristina, and I do running aerials toward the sidelines, all in a row. Kiara does three backflips. Big Bob and my parents stand and cheer—even my dad. Eileen bounces up and down with her stupid camera. And Grove. Grove is standing. And clapping. And looking at me.

We're off to sectional finals.

The week is just one long sigh while we wait for the next game. I'm itching to crash another party, because the high of kicking some jerk's ass would be the cherry on top of winning semifinals, but I don't even suggest it. I think of what Nikki said. We just have to wait.

The boys' soccer team heads off to their semifinals on Thursday. Since it's during the week, we're thankfully not expected to go. Because even though that night feels more clear now, I'm still not sure I want anything to do with Grove. Or any boy. Still, I'm glad they win. They're heading to sectionals too.

Friday night is Halloween. I so want to dress in black and parkour our way through the parties that are bound to happen, but Ava suggests we rally around Sasha. So we crowd into the Dobsons' kitchen and eat pizza, taking turns running to the door to feed candy to the young goblins, princesses, presidents, and sports heroes from their neighborhood.

My favorite costume has to be the trio of girl soccer player zombies with scooped-out soccer balls as their candy buckets. After the doorbell quiets, we pile into the triplets' basement, surrounding Sasha on the big blue boat of a couch watching all the cheesy rom-coms she loves and knows by heart.

As we board the bus the next morning, clouds hustle across the new November sky. The sun glints on candy wrappers blown into gutters. One tree, festooned in toilet paper, looks like a crazed bride. We're off to play Greenville in Rome.

This time, with Sasha. She's been cleared to play, but you'd never know it by looking at her. She's ghost-pale. Her sisters sit on either side of her squeezing her hands, but her eyes look far away.

I think she'd be fine if it was any team other than Greenville.

Even in the locker room she doesn't look right.

Ava crouches in front of her, resting her hands on her knees. "You can't let this psych you out, Sash."

Sasha nods, but I can tell she's not with us. She's reliving that moment on Greenville's field.

"I mean, you came back," Dylan says to her.

"What?" Sasha focuses on Dylan's face. Dylan's roots are growing out, and her hair is half natural and half bleached as she smooths it into a ponytail.

"You came back," she repeats. "*They* should be scared of *you*." Dylan tugs her ponytail tight.

Dylan lifts her foot up onto the bench to tie her cleat, completely oblivious to the effect she's had on Sasha. Sasha's eyes are focused. She's back. "Thanks, Dylan. I never thought of it like that."

"Yeah." Bella pats Sasha's knee. "You're stronger because of it."

Dylan smirks. "Let's kick some ass. We owe them a beating."

We jog out onto the turf. It's cool—autumn-perfect game weather. The stands are dotted with family: Mrs. Liu, Ava's folks, Mrs. Dobson, Mrs. Morrison, Mr. Walker, and Cristina's whole family, with her bouncing little sisters dressed head to toe in blue and green. But this time my parents didn't come, or the soccer team. Just Uncle Bob, Eileen, and the camera.

At the huddle, Ava says, "Let's return to our roots."

So we do. We scream, "Sticks Chicks!" and smash our sticks together.

Right away, Greenville takes the ball and races it downfield toward Ava, guarding the goal. Dylan steps in and drives it back upfield. I stop, turn, and pass it toward Sasha. But she hesitates, and they steal it again. Liv nabs it this time, passing toward Quinn, but they intercept it and sprint toward the goal. They're racing, outpacing, out-dodging us until somehow it deflects off Ava's pads into the goal.

They score.

Coach screams us back to position. "Cristina! You want your camera? You're not taking selfies. Move, girl! Michaela! Lay down the coverage. Zo! Run. Get there yesterday!"

Greenville grabs the ball off the break but they bungle a

pass, and Liv snaps it away, passing it to me, and I sprint. I tear up the field so hard I could beat Liv. I swerve around their sweeper and push it to Quinn, who slams it home.

But I can't help but feel like it's luck—luck that they bungled the pass, luck that I raced so fast, luck that Quinn hit it just right.

Luck doesn't win games.

They score another. And while we keep them from scoring any more, we can't lift off our one point.

It's 1 to 2 at the half.

I refuse to be this close and not take it home.

TWENTY-EIGHT

AT HALFTIME, COACH PULLS US into the huddle. "Look. I know I'm hard on you. You've been through a lot." She puts a hand on Sasha's shoulder. "You girls have taken this team further than it's ever gone. You've practiced hard, played big, dreamed bigger." She looks around the circle, meeting our eyes. "But this isn't the end. You don't get to rest. You need to play as big as you dream. You owe yourselves that. You are going to States."

"Let's stick it to 'em," Ava says.

"Fock yeah!" Kiara yells, and Dylan laughs.

When we race out, we're smiling, determined. They make it tough. They make us tougher.

But this time the ball knows we're home, and it always comes back to us.

We win: 3 to 2. We have just one week to prep for Regionals.

Ava wants to celebrate with parkour. Which is exactly what I need. She picks a new playground, near Dylan's. But when I get there, I realize it doesn't matter that it's new. It's still a playground and I've grown tired of playgrounds.

But I leap, twist, and flip with the others, trying to pretend this was exactly what this dark, cool, moonlit night had in mind.

Despite being closest to her house, Dylan shows up an hour later than everyone else. And when she steps out of the shadows, her entire right side's caked in mud from her sneakers to her hair. Her cheek is bloody.

"What the hell happened?" Kiara asks.

Dylan starts to tear up, but instead she shakes her head and screams. "I swear I'm going to kill that fucker."

"Who?" Nikki asks.

"Kups. This is the third time he's tried to run me over this year."

"Wait," Liv says. "What do you mean he tried to run you over?"

Kiara pours water onto the sleeve of her hoodie and tries to wipe Dylan's cheek, but Dylan swats her away. "I *mean*"—Dylan's jaw tightens—"that I'll be walking on the sidewalk, and he'll drive over the curb and try to hit me with his fucking truck." She smiles a tight line. "It's a little game we play."

Kiara drops her hand, and we all just look at one another. And all the bottles of rage inside me rattle on their shelves.

We've got to do something. We're the only ones who will.

I don't bring it up. I wait. I look at Nikki.

There's a snake in me coiling, shifting, ready to spring free of its skin.

"We need to do something about Kups," Kiara finally says. "This has to stop." It makes sense that it's her. She's Dylan's best friend.

"What if we embarrass him?" Cristina asks.

"How?" Michaela says.

Every cheesy thing I've ever seen in a movie zips through my head, like screwing with his shaving cream or jockstrap. But none of that feels important enough. And I have no desire to go anywhere near his jockstrap.

Liv tilts her head. "What does he love?"

"His truck. The one he always runs me down in." Dylan kicks a rock off the path.

"That pickup with the camo flames and huge tires?" Sasha asks her sister.

Bella nods.

"Blech." Quinn wrinkles her nose. "I hate that truck. It always takes up like three spots in the student lot."

"And what's up with camouflage flames?" Liv asks. "Doesn't he get that the whole point of flames is to stand out and the whole point of camouflage is to blend in?"

I laugh.

Dylan jumps onto a monkey bar and hangs for a beat. "One of my friends works at an auto shop. He could loosen—"

I shake my head. "We need to keep this quiet. Just us."

Michaela raises her eyebrows. "Plus, we want payback, not a murder charge."

I pull my hoodie tight against the cool November air.

We go home. That night, revenge and rage weave themselves into my dreams. And this time, I won't let them talk me out of it.

On Wednesday, after Coach has run, yelled, and driven us into the ground at practice, we lie on the grass at the edge of the field, looking up at the leaves in the fading light. Cristina's snapping pictures, and I wonder if the colors can possibly be captured. It's so strange that the leaves are dying, and yet the way they go out is in these bold colors. It reminds me of this poem we read once in English—something about raging against the dying of the light. That's what fall does. Every year. Again and again.

I want us to rage bold like the leaves. But I want it to be the beginning of something, not the end. We've been brainstorming for days, but so far we've got nothing.

Cristina lifts up on her elbows. "We could plaster his truck in gay pride stickers and pink unicorns."

Liv shakes her head. "That's insulting to gay people and unicorns."

"Yeah. Not. A. Chance," Dylan says.

Bella pretends to gag. "You straight people can keep him."

"We don't want him either," Nikki says.

We laugh.

A bird spreads its wings across the pinkening sky. A black silhouette slicing through the streaks of sun.

I close my eyes. Put myself back into that hallway, Reilly's hands everywhere he didn't have permission to be. I didn't feel embarrassed. I felt scared. I felt ashamed. I felt ashamed that I couldn't fight back, that even though he didn't finish he still scared me so much.

I still feel scared.

I sit up. "What if we scare him?"

"What do you mean?" Michaela asks, but the look in Nikki's eyes, in Dylan's eyes—even in the eyes of some of the others, fuels me.

"Well, when guys do this to girls, it doesn't *embarrass* them. It *scares* them." I breathe deep. "*I've* felt scared."

Everyone's silent. I shiver in the now-night air. I feel more exposed with every moment they're quiet.

"Hmm. Scaring him might teach him a lesson," Michaela says. "Maybe."

"That's reason enough for me," Sasha says.

"How in the hell do we scare Kups?"

"He's the size of a house. It's not like we can just jump out and say *Boo*."

"We could fill the inside of his truck with bugs—fake bugs. Or snakes." Sasha shudders. "I hate snakes."

"Oooh!" Michaela's eyes widen. "What if we sneak into his bathroom and write 'We're watching you' on the mirror and then when he takes a shower and the mirror fogs up the words will appear."

We all just look at her and bust out laughing.

"What? I read it in a book!"

"Of course you did," Ava says. "And there's no way in hell I'm sneaking into any room with a naked Kups."

"It's gotta be something that'll stay with him. Something he won't get over in a hurry."

"We could call him every night at three a.m."

"We could follow him everywhere, so he thinks he's being stalked."

"I know where to get a gun," Nikki says, looking up at us.

The silence is absolute. Even the trees hold their breath, the last leaves clinging to the branches, still.

TWENTY-NINE

A GUN.

Nikki rushes to fill the quiet: "Of course, it won't be loaded. We'll be totally safe."

I imagine the cold steel against my neck. It must be the scariest thing in the world—one click, and your life could end. Everything stops.

It's perfect.

"No," Ava says. Ava, the one who pushed for parkour to begin with, the wild to my tame, says no. She turns away from Nikki to look at me. "It's the wrong move, Cap'n."

"He attacked Dylan on the first day of school! Now we find out he's been tormenting her ever since and you want him to get away with it? He could've killed her!"

"That's not what I'm saying, and you know it."

"He said shitty stuff about Sasha and me too," Bella adds.

"Saying 'shitty stuff' doesn't mean he deserves to be a target," Michaela says. "I thought we were talking harmless stuff. Not guns."

I turn to her. "Dylan could've ended up in the hospital—or

worse. Nothing about what they do is harmless. Nothing about what they do *deserves* harmless. They wait till we're alone. They see us as weak. They touch us wherever they want, whenever they want. They do *not* deserve our sympathy. We are in the right, you guys."

"Not if we start joining them, we're not." Liv's voice. I can't believe she's on their side. "Look, Zo. I know you've been through—"

I glare at her. "This isn't about me. This has nothing to do with me. This has to do with Dylan and the fact that Kups is a certified dickhead. If assholes had to register with the state like pedophiles, he'd be first in line."

"Truth," Dylan says.

"I know." Liv sighs. "I just think there's a difference between what we've done before—which is help people who are in active danger—and what we're talking about now." She bites her lip. "Zo, it's a big difference. I mean, guns? Really?"

"Why not?" Nikki asks. "We wouldn't actually shoot it or anything. We'd just scare the crap out of him. It's like Michaela said: We'd just teach him a lesson."

"Don't bring me into this." Michaela puts her hands up. "This is not what I meant."

Nikki shakes her head. "We'd be giving a gift to the whole school. Why do we have to wait until someone's about to get hurt to do something? If you knew someone was going to murder someone else, would you just"—Nikki throws her hands up—"I don't know, go back to watching *The Real Housewives of I Don't Give a Fuck*, or would you get off your ass, call the police, and do something about it?" Nikki's almost out of breath.

"Exactly," I say.

"Nikki," Michaela says, her voice gentle like she's talking to a wild animal.

Which pisses me off more. *We* are not the wild animals here. *We* are not the ones who need the cages.

"You have to see this is different from premeditated murder."

"Come on, Michaela," I say. "We're just scaring him."

Michaela shakes her head. "We don't know if Kups is going to—"

"Oh, please," Dylan says. "*I* know. Kups is going to hurt people. He's going to do it today and tomorrow and the day after that. He'll keep doing it until someone stops him. Why can't we be the ones?"

"Because," Kiara says, "it's not right, Dyl." We're all quiet. I've never seen Kiara go against Dylan.

Dylan just blinks at her. "Wait, what?" she finally says.

Kiara's lips are tight. "This is going too far. It's wrong, Dyl."

"*He's* wrong!" Dylan shouts.

"I understand wanting revenge, Dyl. I do. But I can't do this with you." Kiara's voice is soft, steady. "You know I can't."

"I *don't* know." Dylan's chest is heaving. "You've seen what Kups is like."

"I have," Kiara says. "But Dyl, I'm Black. You're white."

"And?" Dylan's face is red. "I'm poor. You're rich."

Kiara's face is so still, too still, and I feel like none of us should be witnessing this because they both look scraped raw.

"Yeah, and *you* shouldn't be doing this. No matter what. But I *can't* do it. You can't be Black and fuck up that hard. You get do-overs. I don't."

"*I* get do-overs? Me?" Dylan stands, her fists clenched at her side. "You know exactly what I've been through. How many—" She shakes her head and I can see her eyes squeeze tight against the tears. She walks away, Kiara close behind.

Even though they're walking side by side, I feel the space between them stretch. It's not a rubber band that will snap easily back into place. It's a crack spreading into a canyon.

I look at Liv.

That can't happen to us. She has to get it. She has to see that Dylan and I—and the rest of us—are right.

Bella's doing the same thing with Sasha. Saying something about how their dad takes them to the gun range every year. How they know how to be safe. I pull Liv aside. "Think about how good it would feel to finally put Kups in his place," I say.

"I *am* thinking of how it would feel. I just think we have different ideas about what would feel good."

"I can't believe you won't do this for me. You're my best friend."

"Exactly. Which is why you should listen to me. Zo, this is a bad idea." She sighs. "Besides, I thought this wasn't about you."

"It's not!"

She tilts her head at me. "This isn't about what happened with Reilly?"

"Of course it's about that. But it's not *just* about that. It's about—" I almost say it's about what happened with Nikki and Jamison. But I don't. That's Nikki's story to tell. I look at Nikki, plotting already with Bella and Quinn. "It's about taking the school back from them. I'm not even sure we ever had it to begin with. But this is the way we can get it back. It's about *all* of us feeling safe."

"It doesn't feel messed up to you that to feel safe you have to make someone else feel unsafe?"

"Um, no. Not if that someone is Kups. He's making Dylan's life hell. The dean said his parents thought about pressing charges against her. Against *Dylan*. Everything is slanted in their favor. We're just—"

"Leveling the playing field?"

"Exactly!"

Liv exhales. "I don't think that's what you're doing, Zo. I think that's what we *were* doing when we were saving people. But that's not what this is. Zo—" She looks at me and I feel like there's pity in her eyes, which is messed up because there's nothing to pity here. "Zo, this is serious stuff. I'm pretty sure it's illegal to threaten someone with a gun."

"Yeah? I'm pretty sure it's illegal to sexually assault people and run them off the road."

"And you're willing to risk everything—your scholarship—for Kups?"

"It's not *for* Kups. It's for Dylan, for us. Besides. What am I risking? It's all of us against him and we'll wear masks and have a gun." She widens her eyes at me. "Oh please, Liv. It's not like it'll be loaded. You're making such a big deal of this."

She sucks in her lips and nods. "Okay."

I squeal and put my hands on her shoulders and jump. "You're in?"

She shakes her head. "No. I'm just done trying to convince you. I'm not in."

We stand there for a minute looking at each other. There's so much distance between us she might as well already be in London.

"Do you need a ride home?"

"I'll catch a ride from someone else." My voice feels quiet.

She walks away, and she doesn't turn around. Not once.

I look back at those of us who remain and realize that we're all white. It's an uncomfortable feeling.

I think of what Kiara said to Dylan about being Black. I remember how Kiara was the first one daring enough to tell her story. It's not that this isn't important to Kiara. It's that she can't be the one to respond. It's just more evidence of how screwed up our society is.

So we'll respond. We'll fight back for every girl who's been leered at in the halls, cornered at a party, run off the road.

I text Dylan.

I was right to push that kid off the bridge, just like I was right to have this whole idea in the first place. If I could, I'd stick that gun barrel in all their faces. Kups. Jamison. Reilly. And anyone else who dares to mess with us.

All this time, we've just reacted. Their game, their rules, their refs.

It's time to change the game.

THIRTY

AVA: You're really going through with this?
ME: . . .

There's no point in answering. I'm not going to convince her, and honestly, I don't even want to. We planned for hours last night, worked everything out to the tiniest detail—thought of every contingency. Nikki, Dylan, and I are the lucky three. After, we'll all go back to the triplets' house for a sleepover that will be the perfect alibi. We don't need the others.

AVA: U remember we have a game tomorrow right?
AVA: Not just any game
AVA: Regionals
AVA: U know, the game we need to win to get to the state semifinals in the dome?
AVA: The thing we've been talking about all focking year?
ME: Of course I remember. Don't do this.
AVA: ME? ME don't do this? How about u?? You're risking everything for what?

Nice. It looks like Ava and Liv have been talking behind my back. But they can talk all they want. I get that this doesn't make sense for them. But it's not just about them. This is for *all* the girls. And it's what's right.

ME: Can we just agree to disagree?
AVA: . . .
ME: U can still come u know.

Silence.

It's okay. I don't need her approval. I'm ready for this. I've been ready.

Wearing our black masks and clothes, we meet in the woods outside the school right after the Friday-night game begins. The November wind breaks at the tree line, but the cool air still finds us. I stomp my feet on the fallen leaves to keep warm while I wait for my turn. Nikki brought her cousin's gun, Dylan brought one from home, and the triplets brought their dad's. So we each get one.

Bella hands me the gun and I expect it to be cold. It isn't. But it makes me shiver anyway. Or it makes the air shiver. It's heavy in my hands, like it knows what it can do. I brace myself to rack the slide the way the triplets taught us. The slide is the thing that's cold. To force the bullet into the chamber, I have to pull the slide, hard.

Kuhcheck.

The sound is loud in the night. I wrap my right hand around the grip and cup its base in my left. I lift it and look through the sight at a knot in a distant tree. Slowly, I squeeze the trigger until I hear the click in my ears. The sound rockets through me.

The chamber is empty. Nothing happens. But in that sound, everything happens.

We run to his truck. Dylan found out that he never locks his truck on game days, and sure enough, when we try the door, there's no lock, no alarm. Dylan crawls into the footwell under the passenger seat, while Nikki and I crouch in the back seat.

"Uck," Dylan says. "It reeks in here."

My legs feel like running, not squatting. "Does he really think some girl is going to sit in *here*? *Naked?* Waiting for *him*?"

"Well," Nikki says, "to be fair, leaving the door unlocked did get a bunch of girls in his truck. Just maybe not with the idea he had in mind." She laughs in nervous, short hiccups. Nikki's usually graceful, but now, clutching the gun in her hands, her shoulders twitch.

I think of the triplets, safe, outside. They're walking around the parking lot. Ready to signal us or create a distraction.

"Only Kups would base life decisions on some movie he saw," Dylan says from the front seat. I wish I could see her.

"What?" I can't remember what we're talking about, and the game is loud outside.

"The whole leaving-the-door-open thing. He saw it in a movie. After a guy made a touchdown, a naked girl waited in his car. Ready to fuck him." A pause. I'm sure she's rolling her eyes. "There is no touchdown that would ever make me want to screw Kups."

Nikki's restlessness is contagious, and I try to look anywhere other than at her. A gun rack eclipses the rear glass. I'm not sure whether it's a good or bad thing that it's empty. "Check the glove compartment," I say to Dylan.

"It's locked," she says. "But I'm in front of it anyway. He can't get to it. Besides"—I hear a click—"I have a gun. No matter what, he's outnumbered."

Inside me the snake is uncoiling. It's shed its skin. Its new skin is shiny, smooth. It's circling, scales against scales, spiraling up up up.

The buzzer signals the end of the game. I glance at Nikki gripping the gun with both hands, the way we did in the woods. Mine is heavy. Thick. It doesn't feel hollow at all. It feels like I'm holding everything in my hand.

I'm hot and cold all at once. I exhale and close my eyes for a beat. *He deserves this. They all deserve this.*

I hear the footsteps of the crowd, car doors opening, engines turning. Lights flash across the night sky, and I wonder what the other girls are thinking. The three of us don't dare to speak.

The snake is filling me up, round and round and round it goes.

They all deserve this.

The lot feels empty around us, the other cars far away. There are no voices anymore. I know the players will come out last, but time feels frozen in here, while everyone outside this truck is moving and living and breathing.

Also, it's really hot.

Then I hear his voice. I look at Nikki, and her eyes are

212

set, determined. I feel bad for Dylan up front. At least I have Nikki.

They deserve this.

We duck deep behind the front seats. Our backs will blend into the car's upholstery. I'm more worried about Dylan being spotted.

Time stretches.

Then the door creaks open and it's so loud I almost scream. It's just another bottled one to add to my collection. The gun is shaking and then I realize it's not the gun but my hands, my hands are shaking, and the gun feels too heavy so I press it between my knees. I hear him toss his bag onto the seat. This would be the moment he'd discover Dylan.

But he says nothing. He turns the key and the engine shakes the floor beneath me. Every sound an explosion.

I look at Nikki. Her eyes are focused.

He turns on music, loud and screamy. The truck rumbles slowly through the parking lot. I hear the beat of his fingers on the wheel, off tempo. I count the stops, feel the turns, picture where we are. We need to do it off the main road. But we don't want to stray too far from school, too far from our escape.

I am not worried. We planned it all out. It's not worry that shed the skin of the snake, that made it uncoil, that made it rattle the bottled screams on their shelves. It's something else entirely.

I look at Nikki. She nods. I risk lifting my head to look out the window. He's turned off the main road, just as we knew he would. The woods bordering the school are on our right. Exactly like we planned.

I nod at Nikki. I lift up and place the barrel of the gun to his neck.

"Shit!" He screams and swerves wild into the other lane. The headlights of an oncoming car blaze across the truck's insides before he jerks back. The car's horn is long and loud as it passes. But it is not worry that's rising in me.

Nikki presses play. Our prerecorded male voice says: "I have a gun. Pull to the side of the road. Slowly." You can find anything online.

He starts crying. Blubbering. Like immediately. I want to laugh. *Look at you now, Kups.* He's a cracked dam, a busted water main, a flash flood.

Dylan pops up holding her gun too.

"Oh shit!" He swerves again. "Oh shit!"

Nikki presses play again: "Keep your hands on the wheel. Pull over to the side carefully. And keep your eyes forward. You look at us, you die."

He slows down. Another car passes, but the rest of the road is empty. All the traffic from the game is long gone. He pulls over.

He parks. There are no cars or streetlights. Dylan holds the gun on him, while Nikki and I get out. I open his door, gesturing with my gun for him to get out. Nikki steps out, her gun at his neck. I put mine at the small of his back. He doesn't notice that we're smaller than his three hundred pounds of stupid. He's too busy crying.

I walk him into the woods, Dylan and Nikki flank us, guns out.

He's really crying now, hands up in the air. His whole body shakes with the sobs. My snake is free now, slithering along on the ground beside us, weaving between our feet, ready to bite if I give the word.

Our feet crunch on dried, dead leaves. There's no beauty in the way they fade and shrivel. This is where he deserves to be. With the dead things.

Nikki presses play again. "On your knees. Hands behind your head."

I rock back my slide. *Kuhcheck*. Then Nikki. *Kuhcheck*. Then Dylan. *Kuhcheck*.

The sounds send him over the edge. With each one, he breaks more. He's bawling, begging. "Please, please," he cries again and again.

I think I see a patch of wet spread across his pants. I think I smell it.

He's disgusting. They're all disgusting. I remember the way he called after us, took her stick, our stick, turned it into something ugly, something his. Eyes like knives cutting our bodies into pieces like they're his to slice. Jamison and Nikki and running onto the beach buttons all wrong, my buttons all wrong. He no buttons no zippers basketball shorts his hands on me on my body not his body his elbow my neck no breath ripping at my jeans him laughing on the stairs my stairs my school. Mine.

He got away with it. They all get away with it.

I move my gun from his back to his cheek. I press the hard

hate into his skin. I want them to feel me in their skin like I feel them in mine. I press harder. He whimpers. I rotate it. I wish it had blades on the end so I'd cut a circle. Leave a mark.

Tattoo my anger on their skin.

Dylan kicks him from behind and his face eats dirt. He's crying so hard he's making mud with his tears. It's so perfect. So perfect that he'll leave here bloody and muddy just like he made her last week.

Nikki presses play again. "You have been found unworthy."

He sobs.

"You are unfit to live."

He wails. "Please, please." He curls into himself. "I'm sorry. Whatever I did, I'm sorry."

"Women do not exist for your pleasure. If you don't change, we'll end you."

His face is a mess of tears, snot, and mud. His fat lips are trembly and weak.

My finger feels heavy on the trigger. The snake is coiling around my ankles and it would be so easy to just pull the trigger. It would scare him that much more.

The triplets said you must never pull the trigger when aiming at someone. Even if you think the chamber is empty. Because you never know. But my finger feels heavy and the chamber is empty. I checked. The snake rustles the dead leaves.

Gunshot.

THIRTY-ONE

TIME STOPS. I AM THE hands on Dad's watch. The snake is gone. The bottled screams are gone. The broken glass is gone.

I look at the gun in my hand.

I didn't. I know I didn't.

I drop it.

I poke Kups.

He howls. Screaming for God and Jesus and who knows who else. So he's not dead. "Please, please don't hurt me." So he's not hurt.

Nikki waves me on and takes off. Dylan tugs my arm. Right. Someone could have heard that. I jump up. I crash across the leaves and remember the gun.

I run back. He's still sobbing, still curled, still a mess. I can't see it. I get down on all fours and search around. With every rustle of the leaves he cries louder. Finally, I find it and grab it off the ground.

I run. I run faster than I ever ran on the field.

I think I hear him following us, but when I turn, I can't see anything. I lift my mask up so I can breathe. But when I do, I trip over a root and fall down. My knee slams against something hard.

I'm sure I hear the leaves rustle behind us.

"Come on!" whispers Nikki as she pulls me up.

We jump over a broken-down stone wall at the edge of the woods and sprint to the parking lot of the dead strip mall next to the school. The triplets wait for us. Part of me wants to collapse into their arms and the other part just wants to keep running and never stop.

"We heard a gunshot."

"Was that a gunshot? It could've been a car backfiring."

"It wasn't a car," Nikki says, glaring at Dylan.

"You shot him?" Sasha nearly shouts.

"Shhh. No, he's fine," I say. "Totally fine. We need to go."

"But—"

"She's right. We'll talk at your house."

We split up. Nikki's driving me and Dylan. As soon as we close the doors on the others, on what happened, on the world outside, Nikki spins to Dylan in the passenger seat.

"What the actual fuck, Dylan?"

"Oh *chill*. He's fine. And honestly? Would it be the end of the world if he wasn't?"

Nikki's eyes go wide and her arms straighten on the steering wheel. Her hands are exactly at ten and two. Just how they taught us in driver's ed.

She shakes her head. She turns the key in the ignition. The car starts. She turns it off.

"You realize we weren't supposed to kill him, right?"

"Whatever. He's fine. Now drive." Nikki still stares at her. Dylan tilts her head back and moans at the sunroof. "Okay, okay. I'm sorry. I didn't mean it. I swear."

Nikki looks at her. Dylan smiles.

"Promise?"

"Promise."

Nikki starts the engine. We pull out of the parking lot. Instead of turning at the light ahead, Nikki makes the right before the light. Skirts around it. I get it. I need to keep moving too.

"Dyl, what happened?" I finally ask.

Dylan looks down at the gun she's cradling in her lap. I look at mine. It's so heavy and real. "I don't know. All this mad came rushing at me. Like everything he's done. Not even just this year. Like since middle school."

"He's been doing it that long?" Nikki's voice is soft.

Dylan nods.

"I'm so sorry, Dyl," I say.

Dylan shrugs like it's nothing.

Nikki reaches out her hand, palm up. Dylan looks at it and then puts her hand in Nikki's for a squeeze.

"Anyway, it was like it was all just filling me up and I wanted to scare him so bad. I swear I didn't know there was a bullet. I just thought if he could hear the click he'd really lose it."

I get it. I felt it.

"Oh, he lost it," Nikki says.

"He really did, didn't he?" Dylan says.

Then we all start to laugh. It's a manic, wild laugh that

takes over so hard I couldn't stop it if I tried. Tears spill down my cheeks. Dylan squeals.

"I mean, I'm sorry about the gunshot, but man, it felt so good to see him like that. To be the one who *made* him like that."

"I wonder if he'll still go to Darcy's party," Nikki says.

"Not a chance," Dylan says.

I'm so damned hot. I put the gun on the floor. I peel off my gloves and sweatshirt. I tug my hair loose from my pony-tail. We turn off the main road into the triplets' neighborhood.

I knock the sunroof. "This baby open?"

Nikki presses the button and there's a sucking sound as it opens and Dylan and I unbuckle our seat belts. We stand and pull ourselves up to sit on the roof. We loop our ankles around the headrests.

The November wind beats against my face until tears stream from my eyes. I raise my arms toward the moon and let the wind rip through me.

Up here, I'm invincible.

I wake at the triplets' house Saturday morning thinking of Kups and field hockey.

We need to leave early for Regionals in Cortland against Sparta.

I wish I didn't remember the way Sparta was a red, angry swarm always ready to attack. I wish I didn't remember the way my shins were covered in bruises from their vicious sticks. I wish I didn't remember the way we played the whole game in our goal, as Ava tried again and again to stop them. I wish I didn't remember the way they destroyed us: 4 to 0.

But I do.

And my knee hurts from last night. It's the same stupid knee I twisted with Jason Stimple. This time I must've scraped it because there was some blood I had to wipe clean in the shower.

I'm in the triplets' bathroom, toothbrush hovering midair, when Nikki bumps me in the shoulder. I spit into the sink.

"You're psyching yourself out, Cap," she says.

"Nuh-uh." I rinse.

"Yuh-huh." Her lips purse. "I don't care who they are or that they won a million years ago. Because it was a million years ago." The others cluster behind us. "You guys"—she looks at all of us—"we did something amazing last night. We've been incredible all fall—on the field and off. We changed the whole course of things." She puts some toothpaste on her brush. "If we can do that, we can beat Sparta."

"Sticks Chicks forever!" The six of us bump elbows and shoulders, dapping and high-fiving and whooping, and the others make their way downstairs until it's just me and Nikki again.

She throws her arm across my shoulder. "You are a true badass."

I hip bump her. "I'm so glad you tried out."

She smiles. "Me too. Absofockinglutely."

The wind that beat against me on the car's roof last night is inside, ready to unleash. We did the impossible last night. And we'll do it again today.

Ava, Cristina, Michaela, Kiara, and Liv meet us at the bus. Ava looks worried and Liv looks ready to cry. Like I'm the one who'll be mad at them. But I'm not. I'm just sorry they missed out. I want them to feel what I'm feeling. I throw my arms around them in a big hug and the others join in until they're gasping for air in the middle of a giant team hug.

Ava comes up to me while everyone else boards the bus. "You good?"

I smile. "We're going to kill Sparta today."

"That's the plan." Ava tilts her head. "Did you kill anyone else I should know about?"

I laugh. "Everyone's fine. But I doubt he's going to be messing with us anytime soon."

She nods. "Good." She fumbles with her stick. "We're good, right?"

I hip bump her and she loses her balance, laughing. "Sticks Chicks forever, baby!"

On the bus, I sit next to Liv. "We okay?"

"I am." She turns from the window to me. "Are you?"

I nod. "Yeah."

"You did what you needed to do?"

I think of Kups, face in the dirt, sobbing. "Absofocking-lutely."

"Good. I'm glad you got that out of your system. Because, honestly?" She looks at me hard. "It didn't feel like you."

"Oh, don't worry about me," I say.

Except her words feel too big to blow away. So I change

the subject. "What did you end up doing last night? Did you go out with Jake?"

"Yeah. We went to Tully's—"

I groan. "I'm already jealous."

She laughs. And she talks about who she saw and the movie and a funny thing Jake did. And I'm listening, I am. But I'm also wondering what "me" is anymore.

We fall silent after a bit and put in our earbuds—we all do—and concentrate on what we have to do in Cortland. If we win today, we get to play in the state semifinals in the Syracuse University Dome. State finals are always in different places, so it's just a coincidence that they're in Syracuse this year. But Ava and I took it like an invitation.

Dad used to take us to SU football and basketball games before the accident, the high seats clinging to the sides, the roar of the crowd so loud I thought it might rip the dome right off. I always wondered how it would feel to run across that turf, look up at all those people in all those stands cheering for me.

And now it might actually happen. In less than a week.

No. It *will* happen. I let the wind from last night swirl around and fill me up again. It's how I storm off the bus. It's how we all storm off the bus.

We're here to play.
We're here to stay.
Our sticks and skills will make you pay.
Your jabs are trash.

Your sticks don't smash.

You wrote a check your skills can't cash.

When we race onto the field, their red kilts and socks don't seem as angry. Away from their home field, they seem a little lost. I imagine they heard how we defeated Greenville, how we leveled Sommersville, the top-ranked team in the league. Every time that counted, we've won.

And then there are all the wins they don't know about—the moonlit dressed-in-black wins.

At the whistle, Quinn pushes the ball away. She passes to Bella. When Sparta swarms, she flicks it back to me. I dance around them and advance a few feet before their middie steals it. She gets a good shot and drives it halfway down the field, sending us all sprinting.

Back and forth, back and forth. The seconds roll into minutes. The minutes roll together. At the half, it's 0 to 0.

I kick a tuft of grass on the way back to the bench. We need to win this. I think of the UNC coach going to States, watching some other team, some other girl. I take a swig of my water.

"There's this AA quote I've always liked: 'Yesterday is history, tomorrow's a mystery, and today is a gift.'" Coach gestures toward the field. "*Enjoy* this."

Maybe she's right. Maybe this moment isn't about two years from now. It's about us, being here, further than we've ever been before.

Then again, Coach doesn't need a scholarship.

I look at Sparta's bench. Their heads are dipped, shoulders

bent, faces drawn. Then I turn back and look at our girls. They're sweaty and tired, but they're not defeated. I smile. I tip my head toward the Spartans. "They're scared. Of us."

The others turn, and I watch the truth of it spread across their faces.

"We did that, you guys." I put my stick in the center. "Sticks Chicks forever?"

The girls add their sticks to mine. "Sticks Chicks forever!"

Coach puts her face in the huddle. "Now kill 'em. Unless you want to walk home."

When we run out again, something clicks. Like I know how it will work. When Quinn passes the ball back to Liv, I know where she'll send it before it's there and I'm on it. My stick connects with that satisfying crack and I send the ball through their forward's legs just enough to pick it up on the other side. I search for the triplets, but they're tangled in Sparta's defense. Cristina doesn't have an open lane. I dance around the reds, sprinting toward the goal. I sweep it so hard my knee grazes the ground, and the ball flies across the green, sailing beneath the goalie's pads.

GOAL.

Quinn hugs me so hard my feet leave the ground, and we scream as we race back to position.

We scramble to hold the lead, but they cut through with a goal ten minutes before the end. Coach calls a timeout and wraps us in a huddle. "*Is this the way it will end?*" she asks. Our NO rises like a lion. I see it in my teammates' eyes. We will not be beat.

We run back out with a roar. Bella takes it right off. They steal it and drive it back toward Ava, but Nikki is there and she swings back and smacks that sucker so hard it jumps out of their grasp and right into Dylan's, who slams it toward Michaela. Ahead of them by seconds, we push it out of their reach until Bella hurls it toward the goal. And it lands.

They can hear our screams back home. They can hear our screams in NYC. They can hear our screams in Europe. Hell, our screams penetrate space and time and confuse the crap out of the people who fought on these fields once upon a time.

WE WON.

Us + This Moment = States.

We scream ourselves onto the bus. We scream to the music. I pull out Big Bob's cooler and we stuff ice cream into our screaming mouths, and we muffle our screams with cold sugar.

"State semifinals, here we come!"

"Even better that it's at the Dome." *Our* Dome: the biggest domed stadium in the northeast or on a college campus or the world or something.

I can't believe I'm going to play at States. In the Dome.

Cristina makes all of us lean into the aisle and click sticks for Coach to take a picture on her phone. Then she goes to post it.

She slumps down in her seat. "Shit."

"What?"

She just shakes her head. Liv nudges me. I look over her shoulder at her phone.

Kups is in the ICU. He got in an accident.

I look up, and we're all quiet, searching one another's faces.

Liv, next to me, gives me this look laced with pity or blame or I don't know what.

Sasha bursts into tears. "We should tell the doctors."

Dylan snaps her head back. "Tell them what?"

"Don't." Bella's eyes narrow at Dylan. "Don't talk to my sister like that."

"Everyone chill," Kiara says. "Sasha, think about it. What good would that do?" Kiara shakes her head. "No. Everyone sit tight."

"Besides," I whisper. "It couldn't be because of us. He was fine when we left."

"But what about the gu—" Sasha starts.

Dylan stands and nods toward the front of the bus where Coach sits. "Shut. Up."

"Down in back, please!" the bus driver shouts. I see his eyes in the mirror.

"Whatever," Dyl mutters, sliding back down. "It's not like he didn't deserve it."

We sink back into our seats.

Kiara whispers to Sasha, "You won't tell, right?"

I look back at Sasha. She just stares out the window, tears rolling down her cheeks. She doesn't say okay. She doesn't say she won't tell.

Whispers clog the bus air but I can't make them out.

The ice cream turns sour in my stomach. We were just supposed to change him. I think of the way he cried on the ground. Of how wrong the gunshot sounded in the night.

I remember Coach's words: *Is this the way it will end?*

THIRTY-TWO

ON MONDAY, EVERYONE WHISPERS ABOUT the accident in the halls, during class, in the bathroom. He was drunk.
Someone else was drunk. He smashed his truck into a tree.
Another car plowed into him. He was texting. He was wasted
when he left Darcy's party Friday night. He was sober. Someone said they even saw him crying.

Kups. The great, unflappable Kups was *crying*.

That's the one that gets me. Of all the rumors, that's the one
nobody believes. Except Dylan, Nikki, and me. Because we
saw him. We made him sob. We made him shake and crumple,
wet himself, and beg for mercy.

We broke him.

No one mentions us.

In class, I try to focus on the teachers' words, their mouths,
but it's reaching through the fog. I pass my team in the halls,
and it's like we're all ghosts.

Everyone but Sasha. She's not in school.

And then we hear a new rumor, one that makes our shoulders curl: He went to the party *after* he was attacked. He

wouldn't shut up about it. He was ranting. Everyone thought he was wasted. Maybe he was? Maybe he wasn't? But he was attacked. At gunpoint.

Hearing it in other people's mouths, the words feel sharper, scarier. *Gun. Point.*

In Mac's class, Liv leans over to Bella. "Is Sasha okay? Is it her concussion?"

But Bella just keeps her eyes down and shakes her head. Michaela and Liv give her this sympathetic look, but it's easy for them to be sympathetic. They weren't there. They're free and clear.

Unlike me.

What if Sasha calls the hospital? What if the cops get involved?

I think of when I banged my knee. Blood. I wonder if any blood got on the ground when I fell.

There's something in my stomach, and it keeps growing. Like a tumor.

All I hear is Kups sobbing on the ground. All I feel is the weight of the gun in my hand. All I see is the way his shoulders shook when Nikki played the recording. All I—

"Zoe? Zoe?"

"Yes?" I manage to say.

"Are you all right?"

The vomit rises fast, and I run from the room and make it to the garbage can in the hall. I throw up into the bag. I see Cheetos at the bottom of the trash, smell them, and retch again. A door opens and shuts behind me, and part of me cares about the whispers that feel like needles at my back, and part of me doesn't care at all.

Because of me, a boy is in intensive care. Because of me, a person might die.

And because of Sasha, everyone might find out.

I want to go to the hospital. But I know I can't. I'm not friends with him. I don't even like him. A few days ago, I loved the idea of a gun held to his head. I hated him so much that I wanted to scare him *to death*.

Oh God. It was my idea to scare him.

My idea.

By the time the nurse comes, I'm sobbing. My sleeves and cheeks are wet with tears, and I have that crying headache that sits low on my eyes and craves darkness.

"You're not going to practice tonight," she says. It's a statement, not a question.

"I have to," I say. "You don't understand."

She shakes her head. "It isn't even a game. You kids think missing sports is like a death sentence. Get some perspective."

But she's wrong. I have perspective. I have the full weight of Kups sitting on my eyelids, pressing against my skull. He could die, and I'm responsible.

I throw up again.

I stay in bed the next day. Texts come in and I struggle to focus on the small screen, on the words. Everything feels too big for a text. Anyway, nobody knows anything new. I call Nikki, but she doesn't answer. I think of calling Sasha, or her sisters, but my finger hovers above a button that I don't press.

I replay the moments before, the way we planned everything down to the minute. Everything so that we would get away with it. Everything except for Kups getting hurt.

But that's a lie.

I *wanted* him hurt. I wanted him to feel what I felt. I wanted to punish him for what he did to Dylan. For the fact that he got away with everything. For the way they *all* got away with everything.

And that's when it hits me, and when it does, I run to the bathroom to throw up. Again. *We got away with everything too.* Night after night we decided who got hurt, and nobody stopped us. Who the hell did I think I was that I could—that I should—hold a gun to someone's head?

All the thoughts I had when I held the gun to him rush back at me. The way all the memories of Kups, yes, but Jamison and Reilly too, blended together, like I was punishing Kups for all of them. Like they were all the same person. Like hurting him was hurting them all.

And now he will have a Before and an After.

I slump back to bed and pull the covers up. But I don't feel the safety and comfort of bed. Instead, I keep reliving the night in the woods: Kups on his knees, on the ground, face in the mud, sobbing for his life.

And I laughed.

I run back to the bathroom, but there's nothing to throw up anymore. I lean my head against the cool tank. I can't believe I was that person. I can't believe I let myself *become* that person.

Liv knew. She knew for herself and she knew for me. And I didn't listen.

I call Liv, but she doesn't answer either.

I check my phone for updates about Kups, but I'm not his friend. My friends aren't friends with his friends.

I call Liv that afternoon. "I love you. You were right. About everything."

"Zo," she says, the line crackling with pity. "I love you too."

And I can't bear the pity, can't bear that I fell so hard, so I make an excuse and hang up.

That night, the doorbell rings. Dad's in bed and Mom's working so I drag myself downstairs. It's Eileen. She's holding a bag. I follow her into the kitchen. She starts unpacking it. There's a container of pulled pork. A bag of rolls. A steaming container of collard greens. Uncle Bob's ice cream. Apple pie.

I start to cry.

"Oh honey," she says. "Come here." She wraps me in a hug. This woman who I've treated like shit since day one wraps me in a hug. "It's just pulled pork. It's nothing to cry about."

I give a half laugh and wipe my eyes. I was so wrong about her. She was never huffy or whiny. She was just trying to help—help Uncle Bob spruce up Scoop Dreams, help my dad by sending him videos of my games, help me right now with dinner.

"Thanks, Aunt Eileen."

She draws back and I see it hit her that it's the first time

I've called her that. I can't believe I withheld this thing, this one simple word that links us. All this time, I've been looking for the rifts, not the ties. That's why I had no idea that hurting Kups would hurt me as much as it did. My cheeks feel hot and wet and my head is killing me.

She lifts my chin with her hand. "It's okay to ask for help sometimes, you know."

I nod. I force myself to concentrate on her. "One day," I say, "I want to hear all about what it was like to play for SU."

She smiles. "I'd like that a lot. Over ice cream."

I manage a smile. "Obviously."

After she leaves, I take Dad a plate. But I'm not hungry, so I get back into bed.

It may be okay to ask for help but I'm pretty sure I waited too long.

Wednesday, I stay home again. But my body is too restless for my mind. So I run—no, sprint—on the lake trail.

This Friday, we're supposed to play in the state semifinals. At the Dome. The fact that they're in Syracuse was supposed to be fate. Fate that we'd win. Now I can't imagine winning anything.

I fucked up everything. In one night. Ava and Liv asked us before we did it: *Are you willing to risk it?* And I'd laughed. What was there to risk? I had no idea.

I run harder. I want my legs to hurt. I want my feet to bleed.

I'm heaving when I get back, my heart so large and fierce that it shakes its cage.

It's nice to know it's still there.

That night, Mom comes back later than usual. She sits on my bed.

"I stopped by the hospital tonight."

I throw back the covers and look at her. She had the night off.

She looks at me, concerned, and then shakes her head. "I thought you said you weren't friends with that boy."

"I'm not." It's true. I could say I hate him. That would be true too.

Her eyebrows wrinkle. "Okay. But you want to know how he is? Is that what this is about?"

I nod, and the tears come all over again, and I'm biting my lip to keep everything from pouring out.

"He's going to be okay."

I sob. I sob. I sob.

Mom gets into bed and wraps her arms tightly around me, and I'm so grateful to be contained because I might just dissolve without her. Slowly, my tears ebb and my cheeks dry, but she still holds tight. She doesn't say anything. She doesn't shush me or tell me everything's going to be okay. She's just here, wrapping her arms around me, smelling like Mom. And I cry all over again. I remember when I was little, when I'd skin my knee or scrape my elbow, how she could make me feel better with just a hug. That it didn't matter that she was a nurse and knew how to stitch me up or even which Band-Aid to choose. It was the fact that she was my mom and she was hugging me better. Just like now.

I go early to school on Thursday to meet with teachers, to make up for the two days I missed. I'll stay after too, and stay late at practice. I'll do whatever it takes to get ready for Friday.

None of that matters because Kups is going to be okay.

But when I get to school, all anyone is talking about is the gang that attacked Kups. It's the same gang, they say, that attacked Jason Stimple. The same gang, they say, that showed up at the cemetery party. We're under attack, they say. We need to protect ourselves, they say.

Never mind that this whole thing started because *we* were the ones who needed protection. But that feels like a lifetime ago too. I can't imagine being that girl anymore either.

The police arrive. They set up in the conference room off the principal's office. Kids get called out of class all day, and the main office becomes a revolving door of scared.

"Nobody wants to admit to drinking," Kiara says.

"Besides," Dylan adds, "no guy will admit they could've been beaten by a bunch of girls."

Maybe I'm safe. Maybe not.

After class, I wait for Sasha, but she lingers too long with the teacher. I try again, but I just miss her. Quinn and Bella go scarce too. I pass the others in the hallway, and our smiles are tight like our knuckles as we grip our bags.

Grove gets called to the makeshift police station in the

main office too. I try not to look at him, but I do. His head is down. People say stupid stuff like "Oooooh" and "Give 'em hell."

"What's this about?" Mac says, but nobody fills him in, and he just starts in about the Bill of Rights.

Michaela, Liv, and I exchange a look. We're not the kind of kids they'd question.

I don't think.

I wonder if they have the right to ask anything. I wonder if we have the right to lie if it's for the greater good. But I don't even trust myself to know what's good anymore.

In the hall, Dylan whispers that they called her in. Of course they did.

"They just asked if I was at any of the parties 'in question.'" She uses air quotes. "I said no." She raises her eyebrows. "I mean, I'm not lying. I wasn't *at* the parties. I was *near* them."

Liv and Ava smile and look sympathetic because they're not feeling any guilt at all. Just worry. But it's the sort of detached worry you feel for a neighbor. Like, whatever's happening, however bad, it's not happening in *your* house.

If I'd been a better person, it wouldn't have happened in my house either.

I get bumped from behind by a group of tenth graders walking in a pack, all pushing around the same gossip about this unknown gang terrorizing Kups. And how Kups is getting justice. Which, fine, maybe he should. But we learned our lesson.

Shouldn't that count for something?

And what lesson did Reilly or Jamison learn?

They're not feeling a thing right now. They have no idea how much a part of this they are.

A group of girls whispering at the lockers looks over at us. I know they're not talking about us.

Probably.

I'm in a glass box. The walls press against my skin, but I can't look like I can't breathe can't move can't think.

Because everyone will see.

THIRTY-THREE

MY EYES OPEN TO MY UNC poster. Tonight, we're supposed to play in the state semifinals, and if we win—*when* we win—we'll play the following night in the actual New York State Field Hockey Championship. And UNC's recruiter will be there.

Even though my room is dim in the early morning, I know exactly what my UNC poster looks like. I know the thick blue ribbon along the bottom that reads *Carolina Tar Heels*. I know the crisscrossing diamond design on either side of the words *Field Hockey*. I know the eight girls clumped in the center, sticks obscuring faces, arms looped and threaded, all wearing Carolina blue. Their hair is caught in imperfect flyaway braids, bands, and ponytails. Sweat shines their muscles. None face the camera, so I see their smiles only in the silhouettes of their round, high cheeks. This is the moment their team won Nationals.

I push myself up to sitting. I roll my neck, the ligaments and tissues and bones and muscles grinding against one another. As always, my hips and back ache, but so do my shoulders, thighs, and feet. I don't know if I even slept last night.

I look back at the poster.

I remember Ava's words at Sasha's bedside: *I don't think we can win States without you.*

It's not just about me getting to UNC. It's about Ava getting her dream. Nikki and Cristina getting the senior season they deserve. The triplets getting scouted. Kiara's bragging rights over her dad. Michaela getting to be valedictorian *and* state champ. And it's about not letting Liv down. Again. Somehow I have to pull it together.

And we still have to make it through today at school.

Maybe the police don't work on Fridays. Maybe Santa and the Easter Bunny go clubbing together.

I don't think we can win without you.

It should feel like a compliment.

I scrunch my bare feet against my carpet and stand. I walk to my door, through the doorway, down the hall, down the stairs. Each step like lugging five hundred pounds.

At the bottom, I'm hit with Dad's singing and the smell of waffles.

I'm pulled right back to the Before, when Dad could celebrate big days and first days and birthdays.

When *he* was the one taking care of *me*.

I step into the kitchen, lights bright, waffle iron on, batter stuck to the side. And Dad. Dad turns, with his big smile, his apron tied around his middle, flour on his cheek.

"Dad," I say, finally. "You didn't need—"

"I didn't need to celebrate the world's greatest daughter?"

If he only knew.

"I didn't need to celebrate the stylins' of the world's greatest field hockey player? The captain who took her team to the Dome? The girl who took her team further than any field hockey team in school history?"

His words should feel like balloons. Like unpoppable balloons that only inflate and fill and rise.

They shouldn't feel like corkscrews. Twisting.

I manage a smile. He's trying so hard. I need to try harder.

He gestures with a flourish at the plate waiting at the counter. I move to the stool and sit. He's given the waffle a face with clumps of blueberries for eyes, a half-strawberry nose, and whipped-cream bushy eyebrows and wide smile.

"Wow," I say. "This is . . ."

"Amazing? Food Network–worthy?"

"Exactly that," I say.

He turns around to get the next waffle out. I look down at my plate. The blueberries bleed blue into the whipped cream. The strawberry stains the waffle red.

Dad dances over to the sink.

I don't have the energy to tell him not to.

The fork feels heavy. I slice off a hunk, careful to get some whipped cream, some blueberries. It tastes delicious. I know it does. But somehow it doesn't feel like it does.

Dad cries out.

I look up. He's braced himself on the sink, his face twisted in pain.

My fork clatters to my plate and I rush to his side. I wrap my arm around his middle and wish my arm were longer, wish I were stronger, wish he'd never got out of bed to make waffles for me, wish he'd never fallen off that damned roof.

I'm pulling up as hard as I can.

But I'm not strong enough.

"I think," he says, breathless, "I need to get back in bed."

"Okay, Dad," I say. "Can you hang here while I run and grab the walker?"

He nods, his lips tight.

I race downstairs to grab it and try hard not to bang the walls as I rush back to his side.

We walk slowly out of the kitchen, to the stairs. The walker butts up against the bottom step with a jolt. He looks like he's going to throw up.

We both look up, the stairs stretching before us.

"Maybe just get me to the couch."

"No," I say. "We're getting you to bed."

"But—"

"Mom!" I shout. "MOM!"

"No, honey," Dad says. "She didn't get home till—"

"And whose fault is that?" I snap.

"Hey," Dad says. He looks dizzy. Like he's about to fall and I am not strong enough to catch him.

"MOM!" I shout again.

She comes out of her room, sleep-disheveled. "Zoe, what is—"

But she stops talking as soon as she sees us and runs down the stairs. "What's going on?"

"He needs your help," I say.

"Okay, okay. I'm here," she says.

I want to say, *About fucking time.*

We maneuver the walker so he can slowly turn and get ready. He grabs both railings, and Mom and I position ourselves a step behind on each side. Slowly, we make our way up the stairs, Dad's breath short, Mom and I trading "You can do it" and "You're doing great" and "You got this."

We get to the top and I run down and grab the walker and we help him to bed. And then I leave them to go back down the stairs, down the hall, into the messy, bright kitchen, my waffle barely touched on my plate.

I sink onto the stool and I think it might break from the weight of me.

I take another bite of waffle but I can't even make myself swallow it. I scrape it into the trash and go upstairs to get ready.

I always liked that I couldn't really see the faces of the Tar Heels girls. That way I could replace their faces with mine. I could pretend that I was in that huddle, that I had just won Nationals, that I belonged with them.

But right now, their backs just feel like a wall without a door.

Downstairs, Mom's leaning against the messy counter, sipping her coffee. She looks tired. She looks like she thinks she has a right to be tired.

"Good morning, Zo," she says.

I push past her to the carafe. It's empty.

"Oh," Mom says. "I thought you'd already had yours. Dad must've had more than usual when he woke up."

"I make the same amount each night," I say. "Every night, *I* measure it out. *I* fill the water. *I* set the alarm. Every. Night."

"Okay, Zo. I get it," Mom says in a stilted voice that doesn't sound like she gets it at all. "I'm sorry I drank the coffee you so kindly made." She holds out her cup to me. "Do you want mine?"

"I want you to be the one who makes the coffee! I do the cooking, the cleaning, the—"

"Excuse me?"

"I do everything while you escape."

"Oh, making coffee means you do everything?" Her mouth is so tight her lips disappear. "You do not get to talk to me like this."

"Oh please, Mom. It's not about the coffee."

She throws up her hands. "You're the one who said it was. I'm just—"

"Don't you get it? Dad needed you this morning and you were lazing it up in bed. Like always. For all I know you were tired because you were living it up with the Rebels. *Like always.*"

Her mouth hangs open and she's shaking but nothing's coming out. "I. Was. At. Work," she finally says.

"Oh, you mean the place where you go take care of other sick people instead of helping Dad?"

She slams her coffee down on the counter, some of it spilling. "I'm going to go upstairs before I say something I'll regret. You're welcome to drink my damned coffee. I don't want it anymore anyway."

She turns.

"Great. You run away now. Like always."

She stops and her shoulders rise like she's going to say something, but then she just keeps walking.

I turn to her coffee, take a sip, and spit it right into the sink. She's ruined it with too much sugar. Typical.

At school, I turn a corner and see Kups. He's standing by the lockers with his crew, all guy-thumping and pounding. He lifts his eyebrows at me, and his eyes travel down my jersey to my kilt and linger on my thighs.

I want to fucking scream. After everything? After all we risked, all we did? Nothing's changed?

I swallow my rage, clutch my books to my chest, and hurry to class.

In AP US History, my phone buzzes. While Mr. Mac turns his back to write on the board, I look down to see a text from Dad:

DAD: Mom just called in tears because you think she hasn't taken care of me?

I glance up, but Mac is still writing on the board.

ME: She chooses work or Rebels over u every time.
And y wasn't she up this morning?
DAD: She's taken extra shifts at work to take the pressure off YOU getting scholarship.

Wait. What? She's been pulling extra shifts for me? That can't be right.

"Alamandar." Mr. Mac's hands are clasped in front of him. "You need me to take that phone?"

I look up at him and back at Dad's text. "I'm sorry, Mr. Mac. It's my dad. There's—"

"Do you need to step out in the hall for a minute?"

I nod.

"Make it fast. I've got to get you edumacated." He turns back to the board.

Liv tucks her car keys in my hand.

I look at them, then at her.

Go, she mouths.

I just stare at her.

"Go," she whispers, more insistent. "It's your dad, Zo. I'll cover for you."

I rush out the side exit to the parking lot. As I drive, I keep seeing Dad's text in my head. That can't be right. She never said a thing. No. She's not working for me. She's working to avoid me, Dad, and everything at home.

THIRTY-FOUR

"DAD!" I CALL, TAKING THE steps at a run. I burst into the dark room, the gray Syracuse daylight a thin frame around the shade-drawn windows.

He pushes himself up in bed, setting his laptop to the side. "What's wrong? What are you doing home? Are you hurt?"

"No. I'm fine. I just—" The bedside lamp casts a cone of dull light. He's lying against the headboard, messy hair, tired eyes, all because he tried to make me a waffle breakfast on game day. Forced into bed. Again. Because of me.

"What's wrong, then?"

And it just hits me. Again. Like a relentless wave crashing against the shore. Nothing I do matters. Nothing I do fixes anything. There's nothing I *can* do. But Mom is *supposed* to fix things, to help people. It's her job for fuck's sake. "Mom should—"

"Hey. You have no right to make your mother feel bad about what she does for us." He sits up higher and the pain spreads across his face and his stupid broken watch catches the light and I can't—I just can't—"She—"

"Dad." He would feel so much better if he just admitted it. Finally. All these times I've seen him swallow his disappointment. It would be better to let it out. Then maybe he and I could get her to help somehow. "You have to admit you shouldn't be doing as much as you do and she—"

"Zoe." His lips are thin, his voice stern. "I know you think you know what I need. But you don't."

"But she's a *nurse*, and she can't even—"

"No," he says. "Listen. You are my daughter. Laura is my wife. Neither one of you is my caretaker."

"But, Dad—"

"Stop, Zoe. Enough!"

I go silent. He's never spoken like this to me. My whole body feels unsteady, at the edge of something deep and ugly. Suddenly the six feet between us feels like six hundred. This room is so damned dark. And I don't know how we got here.

"Nurses aren't superheroes. Neither are doctors. Neither are any of the healers and specialists I've seen. They don't have all the answers. Some don't even ask the right questions. But your mom has never given up—not on me, not on you, not on us.

"And none of these doctors and specialists are free. Your mother works her tail off to make sure that I have access to all of them, even if our insurance won't cover them. And on top of everything, she works extra shifts so that *you* don't have to worry about college. Do you know how hard it is for me to see her work like this and not be able to help? And then you blame *her*?"

This room is so dark. Everything's shifted. Nothing is where I thought it was. I'm not where I thought I was. I want to slip into the darkness, become invisible. The lamplight shows me his face and it's twisted with anger, disappointment.

At me.

"It's not her job to fix me, Zoe, but she's doing everything she can anyway. And you know what? I've been to fifty doctors and specialists and physical therapists and nurses and massage therapists and acupuncturists, and guess what? Not one has 'fixed' me." He sighs big. "This is just life, Zoe. You can't control all of it. You can barely control some of it."

I can't control anything. Not my team. Not school. Not myself. Not my scholarship. Not Grove. Not Kups. Not Reilly. Not Dad's face right now.

"Do you know why I think you get so angry at your mom?" His voice is softer but his cheeks go blotchy. Like *he's* going to cry.

I don't think I can take it if he cries.

"It's because you're so angry that I got hurt. And you can't be mad at me so you get mad at her." Tears arc down his cheeks. "And your mom"—he sniffs—"the wonderful, generous woman that she is, just takes it. I wanted to say something to you, but she always protects you. She just lets you use her like a human punching bag because she says you need something to punch." He shakes his head. "But no more, Zoe. It's not fair."

Inside, a tidal wave surges, threatening. "I—"

"Oh honey," he says, waving me over, "come here."

I walk slowly. They thought *I* had to be protected. They thought *I* had to be handled. It's like a compass I've been following all this time just up and switched north and south. I lean over and hug him, careful not to put my weight on him like always, but he holds me tight, holds me until the tears roll down my cheeks anyway.

"I love you, Zozo."

"I love you too, Dad."

He releases me. He nods at the chair and I pull it over. He takes my hand in his. "I think we let things go too far. And that's on us. Not you. But I need you to start seeing things the way they really are."

I swipe my cheeks. "I'll tell Mom I'm sorry."

He nods. "Good. But there's more, Zoe. It's me too. You see me as sick. Ever since the accident. That's all you see." He squeezes my hand. "I am so much more than this injury, Zoe. But you behave as though you've forgotten who I am. You only see me as a burden."

I lean forward, clutching his hands in mine. "Dad. That's not true. You're not a burden. I love you. I just want to help you feel better."

"I know that, honey." His voice softens. "You've done so much to help out these last few years. Too much."

"It was nothing."

"No. It was a lot. And I am so grateful. But that's not what I mean. It's the way you treat me now."

"I—" The tears gather behind my eyes, my cheeks, my nose. I sniff. I refuse to cry again.

"Trust me, I know it's coming from a good place. But—"
He exhales. "It makes me feel like crap half the time. Sometimes I just want to forget about my accident, you know? Sometimes I just want to be your dad. I just want to bake cookies and listen to Marvin. I want to dance with your mom. I want to make you a waffle. I don't want that accident to define me. Or you. Or your mom. I don't need your pity, Zoe."

Every part of me is working to dam up the tears. All this time, *I've* been the one holding him back. *I've* been the one making their lives harder. *I've* been the one not seeing what's in front of my face. Not them. All this time I thought I was in the right. And I was so far from it.

"I'm so sorry, Dad."

"I know, pumpkin. I love you so much." He pulls me in for a hug and I hear the soft music from his earbuds. He laughs softly. "I can't believe you came home in the middle of the day. Did you leave them a note?"

I sit up and let out a half laugh. He rubs the top of my head.

"My little rebel."

It used to be this joke. Me and my notes. Me and my rules. But there are so many rules I've broken I don't even know where the line is anymore.

"You better get back. You've got a big game. That's what you should focus on. Don't worry about me. Enjoy being a field hockey player going to States, okay?"

"Mm-hmm," I manage. I stand, my legs somehow walking me to the door.

"Do me a favor?"

I turn back. "Yeah?"

"Don't forget to shoot your mom that text, okay?"

"Definitely," I say. "I'm sorry, Dad."

"Honey, it's okay. Really. It's on us. Your mom and I made a lot of mistakes. Don't worry, we'll make more." He smiles. "Now go back to whatever passes for learning in that fine institution."

I slam the car door, and the clang rips right through me. I put my hands on the wheel and run them along the ridges. I lean my head back against the headrest. The daylight is the color of concrete, but it still feels too bright, too much after the dark of his bedroom. All this time, it's been me.

Help and harm are too close.

I take out my phone.

ME: Sorry about this morning, Mom.
ME: I'm sorry about a lot of things. I was wrong.
I love you.

I also toss a quick text to Liv.

I wipe my face and start the car. All this time, in so many ways, I've been in the wrong.

I am a complete and total shit.

THIRTY-FIVE

BACK AT SCHOOL, IT'S BETWEEN periods and the halls are thick with people and my throat feels jammed and my chest feels tight and I'm trying to remember where Liv would be but—

"Whoa."

Great. I just ran into someone.

"You okay?"

I look up.

It's Grove. Of course.

"I—"

"Come on." He pulls me toward the lockers, away from the rush of bodies. "You don't seem—are you okay?"

"Don't." I look down, over his shoulder, anywhere but at him. "I'm such an idiot."

Grove shrugs. "Funny. Jake said the same thing about me."

I look at him. "Excuse me?" I think I forgot how gorgeous he is. But man, right here, up close, it's like he's made of gorgeous. Like gorgeousness is a place, and he has a house there. Not a summerhouse. A *house* house.

"I owe you an apology," he says. "I was mean and stupid."

"No, I—"

"No, I was. I liked you, I got hurt, and I didn't treat you well."

Liked me. Past tense.

"And I'm really unproud of that."

My lips tilt up, despite everything. "Unproud?"

He nods. "It's definitely a word."

I sigh. *Unproud* isn't a big enough word for all the mistakes I've made.

"Hey." His voice is soft. "I get that something happened. And if you want to talk about it, I'm ready to listen."

I look down and my hands are shaking. I don't even know where to begin.

"Are you the sort of person who likes to run?" he asks.

"Yes." At least that's a question I can answer.

I text Liv that I'm back, that I'm okay, and somehow, minutes later, Grove and I are on the track. I don't know how he did it. He talked to a PE teacher, a security guard, and then we're here, outside where the air is sharp and cold. Snow feels as though it's waiting, just out of sight. The ground is gray and bare.

I break into a run. He catches up. He doesn't say anything, just runs beside me. At first, it's stressful. I'm so aware of every breath, of the way my boobs look when I run, of the way his legs look as they pound the ground. I go too fast. I go too slow.

But then it's not stressful at all. It just is.

I hear the bell in the distance, but we keep running. I like the rhythm of his breath. It's like waves lapping a shore—steady and sure—and my breath calms too. I don't know how long we run, but when we finally stop, there's more space inside my rib cage.

"Want to talk about it yet?" He bends down to get his water and take a sip.

"Do you miss your dad?"

He looks at me sideways and caps his water. "Are you the sort of person who answers questions with questions?"

"Are you?" I smile.

He shakes his head and puts down the water and nods to the track. We walk it slowly. "I love my mom," he says. "And she does this amazing job with us, you know?" I nod. "But sometimes I feel like she asks a lot of me. Like I'm supposed to be the dad replacement or something." He looks at me. "That sounds messed up. I don't mean—"

"I think I get it," I say. "My dad had this accident a few years back, and ever since then I've tried really hard to get everything right, to be a good student, to take care of things—"

"Before anything goes wrong?"

"Exactly."

"It's exhausting trying to anticipate disaster."

I stop. "Right?" And I realize how tiring this has been. And for what? I shake my head.

"What?"

We start walking again. "It's just that all this time I thought

I was doing the right thing, but it turns out I was hurting him. And my mom."

"What do you mean?"

"I think I was trying to protect him or something."

"I do that too." His voice is quiet.

"I guess my dad felt like whenever I'd do that, I was just seeing him as someone to be pitied. But I do feel sorry for him. I can't imagine what it must be like to be in pain all the time, to be tied to the house, to give up the things he loved."

"That would definitely suck."

"Exactly." I walk a little faster.

"So what's the problem?"

I think about when I thought someone pitied me. When Liv looked at me, I felt like she didn't think I was strong. Like I couldn't handle what happened. When I wouldn't tell Dad about Reilly, it was because I couldn't bear for him to think about me in that situation. But also, I didn't want him to pity me. I didn't want him to see me as weak. I stop. "If you pity someone it's like you don't see them as capable."

Grove is quiet for a minute. "That makes sense. It's sort of like what Mac always says: It's all about—"

"Power," I finish with him. I felt powerless when Liv looked at me that way. At the thought of my dad seeing me that way. It was one thing for Reilly to make me feel that, but to feel powerless in the eyes of someone I love and respect? Awful.

"I mean, if your dad felt like you only saw him as this powerless sob story, he might start to see himself that way too."

My insides sink. "Wow. I'm a complete idiot."

"No, you're not," he says, putting his arm around me in a side hug. The kind of hug guys give to girls they're just friends with. He drops his arm.

And I feel like an idiot all over again. An idiot for everything with Kups, for fighting with Ava, and right here, right now, an idiot for letting Grove go. "No. Trust me. I'm a total idiot."

He tilts his head and looks at me. "Wanna know why Jake called *me* an idiot?" His voice does that rumbly thing I can feel in my knees.

My mouth is dry. I nod.

"Well." He looks down. "I guess Liv told him you were going through something, but that it didn't have anything to do with me, and that if I wasn't a total idiot, I should"—his voice gets lower, softer—"try again."

Right here, looking at Grove, I remember our talk on the dock, our paddle on the lake, our kiss in the canoe. I remember the millions of stars above us and the fireflies between us. A smile rises from my toes, lifting everything else with it. I put my hands on his chest. He smiles right back. I grab his shirt and pull him close to kiss him.

His lips feel soft and strong all at once. He cups his hands around my face and runs them down my neck and shoulders, and I throw my arms around him. I can feel his smile through his kiss. I missed this. I missed him.

I feel something wet on my eyelash and I open my eyes and laugh.

The first snow.

THIRTY-SIX

IT DOESN'T MATTER THAT WE'RE in high school. It doesn't matter that we live in one of the snowiest places in America. It doesn't matter that this is what November always looks like.

The first snowfall is the stuff of magic. And Grove and I kissed our way right into it.

I'm practically skipping when I get to Liv's car at the end of the day.

"I guess you saw that Kups is back, huh?"

"Can I be glad he's alive and still hate him?"

She laughs, opening the car door. "Absofockinglutely. And how about Sasha?"

All the lightness evaporates and the weight in my stomach returns. With everything that happened with Dad, Mom, then Grove, I completely forgot about Sasha.

It doesn't matter that I regret everything. It doesn't matter that I will never touch a gun again. It doesn't matter, because if Sasha breaks, I'll lose everything. I edge into the passenger seat, my whole body rigid. "What about her?"

"She didn't tell. She was just super-upset. You know how nice she is to everyone. She just felt like she let her sisters bully her into . . . not being herself, I think."

"I get that."

"But I guess she decided telling wouldn't make much of a difference. Thank goodness. Can you imagine?" Liv starts the car.

I can. I did.

In front of us, the snow has begun to stick, already blanketing the steps. I remember what Nikki said about parkour and the steps—about parkour teaching us that there are a million ways to get to the next level and not to settle for the one they give us. I twisted that. I took it to mean no rules. But it's not about anarchy or order. It's about seeing all the possibilities in a thing—the way Aunt Jacks does when she carves.

Liv pats my knee. "I'm so glad you're back to you."

"Me too, Livvy. I'm so sorry for all the ways I stressed you out these last few weeks."

She laughs. "We're good, Zo. You and I will always find our way back to good." She turns out of the parking lot. "You had quite the day of epiphanies, huh?"

"Absofockinglutely." I watch Liv's hands move easily from the gearshift to the steering wheel, her eyes scanning the road confidently. "You're amazing, you know that?"

Liv laughs. "That another epiphany?"

"Nah. I've always known it. I just . . . maybe took it a little for granted lately. I'm sorry."

Her globe pendant is caught beneath her seat belt. I untangle it for her.

"Thanks," she says.

"Do you"—I pause—"do you want to talk more about having sex with Jake?"

She's quiet and I think maybe I've messed this up too. That I waited too long. Because I know now that our friendship is bigger than whether or not she has sex or moves to England.

She pulls up to a red light and looks over at me. "Yes. I do. Next weekend, you will spend all weekend at my house and we will bake ten kinds of cupcakes and you will listen to all the things that could go wrong and tell me what to do."

"That sounds perfect," I say. "Except you're the one who tells *me* what to do."

The light turns green. "Only lately. And you didn't listen anyway."

"See where that got me?"

"Exactly. Neither of us should be allowed to do this life thing alone."

I laugh. "Deal."

"But we have to win States first. I plan to do my part and stop by the store to grab some blue and green nail polish. And maybe hair ties. Want me to drop you home first?"

"No way. I want to hang with my bestie. Besides," I say, getting an idea, "I think I'll pick up something for my dad."

I hesitate before Dad's door, clutching the thin box in my hand. I worry that I don't even know him now. I had all these ideas *about* him but, it turns out, they weren't about *him* at all. They were more about me. This time, when I walk into the room, I want to see him.

I knock.

"Come in," he calls.

The room is still dark. He's propped up in bed against his pillows, his legs elevated as usual. He's typing on his laptop. He closes it and puts it aside. I cross to the wall of windows and pull up the shades, one by one. Snow clings to the bare branches, redefining them.

I pull the chair to his bedside. "I suck."

He reaches for my hand. "No, Zoe. You don't."

I wrap both hands around his. "I just wasn't thinking about it right. You have to know I was only thinking about you and trying to help."

"I know, honey. I do." He sighs. "I'm not saying it's fun to be in pain. It's not. But I feel grateful that I have a wonderful wife. I have a daughter who kicks butt on the field and cares about me—to a fault."

"But that's just it. It's all about us. You lost your work, your—"

"That's not true, Zoe. I mean, sure, I can't work the way I used to. But I've started a blog and—"

I lean back. "You started a blog? About what?"

He reaches over, opens his laptop, and passes it to me. On

the screen I see *Hammers and Tunes, a blog by a music-obsessed recovering contractor.*

I look up at him. I had no idea. No. Idea.

He shrugs. "It's just something I started. It's been fun, listening to new songs, thinking about how to curate them, how—"

"Curate them?" I smile. "Who are you and what have you done with my dad?"

He smiles. "This *is* me, Zo."

I think of the CD he made me, still sitting on my bureau, unlistened to.

I close the computer, lean over, and give him a big hug. "I'm so, so sorry, Dad."

He pats me on the back. "I know."

I sit up and hand him the thin box. He raises his eyebrows. As soon as he opens it, he busts out laughing. "Oh, Zoe." Then his face hesitates between a laugh and a cry. "I kind of love you, you know that?"

"I know." I undo the watch on his wrist. I rub the smooth patch of skin where the broken watch face sat for all these years.

"I still love that watch," he says, watching me put it down on the nightstand. "Because you gave it to me."

I smile. "I just thought it was time. For us." I buckle on the new watch, its face full of fierce cartoon superheroes. "I owe you a superhero movie."

He smiles and his whole face crinkles up. I can tell he's

trying not to let the tears fall, but I'm not even trying anymore. I just let them run as I rest my head on his chest, his thin T-shirt soft against my cheek, the weight of his arm around me, the hushed music from his earbuds.

"Oooh," he says after a while. "So beautiful."

I turn to face the windows to see what he sees. A wind has come through to shake the snow from the branches. Some falls in clumps, sending giant snowballs to the ground. But some falls in a swoosh, a drifting veil of white dropped over the world for just a few seconds. Then, when it's gone, everything is crisp and clear.

"Snow-covered branches always make me think of frosting," Dad says. "Mmmm. Wegmans cupcakes."

I laugh and wipe my cheeks. "Of course they do."

Later, when I hear Mom open the garage, I abandon my AP US History homework and run downstairs so I can meet her at the door.

"Oh!" she says, her hands full. "Do I have you to thank for the shoveled driveway?"

"Yeah," I say.

She drops her purse on the floor and shrugs off her coat. "I hate knowing that we'll be shoveling for the next five months. There's something so depressing about that."

I give her a huge hug. Her arms take a second to catch up, but soon they do, and I'm reminded of how safe I feel in her arms. How sometimes she's exactly the container I need. "I'm so sorry."

She pats me on the back. "Can I get a recording of that?"

262

I step back. "I had no idea you were working extra shifts to—"

She holds up her hands. "Honey, it's not your job to worry about that." She shakes her head and puts her hands on my shoulders. "I think—I think we've put too much on you these last couple of years and you've forgotten how to be a kid. It's just that you were so capable and good at being a grown-up. We forgot to take care of *you*."

It was never about the cooking and the cleaning after all. It's like she flung open all the shades the way I did in Dad's room and let the light pour all the way down.

"Thanks," I finally say. "Also"—I take a deep breath—"I didn't realize I was taking Dad's accident out on you."

She's quiet. She exhales and her cheeks puff out from the force of it. "That—that means a lot." She nods. "A lot." She exhales again. "I just hate how much all this had to affect you too. Nobody lives in a vacuum I guess, huh?" She shakes her head. "We're all just ripples in a pond, no control over the rock that made them."

I half laugh. "That should be on a T-shirt."

"That's me, Zen-Master Mom."

"I love you." And it feels so good to say. I've missed saying it. I've missed feeling it. So I say it again. "I love you, Mom."

She sniffs and puts her hands on my shoulders. "Now, what do soon-to-be state champions have for dinner?"

I shake my head. "I already ate. Liv's on her way to get me."

"No way, honey. We're driving you. Dad and I are coming to the game tonight."

All geared up, I tap my Tar Heels poster for good luck and zip downstairs. Dad's footsteps are slow as he navigates his way down. I fight the urge to help. If he wants help, he'll ask for it.

All three of us pile into the car and it feels like the weirdest thing in the world to be in the back seat again after all these years. Mom puts the car in reverse, carefully easing onto the street, and then we're ready to move forward.

THIRTY-SEVEN

WE'RE ALL IN THE SCHOOL'S parking lot. I keep looking at Dad because I can't believe he's here, but also because I'm trying to see him differently. Mom keeps rearranging the pile of cushions in the front seat. Liv's parents are equally weird, taking apart a huge fancy camera only to put it back together again. Liv, meanwhile, keeps rattling off random facts about the Dome, like if she knows its whole history, she'll be able to predict our future.

Then the 1978 green Triumph Spitfire pulls up.

Jake jumps out of the passenger side and twirls Liv in the air until her anxiety dissolves into laughter. The driver's door creaks and slams. Grove walks slowly so I have time to admire his stride. I move toward him and take his hands in mine. I kiss him quickly on the lips. But just as I'm rocking back on my heels, he pulls me in again for a real kiss.

My team whistles and bangs the side of the bus. I redden and pull away, grinning.

"Go Captain!" Quinn screams.

He smiles as he lets go and tilts his forehead toward mine. "I had to do that before you left."

"Yeah?" My voice goes low.

"Well." He leans back and stretches our arms wide with our clasped hands. "I have to make sure you don't forget me when you get all famous."

I laugh. "There'll probably be twenty people who show up. It's *field hockey*."

"I'll be there," he whispers in my ear.

I step back and realize that in addition to a packed bus, my parents, Jake, Liv, and Liv's parents are all watching us, open-mouthed.

Of course, this is the first time Grove's meeting my family and friends, and they look like a bunch of wide-mouthed Muppets.

Jake does a slow clap, and Liv elbows him, while Dad laughs. Mom nurse-walks up to us, ever speedy and efficient, and pumps his hand. "Nice to meet you."

"Mom, everyone"—I exhale—"this is Grove. He's . . ."

"Your friend?" Mom rushes in to save me.

"Boyfriend." Grove shakes her hand. He raises his eyebrows at me, and I nod. And blush. And smile. And blush again. I'm about two seconds away from erupting into flames.

"Well, come on over here, Grove," Dad says. "I've got to shake the hand of the guy who was finally good enough for—"

"Dad!" I yell. And he bursts into laughter and just claps Grove on the back.

"Okay!" Liv yells. "If we don't go soon, I'm going to leave you all and just run there myself. I can't take any more waiting."

266

Liv and I race onto the bus. To Syracuse. To the Dome. To the biggest stadium I've ever seen, and ours for the night. Even the Motown can't steady me. I'm a Jell-O bowl of giddy.

We pull up to a giant garage door on the side of the Dome and step off the bus. Security types wave us over and lift up the door on some kind of huge pulley system, and we race in before they close it again. We walk down a long concrete hallway lined with tackling dummies and football sleds. I smile. Our football team won't get to States. But we did.

We push through the doors into our locker room—the away team's, since we're the lower seed. The "lockers" don't look anything like at our school. They're wooden cubbies, with hooks, a shelf, and a bench below that runs around the room. A magnetic strip sits above each one where they put the players' names.

It smells like dude. But *we're* here now. Quinn braids blue and green ribbons into our hair, and Ava and I streak our cheeks in glow-in-the-dark paint. I bet the boys don't do that.

Coach pulls me aside. "Look, Zoe, I haven't heard anything else from the UNC coach. Given the last email, if we bring it home today, we can expect her at the championship game tomorrow night. So just get through this game and everything you've been working for is on the other side."

I raise my eyebrows. "Oh, is that all?"

She laughs. "Remember, you can eat—"

"—an elephant one bite at a time. Yeah, yeah. I remember."

She pats my shoulder. "You done good, kid."

Finally, it's time. We push through another set of doors and walk across an orange-splashed hallway with giant posters of players on the walls. But I'm focused on the ramp.

A legion of drummers beats their rhythms into my bones. Pound. Pound. Pound. I've watched a hundred games here, but I've never seen this view. When the hall slopes up and the ceiling disappears to reveal the giant curved dome above, I still can't believe it.

We break into a run, and the second my feet touch that turf, it feels as good as kissing Grove, as good as parkour, as good as being a hero, as good as being a part of this sisterhood.

We've got this.

I look up into the stands to find my parents. When I find them, I find everyone else. Even the Rebels. They've made a huge banner that reads SHOW 'EM HOW REBELS ROLL, ZO! with all different-colored letters. Uncle Bob is here with Aunt Eileen. She's got a big tub of popcorn along with the camera. She swats him when he starts jumping and waving, threatening to knock down the poor family in front of him, but she's waving too.

Grove, Jake, and a bunch of the soccer guys are here. Their Regionals game is tomorrow in Albany, so even if we win tonight, Grove won't be able to be here for the championship game tomorrow. They turn around at once, letters clustered across their backs: UNLASH THEE HOLE HULNDS. I bust out laughing.

"Pretty sure that's supposed to say 'Unleash the Hell-hounds.'" Liv laughs.

We cup our hands to our mouths and howl.

Three Rivers is from somewhere downstate. They're stuck with the parents willing to drive five hours. We've got a wild home crowd. We've got anyone bored on a snowy Friday. We've got our *family*.

The crowd stamps their feet for *us*. They stand and scream for *us*. They wave their banners and shake their fists.

For *us*.

When the anthem plays, it booms off the dome roof and walls, the vibrations thumping through us. All the cells in our bodies soar in tune.

The whistle blows.

The game is a mess of sticks, a blur of kilts. We fill the arena with our yells, intertwining with the crowd's. We're at our goal, we're at their goal, we're back again. I try to direct the chaos, but their sweeper and goalie block us every time. Still, Dylan and Ava are a wall at the end of the field, keeping them at bay.

I sprint up and down the field, passing and pushing, calling and conducting, but the ball refuses to land on either side. By halftime, it's still 0 to 0, and we're panting in our locker room.

"Any other year, this team would have us crying into the turf by now."

"Aw, Coach." Cristina clasps her hands and bats her eyelashes. "You're such a sweet talker."

Coach shrugs. "You know this year is different. You know you're different. And you know what you know—nothing I say will change that. But just look around." She throws her arms wide. "We're in the *Dome*. Some of the best athletes in the world have played here. All I want—"

"We know, we know, *enjoy* it."

Coach side-eyes the triplets. "Yeah. That. *And* stick it to 'em."

We run out and the whistle blows again, blasting off the dome and back down. It's a tumble of legs and hits and calls and passes, but nothing gets through on either side. Field hockey turns into tennis. It's all volleys and no landings.

A Three Rivers girl slams her stick into Dylan's leg, and she screams, "*Fuck!*" But instead of calling the girl, the ref hands Dylan a yellow card for the swear. Coach sends in the sub, but the sub isn't Dylan, and the panic rises. I look at the others and see my fear in their crouches, their drawn mouths.

No. This is our year. Our Dome. Our championship.

We run to position. As soon as the whistle blows, we don't hold back. We charge and get a penalty corner. They block it. There's 1:26 left on the clock. We get another penalty corner. Bella inserts the ball from the left to Quinn. The ball disappears in a jumble of sticks and shins. I hear the taps but I can't place it, and then there's a crack, small but sure, and I see it rest in the back of the goal.

We scream. Quinn did it. And we're hugging and jumping and yelling, only seconds on the clock.

We get to play in the finals.

We get to play in the State Championships.

Us.

As we skip back to the locker room, the concrete walls echo our replays, our shouts, our cleats, our sticks—until the noise doubles and triples and quadruples, until we're not just a team, we're an army. Headed for States.

We pull up short. Two police officers stand outside the locker room.

THIRTY-EIGHT

THE MAN POLICE OFFICER STEPS forward. "Dylan John-son?"

Dylan's face pales. She nods.

"We'd like you to come with us." The woman officer is silent.

"What for?" Dylan's voice holds steady, but her eyes are scared.

"We just need to ask you some questions at the station."

"What if I don't want to come?"

The woman officer steps forward. "Then we'll get a war-rant for your arrest."

"Arrest!" Kiara says. "For what?"

"The menacing, assault, and kidnapping of Lance Kup-perton." The officer cocks his head at the exit, and Dylan fol-lows, muttering "Bullshit" under her breath.

Oh no. It's happening.

"Coach." Kiara's voice is tight. "I'm going to run and get my dad, okay? He's a lawyer." At Coach's nod, she races off, yelling after Dylan not to say anything. That her dad will

meet her at the station. Wordless, the rest of us walk inside the locker room. Without Dylan.

Coach sinks onto the bench with a loud thump—like she didn't sit at all but fell.

Quinn starts crying and so do some others, but not me.

We made it through the day. We made it through the game. I thought we were on the mountaintop, ready to place our flag.

But the floor yawns open, sucking me into a great, dark hole. My friends far above me. Dylan out of reach. The mountaintop a mirage.

And it's all my fault.

Someone touches my shoulder, and I flinch.

Liv. "What do we do?" she says.

But I'm in the hole and I can barely hear her through the distance.

That night, we cram into Kiara's living room, her dad reaching toward his computer perched on the coffee table, papers scattered by his feet. He sits on the edge of a cushy chair, his back rigid.

"I don't get why she's there overnight," Ava says. "What happened to 'We're just taking you in for questioning'?"

Mr. Walker raises an eyebrow. "Well, it didn't help that she said 'F you' to the interrogating officer—five times, no less."

"Oh," Ava says.

"Or that she has priors on her record. Or that Lance's parents already thought about pressing charges against her for her earlier assault at school. Holding her overnight was a fore-gone conclusion, I'm afraid."

"Did she seem okay?" Kiara bites her nails, then tucks her hands under her thighs.

Mr. Walker looks at her, his face wrinkled in worry. "She didn't seem hurt or abnormally upset." His voice is soft, and Kiara nods.

I lean forward. I have to lean so far to reach my way out of the hole. I have to get Dylan out of the hole. "How can we help?"

He tidies a stack of papers. "Dylan has given me permission to be fully transparent with you all. She seems to believe she should plead guilty, and I don't agree." He runs his hand over his tight gray curls. "She doesn't have faith in the system, so she's giving in, which is understandable given her history. But these are serious charges, and I don't think we should let her do that." He clasps his hands together. "I hope that through our conversation we can arrive at a better decision for Dylan.

"Here's what we know. The school told the police that, at the start of the year, Dylan threatened Kups—"

"What!?" we shout, and all start talking at once.

Mr. Walker pats the air with his hands. "Okay, okay. One at a time. Tell me what happened."

We tell him how Kups assaulted her, and she defended herself. How we did the right thing, and went to the dean, but she didn't believe us—or care. Kups continued to harass her. He chased her with his truck onto sidewalks, forced her into ditches.

274

We don't tell him about parkour. We don't tell him about our evening activities. We don't tell him about the guns.

His face is grave. "Girls, I can't tell you how this breaks my heart—the way she was treated and the way you tried to support her. But I'm afraid this won't help her case. It only makes it seem more likely that she'd want revenge."

We *did* want revenge. And I wonder why the world lets that happen. Lets all the words and touches and abuse pile up on one another, pile up on us, until we can't breathe and we have to push our way out, break our way free. Of course there's an avalanche. Of course people get hurt.

"But why do they even think she did it?" Michaela asks. "What evidence do they have? Is there DNA?"

There isn't enough air in my chest.

"Of course there's no DNA!" Kiara glares at Michaela. "Why would there be any DNA?"

I count my breaths. In. Out. I see my bloody knee. In. Out. I feel the sweat on my skin in that hot, hot truck. In. Out. My DNA on a jagged branch. On Kups's dirty truck floor.

Breathe. I am not suffocating.

"No one's talking DNA." Mr. Walker sighs. "But when the police followed up with Dylan's foster parents, they told the officers that she's often out at all hours of the night without explanation. And it doesn't help that she's been in trouble before. Nothing major, more wrong place wrong time. But her foster parents brought up her late nights and previous record."

I think of my own mom, sucking up all my shittyness and never saying a word.

I don't understand how the world gets away with being so unfair.

"But she was with us." Bella's voice is firm.

"Are you sure?" Mr. Walker asks. "Are you absolutely sure? Where were you that night?" He looks down at his notes. "It was just last Friday. What were you doing? Can you remember?"

We all remember.

I don't look at Nikki across the circle. I don't notice that her cheeks are an ugly pink—like someone hit her.

"Isn't it enough that we were together?" Quinn asks. "We've been pretty much inseparable since tryouts."

He shakes his head. "I'm afraid 'pretty much inseparable' doesn't cut it."

"Dad?" Kiara asks.

"Yes?"

"I think we're too hungry to think. Would you and Mom order us some pizza? Please?"

He pats his knees and stands up. "Of course. You must be starved after that incredible game." He walks to the door, then pauses. "You girls should be so proud of yourselves. You made it to States, after all."

Proud is me and Dylan and everyone together on the mountaintop planting our flag, claiming our win, looking back over the steep upward climb that got us here. This isn't proud.

Kiara tiptoes over to the door and closes it, sealing us off from the rest of the house.

"Michaela," Kiara whispers, "what the hell was that about DNA?"

"I'm sorry." Michaela runs her hands down her kilt. "It just came out."

"Well, don't let anything else 'just come out,' okay?"

"We should've told someone," Sasha says. "We should've—"

"Then we'd all be in jail," Bella says. "Or half of us would." She eyeballs the ones who stayed away, the ones who knew better.

Sasha looks at the lucky five. "You were smart."

Ava waves her hands. "It doesn't matter. We stick together. Focus. We'll all figure out how to get Dylan out of there. Sticks Chicks forever, right?"

Everyone nods, but we're not in this together. Dylan's in a hole. Nikki's in a hole. I'm in a hole.

And those holes are drenched in our DNA.

THIRTY-NINE

EVERYONE "RECONSTRUCTS" THE NIGHT FOR Kiara's
dad. "We" didn't go to the football game because we were
playing Sparta in the Regionals that Saturday morning all the
way in Cortland. Instead, "we" went to the fields behind the
elementary playground to practice where nobody saw us.
Then "we" went to the triplets' house.

The "we" is a lie that churns and groans inside me while
the others talk. It's flimsy. The others had dates. They were
home. They worked. It won't stand up.

More important, I know they want to help and support
Dylan, but this shouldn't be on them. I remember Kiara's words
that night. It's not just that she thought we were wrong. She
said that as a Black person, she wouldn't get a do-over. And
maybe Dylan won't and maybe I won't either, but we were
the ones who made that choice. Not her. Not the rest of them.

This is on me.

I look at Nikki. Her cheeks are flushed and she's focused
on her sneakers.

Please, please look at me.

Finally, she does.

After Mr. Walker leaves us with his arms full of lies, and the others claim their spots on the floor to sleep, Nikki and I put on our coats and boots and sneak out to the Walkers' patio. Their pool is closed for the season, the green cover pulled taut. But two lone plastic lounge chairs remain. We cross to them in silence.

We use our sleeves to brush off the thin layer of snow. The plastic slats are cold through my sweats. I don't lie down. I don't think my body even knows how to rest anymore. I rub my fingers. There are holes in the pool cover.

I wonder what would happen if I turned myself in. Would they let Dylan go? Would they leave Nikki alone? Would I be able to breathe again?

Nikki takes her feet out of her boots. Dips them into the snow up and down, until her toes are shiny and red.

Do sixteen-year-olds go to jail? Or juvie?

I think of the UNC girls on my poster. Maybe I was never supposed to see their faces, never supposed to be in that huddle. Maybe I'm supposed to be happy with just having gotten this far. Maybe that's what a better person would feel.

I think of my stick, my beautiful beat-up stick. If I turn myself in, I'll never play another game again. Tonight was it. My stick will sit in the mudroom, get moved to the basement, maybe eventually get sold in some garage sale. My hands feel empty.

I wonder how often Dad would feel well enough to visit me in jail. I wonder if not paying for college would mean Mom could work less and take care of him more.

There are holes in the pool cover. What good is a cover with holes?

Tears burn the edges of my eyes. All this time I was disappointing my parents and I had no idea. This time, I know I'd be disappointing them. And it would be worse than ever.

Nikki takes a small bit of snow and rolls it between her fingers, rolls it until it disappears.

I wonder if my existence will be that easy to erase.

At the beginning, I thought Dylan was the one who was going to bring the team down. But really, it was me.

I don't want to be erasable.

Nikki lifts her legs and leans back against the chair. "You know, I was really looking forward to college. To getting the hell out of here."

"Me too," I say.

"I just want a good art program more than two hours away. And junior year in Italy. That's what I really want. Or wanted."

I look at her, this girl whose face I wouldn't even have recognized before this season. Now, after everything, I know what she's thinking.

The erasables are the ones who don't speak up.

I lift my feet up and look at the stars, the November night air making me shiver.

"I'm going to turn myself in," I finally say.

"Me too," she says.

"Okay," I say. "We'll go to the police station in the morning. Before Mr. Walker."

I look over at her. She looks back at me and reaches her hand between the chairs. I grab it and squeeze.

"So weird," she says. "That we ended up here."

"I know," I say.

"I thought we were going to change everything."

"Me too," I say.

We let our hands go and I pull my coat tighter and realize that even though it's November and nighttime and there's snow on the ground, it's not actually as cold as I thought.

"I regret a lot of things," I say, "but not becoming friends with you."

"Absofockinglutely," she says.

I wake to the quiet alarm I set for 7:15 a.m. It takes me a second . . . then I remember.

Nikki's curled beside me. I shake her shoulder. "Nikki," I whisper. "Wake up."

She turns over and squints at me. Her face tightens, then falls, and I know she's remembering all that we have to do this morning.

We stand and my muscles pop and creak courtesy of last night's tough game and sleeping arrangements. But it doesn't matter. I won't play tonight. Or ever again.

Silently we gather our things, careful not to wake the others. When we sneak through the house to leave, we find Mrs. Walker in the kitchen, sipping coffee.

"Good morning," she whispers. "You girls are up early. Mr. Walker made coffee before he left so—"

"Mr. Walker left? To see Dylan?" I ask.

"Yes," she says, putting her mug down. "Is something wr—"

"We're just going to run out real quick," Nikki says. "Will you tell the girls we'll talk to them later?"

"Of course. But—"

"We have to go," I say. "Thanks for everything, Mrs. Walker."

The police station is an unassuming one-level building that looks more like a mom-and-pop restaurant than a place to store criminals.

We get out of the car and walk, our feet slow. With every step, I'm picking each foot out of the deep, dark hole, hefting myself up, and doing it all over again with the next foot.

I am doing the right thing.

But as I look around the lot, I imagine what it would be like if Reilly and Jamison and even Kups were here too, to turn themselves in. Just because I'm not the right person to enact justice doesn't mean it shouldn't get enacted.

The windowed door reads VILLAGE OF NORTHRIDGE POLICE DEPARTMENT.

We push open the door.

I am doing the right thing.

FORTY

WE NEARLY SMACK RIGHT INTO Mr. Walker and Dylan.

"Girls!" Mr. Walker says. "What are you doing here?"

"We—I—" I look back at Nikki. I look at Dylan, whose eyes grow watery. "We wanted to be with Dylan."

Which is exactly, entirely true.

Mr. Walker holds the door and waves us back outside. "Well, now you can. Outside."

"But—"

He pushes us out the door. "I never like to linger too long after I've won. You never want to give the other side time to change their minds."

"Change their minds?" Nikki repeats.

Mr. Walker smiles, and it is so Kiara's smile. "They didn't have a shred of evidence. And even this Lance Kupperton boy says it couldn't have been Dylan. He says they were definitely big guys." He leans in. "If you ask me, the Kuppertons wanted someone to blame and saw poor Dylan as an easy target." He wraps his arm around her. "But that stops today, right, Dyl?"

She's stiff for a minute, then leans into the hug. "Yeah. I guess it does."

"In some ways, this was a blessing. It sped everything up."

The door opens and out steps a woman with salt-and-pepper hair. She comes over and squeezes Mr. Walker's arm.

"Jesse," she says, "we did good."

"Yes. We. Did." He stretches each word out with a grin.

Dylan blushes.

"Now," the woman says, looking at Dylan, who has her eyes trained on our feet. "You need to stay out of trouble. There's only so much magic your fairy godmother and"—she looks at Mr. Walker—"your fairy god*father*'s got."

"Yes, Mrs. Malone," says Dylan. She looks up. "Thank you."

Mrs. Malone smiles crooked like she's trying to plug up the tears. And Mr. Walker does too.

I look at Nikki. What in the actual fock is happening?

Mr. Walker laughs. "I'll let you fill in your friends. Do you want to catch a ride with them or come home with me?"

"I'll . . ." She looks at us. "Can you guys drive me back?"

"Of course," Nikki says.

"Right." Dylan turns to Mr. Walker. "After we talk, I'll come . . . home."

Mr. Walker stands a little taller. He sucks in his lips like he's trying not to cry. "It's good to hear you say it." He exhales a quick breath. "Now. Don't forget we're going to have a celebration dinner tonight, right? Early before the game. Home by three?"

"See you then."

Mr. Walker throws out his arms wide like he's going to give her a big hug and they do this awkward dance and finally he just pats her on the shoulders.

"Right," he says, and walks toward his car.

"Thank you!" Dylan calls after him.

"What the—" and "What's happ—" Nikki and I both start but Dylan shushes us.

"Please, let's get the hell out of here," Dylan says. "I'll explain everything."

The three of us take our cones and sit at the picnic table at the shuttered Scoop Dreams. Yesterday's snow didn't stick, but the tabletop is cold, the 9 a.m. sun barely having had time to warm anything. The shack closed for the season a few weeks back, but Uncle Bob's waiting until I'm done with fockey to help him move all the remaining tubs of ice cream into the megafreezer at his house. I fix Dylan her s'mores and Nikki her PB and caramel. I get cookie dough. The whole time I'm scooping, I'm thinking of what Dylan told us in the car: She's getting adopted by the Walkers.

Apparently, the Walkers filed the paperwork months ago, but it takes a long time for the officials to do all the background checks and process the paperwork. Dylan never even believed it would happen. Mrs. Malone, her caseworker, and Mr. Walker were able to argue that the way Dylan's foster parents offered her up to the police with no evidence not only revealed their bias but also demonstrated that their home was unfit and unsafe—not just for Dylan, but for future foster kids. So even though the adoption isn't finalized, the Walkers got permission to become Dylan's new foster parents in the meantime.

Dylan looks at her cone when I hand it to her. "It is hella weird that I'm eating ice cream for breakfast before moving to my dream home, when yesterday I was in jail and thought my life was over."

"Beyond," says Nikki.

"So," Dylan asks, "what was *your* plan when you showed up?"

I look at Nikki. She shrugs. "We were going to tell Mr. Walker that it was Nikki and me."

Dylan drops her hand, the scoop tilting dangerously sideways.

"Careful!" I reach out and right the cone.

She grabs my hand. Nikki puts hers on top of ours. And we just sit there for a minute, hands stacked.

A bit of ice cream melts onto my hand and I lick it.

Dylan lets out a burst of a laugh. "Way to break the mood, Cap."

"It's Big Bob's ice cream. It's here for every mood."

"Thank you," Dylan says, her voice fuller than I've ever heard it.

"Thank you, too," I say.

"Is it weird that I feel a little deflated?" Nikki asks. "Like, Zoe and I were gearing up all night to turn ourselves in, to face the consequences. And it feels off somehow that we're sitting here eating ice cream."

I nod. "Same."

"I don't," says Dylan. "One night was enough to teach me my lesson. You heard Mrs. Malone. I am not messing up my shot with the Walkers by getting into more trouble."

"It's not about never doing it again," I say. "It's that I feel . . . guilty."

"Maybe that's our punishment," Nikki says, looking at the road. "The guilt we don't get to ditch."

We're quiet a moment, eating our ice cream, watching the traffic come and go at the intersection.

Nikki's phone vibrates. She looks at it. "Are we sure about turning over a new leaf?" she asks sarcastically. "Reilly's hosting a Day Drink Olympics this afternoon."

"Of course he is," I say.

Dylan shakes her head. "I know what we did was wrong, but it sucks to just sit here knowing they're gonna fuck up and hurt someone else. Because they will."

"They will," Nikki says.

"I'm sure they don't feel any guilt at all." I wipe my hands with the napkin and ball it up. If I thought they did feel guilty, or even *could* feel guilt, it would be so much easier to let my anger go. "I still think we were right." I sigh. "I mean, not the way we did it. We messed up. *Big.* But our intentions were good. We wanted to change things for other girls."

"But we didn't," Nikki says.

"No," I say. "We didn't." I hold up my phone. "I'm sure in a few hours there will be photographic evidence of all the awful ways nothing's changed thanks to the Date Rape Olympics."

Nikki groans. "That would be funny if it weren't true."

"I just wish we'd won," Dylan says.

"Me too," I say. But then that doesn't sit right either. "The thing is, the whole time, I was keeping score. Clocking wins. But if I think about it, we were playing *their* game with *their* refs. I thought we were inventing something new. But we were just new players on *their* field."

"That's Grand Canyon deep," Dylan says.

I laugh. "You're Grand Canyon deep."

Dylan grins. "That's what she said."

I throw my napkin at her.

"I'm glad you guys are here," I say. "This is a good distraction from tonight."

"Oh, fockity fock," Nikki says. "I think because of all our talk last night about turning ourselves in I kind of forgot about the State Championships."

"You forgot?!" Dylan laughs. She shakes her head. "It's half of what I thought about last night. I was just so bummed I wouldn't get to play."

"I am so bone-tired I hope I'll be able to hit the ball," I say. I turn to Dylan. "But I'm really, really glad you're going to be there. It wouldn't work without you."

Nikki's phone pings. Mine too. And Dylan's. We all look down. "The team," we say together.

Within half an hour, everyone's at Big Bob's picnic table. Kiara and Dylan hug for a long time and everyone's clapping them on the back. I scoop cones for everyone, and when Ava asks for cookie dough, I remember something.

"Hang on," I say.

"Don't tell me you're out! Oooh, that's a bad sign for tonight!" She starts to pull her cross necklace from under her shirt.

"Don't worry," I say. "We're not out. I'm just checking to see if we have something better." I open the back freezer. Sure enough, I see the small container I hoped would be there. I lift it down and take a sample spoon, making sure everything good lands on it.

"You are not giving me some shady garbage—"

I shove the spoon at her and she takes a tentative bite, her eyes growing wide.

"Doritos ice cream?? He actually did it??"

I nod and laugh.

"Big Bob is a focking genius."

"Agreed," I say. "Want a whole cone?"

"Absofockinglutely!"

"Except it's not called Doritos ice cream," I say. "It's called the Ava."

Her mouth goes wide in this huge openmouthed smile.

"You're famous!" Cristina says.

Ava eats a big hunk of her ice cream. "Ohhhhh," she says. "We are so winning tonight, my friends."

We're crowded around the picnic table, everyone eating their cones, talking about tonight, when Nikki's phone pings again. She looks at it and makes a disgusted face.

"What?" I ask.

She looks down, reading: "'What's better than sunshine? Sports. What's better than sports? Beer. Combine all three and you get Reilly's Day Drink Olympics. Winter is coming, Ridgebacks. Party before it hits.'"

None of us speak.

"So," Dylan asks, "we're just going to go play our game and pretend that's not happening?"

Ava gives me a look.

"Don't worry," I say, "we learned our lesson. We have no desire to go down that road again. I just . . . I wish there was something we could do to change things."

We're quiet, watching the traffic. Maybe it's enough that we tried. Maybe it's enough that we're all still here, together.

"The #MeToo movement changed things," Nikki finally says, her voice quiet. "I mean, that's what led to all those arrests. All those TV guys lost their jobs."

"Because women came forward," I say.

Nikki shakes her head. "Not just that. It wasn't just that a few women came forward. It was a flood of women's voices. It was the force of all those women together that did it."

I look around the table at all these strong girls. Weeks ago we sat on a dark playground and shared pieces of our stories. Then, I wanted the stories as a means to an end. I didn't get that they were valuable all by themselves.

And I never shared mine.

Nikki begins to talk and Ava wraps her arm around her. Liv takes my hand and squeezes. I listen. Others talk.

I'm amazed by these girls that I get to call my friends. These girls who have been forced to question too many times whether their bodies are even their own. These girls who must fight to reclaim their bodies every time they take the field, or even get out of bed. And yet, each day, they rise.

Finally, I tell my story. They hold my words, my truth, and it's unexpectedly ... powerful.

I remember the flyer Nikki and I saw for the SU Speak Out. Even though it feels forever ago, I still remember the words:

> Stand Up. Speak Up. Be Heard.
> Heal.

Speaking up and speaking out heal.

Voice not violence. All these weeks, we fought in masks, at night. Voices silent, faces hidden, stories buried.

Nothing changed.

I wanted to be the lit match to their gasoline. I wanted to level their world. But I didn't. And I'm not sure I realized how much being on fire hurt me.

"I have pictures," I say. "Of some bruises. After Reilly. I could post them."

"Wow," Nikki says.

I wish I could swallow the words back down. Because speaking out could hurt even more than what we've already been through. There'd be no broken bones or fear of arrest, but I would be unzipping my rib cage, exposing my heart, leaving it bare.

"That's really brave," Dylan whispers.

"I'll post too," Nikki says, nodding.

"Me too," Dylan says.

"Me too," Kiara says. And soon they're all saying *me too, me too, me too.*

"What if people call us sluts or troll us?" Sasha asks.

Michaela nods. "They might. But maybe more will be on our side."

"And," Dylan says, "if even one girl doesn't get hurt because of it, isn't it worth it?"

I think of that burl that Aunt Jacks showed us. How it looked like all the words and secrets were caught in the tree's throat. How it was an ugly mess of a thing, and yet so powerful. How when Aunt Jacks finally opens it up, and lets it speak, it will be the most beautiful version of itself.

Nikki's staring at her phone, her face all blotchy. "I took a picture too," she says, holding it out to us.

In the picture, she's wearing the white blouse I remember from that night, buttoned all wrong. She's pulled it to the side to show her upper arm, near her shoulder. The bright red mark is ragged and swollen, angry and ugly against her skin. Purple creeps in all around the edge of the bruise.

"Oh, Nik," I say. "I'm so sorry." I put my hand out and she takes it. Ava tilts her head onto her shoulder. Cristina wraps her arms around her.

"Thanks," Nikki says. "But we don't have to do this today, you know. If you think it'll mess up the game."

I look at Ava. And Michaela, who wants this win as badly as she wants valedictorian. And at Cristina, who, like Nikki, will be playing the last game of her senior year tonight. I look at my whole team.

292

"It's not my choice," I say. "All of us need to be on board."

Ava smiles at me and looks around.

"I think," Liv says into the silence, "it's really about you, and Nikki, and the others who choose to put their stories out there. Will it drain you too much?"

I think for a minute. "I didn't feel drained after I told you. Weirdly, I felt—I *feel* stronger than ever."

A smile spreads across Ava's face. "Then maybe this is exactly the power we need to win tonight."

We all look at one another and it's a buzzing, alive kind of silence. We are not hiding in the dark under masks. We are on a busy intersection, on a sunny morning, the cold November air whipping our hair, and we are about to get loud.

We write:

#BoycottDDO
Day Drink Olympics or Date Rape Olympics?
They can't assault us if we don't go.

Ava counts us off: "One, two, three—post."

And we wait.

FORTY-ONE

I LEAVE THE OTHERS WHILE I lock up the ice cream shack and make sure everything's put away. It's not even noon and I feel like I've lived a lifetime since Dylan got arrested last night. And we still have hours before our championship game tonight.

When I return to the table, they're all looking at Dylan's phone.

"What?" I ask.

"Well, there were some really nice reactions," Ava says, "fists-raised, girl-power-type stuff."

"So why do you guys look like a puppy died?"

Dylan passes me her phone, her finger pointing to one comment.

johnstowniez: who wants u anyway tired slut

"Wow," I say.

She turns it back around and squints at the phone. "You should see his picture. As if I'd want YOU, Johnstowniez."

"Let's turn off our phones," Quinn says. "We don't need this negative energy clogging our pores tonight."

"Wait," Liv says. "We have hours before our game and I plan to send all of you at least three thousand bored texts. Let's just delete the app instead. We can reload it after the game."

"Smart," I say. "Just like they can't assault if we don't go, they can't hurt if we don't look."

Once we delete the app, Ava says, "If we helped one girl not go, not get hurt, then we did what we meant to do. So tonight we can focus on winning."

And for the first time since I saw those cops waiting for us in the hall outside the locker room, I let it fully sink in.

We are going to the State Championships.

When Liv drops me off, my parents, weirdly, are waiting at the front door. At first, I think they're excited about the game. And then, as I walk up the path, I see their faces.

Something's happened.

I jog the last few steps. "Is everything—"

Mom goes to put her arms around me, and then she pauses. "Can I hug you?"

"Of course," I say.

"Is it okay if I hug you too?" Dad asks.

I pull away from Mom and look between them. "You guys are auditioning for freak parents of the year. What is going on?"

"Let's go inside," Mom says.

I follow Mom into the living room, Dad on my heels. Mom sits on the couch and pats the seat next to her. Dad sits in the chair facing me. He sits forward. He leans back. He's a Ping-Pong ball of weird.

"Seriously," I say. "Are you pregnant?"

Mom smiles. "Happily, that ship sailed a long time ago." She puts her hand on the couch cushion between us. "This is about your post. We saw it."

Oh. Shit.

I completely forgot that they could see that. Years ago, that was the deal when I signed up. I could get an account if I let them follow me. And it has literally never, ever come up. Because I post pictures of blue skies and empty roads and field hockey sticks. I barely even post selfies.

I need to end this conversation. Fast.

"Mom, I'm—"

"First things first, are you safe?"

"Yeah." No. I don't know? I don't know if any girl is safe.

"Are you in a relationship with the person who did this—"

"What?!" I recoil. "No. No way."

"So this Grove boy we met last night," Dad says. "He—"

"He is a good guy." I look down at my hands. "A really good guy. And definitely not the guy who did it."

"Would you prefer to talk about this just with me?" Mom asks.

I would prefer not to talk about it ever in the history of the world.

"Yeah." Dad makes a move to stand. "I can go."

"No, stay." I surprise myself. I'm tired of hiding.

"Okay," Mom says. "If this happened recently, sometimes

when we think there might be enough evidence, we ask people to do something called a rape kit. Do you think there might be any semen on any of your clothes?"

I think a field hockey ball might've slammed into my chest. Dad's frozen on the edge of the chair. In between us there's a *Sports Insider* magazine that's been there for more than a year. Longer. Nothing in this room has changed for years. The same pictures on the wall, the same furniture, the same rug. And yet none of us are going to be the same after this moment right now.

My cheeks are wet. I don't know when that happened. Mom passes me a box of tissues.

And it's like that ball's slamming into my chest again. Because in the moment she passes me the tissues, I realize Mom has done this before. She has had this same conversation with other girls. She has asked them about semen. She has talked about rape kits. She has passed them tissue boxes. I had no idea.

Mom's eyes are so kind. She has small wrinkles at the sides of her eyes, her mouth. Those girls are so lucky Mom was on their side.

"I wasn't raped, Mom." I risk a glance at Dad. His face is calm but his eyes are puddles. "I wasn't. It happened . . ." I calculate in my head. It feels both forever ago and yesterday. "About two months ago. There was no . . . semen or anything. He just . . . grabbed me and scared me . . . and . . . I ran away. He never got that far."

She nods. "Okay."

"I'm . . . better. Than I was," I say. "I just posted it because . . . because I wanted to stop it from happening to other girls."

I suck in my lips, trying so hard to keep the tears back but they're pooling in my eyes.

"You're amazing," Dad says. I look at him. I never wanted him to pity me. And I can tell by his face, he doesn't.

"Can I hug you?" Mom asks.

"Yes." I wrap my arms around her and she holds me.

"I'm so, so sorry, lovebug. Nobody should have to go through what you went through."

I pull back. "I know."

Mom holds out her hand and I take it. "Just because he didn't get that far doesn't mean it wasn't real or illegal. It was dehumanizing and reprehensible. And, if you want, I will help you make him pay."

"*We* will help," Dad says.

"Right," Mom says. "We can talk about that later or tomorrow or next week. The most important thing is that you're safe now. And for you to know that we will do anything to help you heal." She squeezes my hand. "And you will heal."

The look on Mom's face is so serious, so fierce. And I realize how like her I am. How like her I want to be.

She exhales. "I also owe you an apology. For not being there for you. For not noticing . . . I—"

I pull her back into a hug. "I love you, Mom. It's okay."

"No." She pulls back and holds me gently—ever so gently—by the shoulders. "It is very far from okay that this happened to you. But I never want you to feel you can't come to us. Life is hard enough, you know?"

Dad comes over and squeezes onto the couch on my other side. "Zoe, we are your original team. The OG," he says.

I laugh despite the tears. "I don't think that means what you think that means, Dad."

"I just want it to mean that I'm in your corner forever and ever no matter what, and you can always come to us with anything."

I nod.

"Can I hug you too? You can say no. I don't want you to ever feel press—"

I throw my arms around him and he grunts as he falls backward.

After I sit back up, Mom looks at me. "Will you let me look at your arm?"

I nod. We go up to my room and I take off my shirt. We stand in front of the mirror, me in my jog bra. I watch her as she brings her eyes close to my skin so she can check my arms and shoulders. Then she moves them all around and checks my rib cage. She gives me the most thorough exam in the history of nurse moms.

As she moves over my skin so gently, I realize she's putting her love into every look, every touch. That the longer she spends examining me, the more she's coating me in her love. And it's the weirdest thing, but it makes me feel full and bright and seen.

"Everything's fine, right?" I ask when she's finally done.

"Physically there doesn't seem to be anything wrong. But there can be lasting psychological effects from an experience like this. I know we said it before, but we will help you through all of it. We will be as present as you let us be."

I nod. I look at her. "I want you on my team. Always."

She bites her lip. "Good. I don't want to be anywhere else." She exhales a big breath and smiles. "You are the most incredible girl, Zoe Thane Alamandar." She looks at me in the mirror, her hands on my shoulders. "I knew you'd be a force, kicking me nonstop the way you did for half the pregnancy. But I had no idea how strong you'd become. Now"—she drops her hands and tilts her head—"do you feel ready for tonight? We can cancel, or—"

I laugh. "You can't cancel the State Championships, Mom."

"I know. I just mean, we're allowed to stay home. I don't care if scouts or your team or your coach or the Queen of England says otherwise. I will make the excuse and it will be fine."

The funny thing is, I believe her. She would make it fine . . . with them. "No. I want to go. I actually feel . . . really ready to kick some ass."

She laughs. "Well then, I am really ready to watch you kick some ass." She walks toward the door. "I'm going to make some salads for lunch. Want one?"

"Definitely," I say.

When she leaves, I look down at my phone. There's a text from Grove.

Shit. He probably saw my post too and I have no idea how to tell him . . . any of this. Or if I want to.

I remember what my parents said about them being my original team. All this time, I've kept my team really small. For so long, it was just Liv. And then it grew to include Ava, and all the girls we chose. Then Nikki.

I can't control Grove's reaction. But I can control what I do once I find it out. And it's probably better to find out now if he's an asshole.

FORTY-TWO

IT'S ONLY AFTER THE PHONE rings that I realize I've never talked to Grove on the phone. But this isn't a conversation to have over text, and there's no way I'd want to do this in person. Thank you, Alexander Graham Bell.

"Hey," he says, and it takes me right back to sitting on the floor of Scoop Dreams, listening to his voice . . . and hiding.

"Hey," I say. "I want to wish you luck tonight at Regionals. When do you leave?"

"In about an hour."

"You feeling good about it?"

"Zoe, for once in my life, I don't want to talk about soccer right now."

I love that he said that. I mean, I don't want to talk about what I called to talk about, but I also don't want to talk about soccer, or fockey, either.

"I . . ." His voice is so close but I want it closer. I roll onto my side, holding the phone between my ear and the pillow. "I saw your post."

I don't say anything for a second. Neither does he.

"That was . . ."

My rib cage is unzipped, my heart beating and bare.

". . . brave."

I smile slow and soft.

"Did it—I mean, who—no." I hear him take a breath. "Are you okay?"

I think for a second. I think I'm better than okay. "Yeah," I say.

"I don't want to pressure you to talk about it, but I also want you to know I'm here. If you want to . . . you know . . . talk about it."

"Thanks," I say.

He's quiet on the other end of the phone and I realize he's waiting for me. Waiting for me to decide.

"It happened that night we got together. At the bonfire."

"Oh, Zoe," he says. "I'm so sorry."

I resist the urge to say *It's okay* or *It's not your fault*. Not that it is. But it's not my job to take care of him around this. And it's not his job to take care of me. Maybe our job is to just be in this together.

"Thanks," I say instead. "I think that's why I got all mixed up after."

"That makes sense," he says. "I completely understand. I mean—I don't because I can't. But I get it. I wish I could punch the shit out of whoever did this."

And I almost laugh. Because so did I. And when he says it,

part of me feels good—like he cares, he's on my side, and he's angry for me. But I don't need him—or any boy—to fight any battles for me.

"Yeah," I say. "I felt the same way. But then I realized it took more guts to speak up, to keep it from happening to other girls."

"You're kind of amazing, you know that?"

I smile. "You didn't?"

He laughs, and I swear I could let that laugh and his voice roll across my ears forever.

"I just want you to know," he says, "that I will never, ever be that guy."

"I wouldn't be talking to you right now if I thought otherwise," I say.

"And if I ever do anything that makes you feel uncomfortable, just tell me, okay? I mean, it shouldn't all be on you or whatever. I'll ask. I mean, we'll figure it out."

"Okay," I say. "I'd like that."

I pull my comforter closer. I like lying here, his voice so close.

"Can we talk about tonight now?" I ask.

He laughs. "Yeah. We can talk about whatever you want."

"What are you wearing?" I croon.

He laughs again. "My very sexy school uniform that has been worn by a thousand sweaty teenagers before me."

"Mmmm," I say. "You really know how to sell it."

"I'm excellent at selling it. I sell it better than you sell ice cream."

"What?" I squeal. "I am Big Bob's number-one employee."

"I bet," he says, and I can hear him smile. "You know, I used to drive past in the summer, to see if you were working. I even stopped in once because I was sure you were there, but—"

"You did not," I say.

"I did!"

"I got a—"

"Chocolate chip Shaken Cookie," I say.

"Liv told you?"

"Uhhh." I groan. "I was there. I was hiding."

"I knew it! I could've sworn I saw you." He pauses. "Why'd you hide?"

"Because I had a massive crush on you and—"

"So hiding made sense?"

"It made total sense. At the time."

"I'm glad you came out of hiding," he says, and his voice is like caramel over vanilla ice cream.

"Me too," I say.

FORTY-THREE

BALON BAY IS FROM LONG Island. I want them to be boppy surfers who shop and tan a lot. But I know they must be fierce. They've won States the last four years in a row.

But we've beaten teams used to winning before. We can do it again.

We sprint into the Dome, and as the door rattles shut behind us, the smell of nachos hits me and so does this: I get to play in the Dome for the second time.

"Anywhere in the World?" Liv asks, as we jog toward the locker room.

"Right here. Even with the nachos smell." I grin. "You?"

"Right here. Even with the nachos smell."

"Not in Yemen? Or Myanmar? Or some other nachos-free place that needs your human rights badassery?"

"Nah." Liv smiles. "I'll fit that in after I'm a state champ."

I smile. "Absofockinglutely."

"What do you think the home locker room is like?" Bella asks.

"I bet it's all riched up," Dylan says.

"They've probably got gold toilets," Cristina says.

"Next year," Ava and I say together.

Quinn rebraids our hair. Ava does the little dance she does to pump us up. And Coach is like a gumball machine that only spits out encouraging AA quotes. She runs off to check something, and I ask her to keep an eye out for the UNC scout.

"And the SU one!" Ava calls.

Everything's coming together. Finally.

Part of me has never felt so connected to my body, the other part feels as though I'm floating above, watching the whole scene from afar. It's 5:15 p.m., and forty-five minutes feels as short as a heartbeat and as long as forever. Soon, they'll let us onto the field to warm up.

Ava's lacing up her shoes for the third time. I go over and sit next to her, leaning into her with my shoulder. "Come outside for a second?" I nod toward the field door.

She raises her eyebrows and grins. "Sure."

I link my elbow through hers and we push the locker room door open to the hall that leads to the field.

"I don't want to go up the ramp," I say. "I don't want to jinx it."

She shakes her head. "Me neither."

We both stand there for a second taking in the noise. It feels louder than it did last night, but maybe that's just my insides screaming.

"We did it," I say.

She turns to me. "We did."

I look down the orange-carpeted hall we cross to get to the field ramp. Giant pictures of athletes hang on the walls. We start to walk along it.

"Oh wow," I say, stopping underneath a picture of Carmelo Anthony, one of the greatest basketball players ever to play for the Orange.

"Carmelo focking Anthony," Ava says.

I laugh. We turn back toward our door. Just to the right of it, there's a photo of a field hockey player in orange. The photographer has captured her lunging for the ball, every muscle in her arms and legs straining, strong. She could be chiseled from marble she's so cut.

I nod at the girl. "That's going to be you in two years."

She crosses herself and looks toward the ceiling. "I will never eat another quesito. At least I won't for a whole year. Or Cheez Whiz. I'll totally give up the Cheez Whiz."

"Doritos?"

She side-eyes me. "Don't push it."

I laugh. "You're the most incredible goalie ever. Any school would be lucky to have you."

She knocks her shoulder into mine. "Thanks, Cap'n. You still determined to run away to North Carolina?"

I start to say yeah, and then I wonder if I'm doing that out of habit. I wanted UNC because it has one of the best teams in the country. But I also loved that it's five states away. Before, I thought Mom worked so hard just to avoid me and Dad. But maybe I wanted an escape too.

"You and me on the same team? We would kill it. SU all the way." She tilts her head. "Besides, you love it here."

"I do." I kick my shoe into the orange carpet. "I think maybe I've been a little hard on the place." I smile. "But I don't have to figure it out right now. Right now, we just—"

"Girls!" We turn to see Coach rushing down the hall.

Ava leans in. "They should probably check her heart before every game."

"Mandatory EKGs," I whisper.

She rushes straight for us, hustling us back into the locker room. "We've got scouts from SU *and* UNC."

UNC. Is here. Now. Waiting to see me.

I sit down in front of my open locker. I look over at Ava. Right above her head, there's something etched in her magnetic strip. I squint. It says, *Trevor*. Someday, I'll have my name over a locker in a college locker room. But it won't be scratched with a pen.

Ava widens her eyes at me and takes a big breath. The others have stopped talking. I don't even hear the squeak of our shoes on the floor.

"Girls." Coach exhales with her whole body. "I am awed by you. There's an AA quote I love, 'Adversity truly introduces us to ourselves.' Adversity just may be our greatest teacher. You have all been through so much this season." Coach looks at all of us and lands on Dylan. "Though adversity doesn't have to mean getting arrested." She winks at Dylan.

"I like to keep you on your toes, Coach." Dylan smiles.

"You are the best at that. And"—Coach gives her a warm smile—"at so many other things."

"My point is that you've grown not only as athletes, but as humans. You've grown not just as individuals, but as a team. You've grown not only as teammates, but as friends. And I couldn't be prouder."

Ava stands and swings her arms around Coach and Coach lets out an "Oof" as she squeezes the air out. Then we all pile on. A great group hug with Coach at the center.

"I think that's enough," she chokes.

We let go.

She looks at us, tears brimming. "It's time."

We push out of the locker room and clump on the orange-carpeted hallway before the ramp. Balon Bay gathers to our right in their crisp navy and white.

We glare at each other.

Kiara yells, "Go 'Cuse!"

Which isn't quite the same as screaming *Northridge*, but it lets them know that while they may have scored the home locker room, this is *our* house.

We get the all clear and run up the ramp, onto the field.

This time, Grove and the soccer team won't be here. Still, I know my parents, the Rebels, and Uncle Bob and Aunt Eileen will. But when we race out onto the field and I look up into the stands, I can't find them.

Because there are too many people. Which has never happened in the history of field hockey.

They call the Dome "the Loud House." It seats fifty

thousand, and when all fifty thousand fans stomp and scream, it rocks the roof. We're not at fifty thousand but we're not at fifty either. Last night, I was surprised to see a couple hundred. But tonight, there are even more. The noise is thick and real.

I turn to Ava. "Are all these people from Balon Bay?"

Ava studies the stands. "No. Look. I recognize a lot of them. They're from school."

I squint. She's right. The stands are filled with kids from Northridge.

And then I hear the cheers—they're yelling for Northridge.

Ava busts out laughing. "You know what happened?"

"What?"

"*We* happened."

"What are you talking about?" I ask.

"I didn't want to distract you, and I swear I didn't look, but someone texted me. Tons of people ditched Reilly's thing." She looks across the stands. "They must be here instead."

"Fockity fock," I say, taking in the crowd.

They're cheering for us. No, screaming for us. Pounding their feet for us. This is so much better than any school pep rally.

And then I catch sight of someone else. Dean Eldrich. She's standing and howling and screaming with everyone else.

"Fockin' nuts," Dylan says.

I laugh. "Fockin' nuts."

We do our warm-ups, we do our coin toss, we do our handshake.

We stand in a row, Ava on my left, Liv on my right. I put

my hand on Ava's shoulder. Liv puts hers on mine. We each do the same, right down the line, linking ourselves.

We are a chain of iron.

The national anthem plays and for the first time, I sing out. Ava's voice and Liv's voice and everyone's blend together and all our voices fill me up.

We huddle at midfield. We scream, "Sticks Chicks!" We race to our places.

Ava crosses herself and hops twice. The announcer counts down: "Ten ... nine ..." The crowd joins in. "Six ..." I chop my feet. "Four ..." Liv jumps with the crowd. "Three ..." Their shouts fill my chest. "One!"

At the whistle, we ignite. We flame. We explode.

Quinn wicks the ball to Bella who zips it to me. Balon Bay presses hard and I pass back to Kiara who knocks it to Dylan who passes to Michaela who kicks it to Liv who passes to Sasha.

They press again and it's back to Liv who flicks it to me.

Balon Bay is a wall of navy so I pass back to Nikki.

Maintaining possession is key but so is making a focking goal.

We keep it but they're just waiting for us to mess up, for the pass to veer a touch off course, for the ball to slow at just the right moment so they can snap it up with their stick like a frog snaps a fly.

Each team is good. Too good. This game will be won on a mistake.

I just hope it's not ours.

FORTY-FOUR

ON A PASS FROM SASHA to Liv, their number 23 darts in and takes the ball. She skates around Bella then Liv then Nikki but Dylan's there ready to stop her, and I'm there when she passes.

I hop it over one stick, then I run.

The crowd goes nuts. "North-ridge. North-ridge. North-ridge." They clap on the beat, and the beat pounds into my run, my stick, my chest.

Two of theirs come in from the side and I flick it over their sticks and keep flying. The crowd is screaming, slamming their feet. I fake right then when their sweeper lashes out her stick, I send it flying underneath. Right in the back corner.

Goal.

I howl at the dome, and Liv flies at me and lifts me off the ground. Kiara and Cristina and the others race up and we're howling and the crowd's howling and stomping and it is perfection.

We rush back to position.

Balon Bay drives hard right off the top. All their passes are tight. Every time we try to snap it up with our sticks, they spin away. Cornered, one of them drives hard against Michaela's stick so the ball goes out and they get the call. Michaela hates that.

She plants right in front, and when the girl tries to fly the ball over her stick, Michaela lifts just right and the ball drops at her feet.

Michaela drives to me and I run. Balon Bay is there and I look at Quinn.

She nods.

I run hard at their forwards like I'm going to crash through while Quinn breaks in from the left. I fake and knock it to Quinn, my energy still propelling me forward so Balon Bay loses sight of the ball for a second, giving Quinn a chance to break away. She takes a shot.

But the goalie's there.

They take a run. But Ava lunges and bats it out of goal.

We get another breakaway—Cristina this time—but their sweeper traps it.

Then they get a run. Ava stops it again.

They're everywhere—my shoulder, my side, and no matter where I spin, they're there.

We get possession, we lose it. They get possession, they lose it.

Cristina has the ball but she can't press forward. Bella's open but Cristina can't reach her without me. I call for it. Fast so they can't steal it, I flick it to Bella.

But they're there. They intercept.

Shit, I should've paused. Should've held the ball. Should've passed back.

314

They race downfield and Liv lunges but they skate around her and the girl drives hard. Right under Dylan's stick. Right under Ava's pads.

It's 1 to 1.

Balon Bay scored off my mistake.

I look at Coach on the sidelines. She looks down, shakes her head. Then she lifts her chin to me. *It's okay, Zo,* she mouths. *It's okay.*

Which only tells me for sure that it was my fault.

I squeeze my stick. I chop my feet. I have made a thousand mistakes this season. I'm not going to let this one be the one that wrecks everything.

The whistle blows.

Quinn and Bella pass it back and forth, spinning, twisting, flicking. Cristina drives up and Bella gets it to her but Balon Bay presses hard again. She knocks it back to me. I spin around one of theirs and send a clear shot to Sasha. She sprints hard up the sideline but she's cornered. Balon Bay swings their stick and Sasha trips and flies.

She pops up, thank goodness. And we just landed a penalty.

We line up around the circle. They cram the goal.

I drive it to Quinn. She pulls it back to me. I flick it to the goal but the goalie is there and it bounces off her pads to me. I slam it again. The goalie is there. I drag it, keep pulling it back and to the left while Bella and Cristina crowd in to give me space and then, I reverse it. Slam it.

Goal.

The crowd goes nuts when the ref makes the goal sign.

We scream back to our spots. And we hold it . . . till the half.

We head back to the locker room.

Our shoes clatter against the concrete ramp, and our laughs and squeals bounce back to us from the walls and sloped ceiling.

Coach leads the way, laughing, Kiara, Sasha, and Ava by her side.

"Wait." I grab Nikki and Liv. "Let's grab one more look."

We race back to the opening, see the bright green turf, the white dome above, and our giant, screaming, beautiful home crowd there for us in between.

"You guys, we're going to do this."

They squeal.

"I know!" Liv says.

We turn and run down the ramp. The rest of the team is already in the locker room.

Liv and Nikki open the door and rush in. But I stop to look at the fockey girl on the wall, slamming that stick against that ball with everything she has.

No matter what color I wear in college, I'll be doing that too, because I just nailed it in front of every scout here.

I grin at the girl.

Then someone steps in front of her. I expect him to keep moving, but he stops. And I register his face.

Reilly.

"Heeeeeyyyy, where you going, my slippery salamander?"

FORTY-FIVE

MY FEET ARE WELDED TO the floor.

I can hear the fans on the field, the team in the locker room, my own quick breath. All of it buzzes in my ears and his voice slithers through the fog of noise and I'm two months ago in his house, pressed against a wall.

Heeeeeyyyy, slippery salamander.

"What?" he asks. "You don't have anything to say now?"

Laughter.

That's when I notice the others. Two guys behind Reilly. The sour stench of beer thick on their breath. The smell of nachos snakes through the walls, and vomit clogs the base of my throat.

Sticky chip-dip-beer breath on my skin, hot on my shoulders hands moving, shoving, pushing, smashing—

"You li'l bitch." His words slur and spit. "Today was a sausage party because of you, you lying slut."

His eyes are wet and unfocused. He pushes off the wall and takes a step toward me.

He was leaning against the hockey girl on the wall. And she looks pissed. The cut of her muscles, the set of her chin, the grip on her stick.

I imagine her here, now, with me. I imagine the faces of all the people who have stood up and spoken out. Who voiced their pain at speakouts and online. I can feel them lining up beside me, one by one by a million, shoring me up with their courage and strength.

I am one of many.

"Get. Out."

"No." He steps closer, thrusting his head at me like a rattlesnake. "I need you—"

"I couldn't care less what *you* need. This isn't me and you alone in a dark hallway in your house." I lift my stick and he inches back. Not much. But enough. "This is you invading *my* house. So I'll say it again. Get. Out."

I clutch my stick across my body. My stick is sweaty and the tape is ragged and the foot is beat up. But it is strong and fierce and mine.

I step toward the locker room and reach for the door handle.

He knocks me away. Hard.

I fall back, and my stick slides beneath me and I come down wrong, my right arm twisted under me. My stick jabs my back, but when I roll off the stick, I realize it's not my back that really hurts, it's my wrist. I try to reach for my stick but I can't grab it right.

Reilly stalks toward me, a sick smile on his face.

Scrambling, I fling my left arm over, grab my stick, and swing it at Reilly hard, cutting his legs out from under him.

He teeters for a second and he must be too drunk to right himself because he crashes right down on the floor.

"What the hell?!"

It comes from one of the guys with Reilly. Shit. He's going to come at me too. I hold my stick tighter.

But he's not facing me. He's yelling at Reilly. He looks toward me. I lift my stick.

"You okay?" he asks, holding out his hand.

The locker room door slams opens and Coach runs out, the rest of the team right behind her.

"Zoe!" Coach yells. She looks at the guy standing over me. "What the hell did you do?"

He puts his hands up and steps back.

"It wasn't him, Coach." I nod at Reilly. "It was him."

"She attacked me with her stick!" Reilly yells.

Some guy in a security uniform runs up, panting. "I just saw her attack this boy with her stick on my monitor," he says to Coach. Then he turns to me. "Young lady—"

My team loses their shit.

"Oh, no. Not today," Kiara says.

"This fucking shit again?" Dylan says.

"Sir," Liv says, marching right up to the guard. "Thank you for doing the hard job of protecting people. But this boy"— Liv points to Reilly, the tip of her finger trembling, and I have never seen her look so angry—"has no reason to be here. *We* are playing a game. *We* are the ones you're hired to protect."

319

"Well," the guard starts, adjusting his belt. "I—"

"Wait." The guy speaks up. "I came here with Reilly. I thought we were just picking up more people for the Day Dri—I mean—the, uh, birthday party. But then he attacked this girl out of nowhere. She was just defending herself."

We all stare at this kid. I'm sure I've never seen him before in my life.

"Fucking pussy," Reilly mutters.

The other guy with them doesn't say a word.

"Is that true?" the security guard asks me.

"Yes," I say. My voice has never felt more clear.

"Hell, yeah it's true," Dylan says. She snaps a picture of Reilly on the ground.

"Reilly has attacked her in the past. She has pictures. Now, he's back to do it again. Just because he thinks he can." Liv walks over until she's standing over him, gripping her stick like she's going to bash his face in. "Well, guess what, dickhead, you can't. Not now. Not ever."

"Okay, that's enough, young lady," the guard says.

"Don't call me that," Liv says, right at the same time Coach says, "Don't call her that."

Liv stands up straight and I've never seen her walk so tall as when she comes over to me and holds out her hand. "C'mon, Cap. We have a championship game to win."

"I don't know about that, Coach. We have firm policies against fighting. We're going to have to get the officials out here." The guard takes out his walkie-talkie.

I hold out my right hand. As soon as Liv grabs it, I scream.

"Oh no," Coach says. She turns to the guard. "We need the athletic trainer on staff. Now. Please."

"No," I say. "I'm fine. I'm sure I'm fine." I push down on my left hand, still gripping my stick, and heave myself up. "I'll just take some Advil." I nod my head toward Reilly because I refuse to even look at him. "I am not letting *him* ruin my game."

The guard's gripping his walkie-talkie like he doesn't know what to do.

"Call the official," Coach says, impatient. "But first please do something to actually protect these girls and get some medical help."

His thick eyebrows come together over his nose, but he calls the trainer.

Reilly's silent friend pulls him up and they start to walk off.

"Oh no," Coach says. "You aren't going anywhere." She turns back to the guard. "I assume you're going to detain him for assault. And underage drinking. And, one would presume, driving while drunk."

The guard gives Coach a look like he doesn't appreciate her telling him what to do, but he walks over to Reilly, turns him around, and wraps a zip tie around his wrists.

I could watch Coach boss this guy All Day.

"What the fuck, man?" Reilly asks. "I'm not—"

Dylan snaps another picture and waves her phone in the air.

Reilly's face whitens. "Erase that, you bitch."

Dylan whistles. "I would think you'd have learned to talk to women differently by now." She looks back at me. "Wouldn't you, Cap?"

I finally look at him. A glob of spit is caught in the corner of his lips, and he looks unsteady with his arms wrenched behind his back. Above his head, there's the picture of my fockey girl. My future.

He lost one friend. He lost his party. Maybe, after tonight, he'll lose even more.

"Nobody cares what you have to say," he says to me.

I step toward him. He flinches. *He* flinches. I smile. I turn to my team. "Did he speak?"

Applause. I look over to see the whole Balon Bay team clapping. I have no idea how long they've been standing there.

The head ref and the lead official run down the ramp.

"What's going on here? Why aren't you out on the field?" The official looks around and lands on the security guard. "What happened?"

The guard nods at Reilly, then at me. "These two got in a fight."

The official snaps her head back. "A fight? Well, that's unacceptable." She looks at me. "You're out the rest of the game."

My team erupts.

I look back at Reilly. Because of him, I'm not going to get to play the rest of this game. I'm not going to get seen by scouts. And I'm—

Coach puts her hands up. "This boy attacked my player out of the blue. This was not a fight. This was an attack." She nods at the mystery boy. "This boy is a witness."

The official looks at the boy.

"It's true," he says.

"We're okay with her playing," says a girl's voice. We all turn toward it. She's one of the Balon Bay captains. She stands tall, both hands on the stick in front of her. Her team stands beside her, same pose. And they look so focking fierce.

The official looks between the boy and Balon Bay and me. She throws up her hands. "Fine. The clock is ticking. Let's get out there."

I look at the Balon Bay captain and she just nods at me before they turn and walk up the ramp.

I feel like laughing. I feel like screaming. I feel like hugging the official and the ref and even Balon Bay, right before kicking their ass all over the field.

The athletic trainer runs up.

Coach sends Ava to run quick warm-ups with the team. Just Coach and Liv remain.

"You, Zoe Alamandar, give me heart palpitations."

"Well, that's a—ow!" The trainer's manipulating my wrist.

"I take it that hurts?" she asks. She shakes her head. "There's no way you can play with this."

"No," I say. "Of course I can."

"What if she just babies it?" Coach asks.

"I just need an Advil. I have some in my bag. It's really no big—"

"I'm afraid not." She bends down to get a bandage out of her case. "No babying or Advil will fix a broken wrist."

FORTY-SIX

"YOU SHOULD GO TO A hospital for imaging," the trainer says. She turns to Coach. "You want to call her parents?"

Coach gives me this look filled with sad, then takes out her phone.

"No," I say. "I want to stay."

"I have to call your mom, Zo," Coach says.

"I'll go to the hospital right after the game," I say. "I promise."

The trainer wraps a splint onto my wrist while Coach fills Mom in.

"I'm giving you a sling too," the trainer says. "To keep it above your heart. That'll reduce the swelling and pain."

Coach puts the phone to my ear.

"Mom?"

"What in the—"

"Mom," I say, and I'm surprised by how level my voice is. "The thing I want most in the world is to be here to finish this game. Right now. The trainer wrapped my wrist really well and we can go to the hospital as soon as the game's over. I promise. It doesn't even hurt."

Mom's silent but I hear people near her in the stands.

"Mom," I say. "Please. I need this."

I hear her sigh into the phone. "Fine. Have the trainer give you a sling."

"She already did."

"And take some Advil. Because it'll hurt like hell when the shock wears off."

"Yes, Mom. Thank you. I love you."

"Yeah, yeah. I love you too. Do not hurt yourself further. If you do, I'll kill you."

I smile. "Okay, Mom."

She hangs up. I ask Liv to run and get me some Advil from my bag.

"You sure about this?" Coach asks. "I mean, I'd love you to stay, but your—"

"I'm very sure," I say.

"Well, you can leave your stick," Coach says.

I look down at my stick, the stick I'm still clutching so tightly. This beautiful stick with its worn grip and ratty wrapping, with its scuffed toe and big lettering. Mine.

"No way," I say. "It's coming too."

Coach shakes her head. Liv runs up and I take the Advil, then we head up the ramp.

I turn to Liv and whisper, "You taking on that guard was a thing of beauty."

She squeezes my left arm.

"I'm serious. You were a legit human rights lawyer. You should just skip college."

She laughs.

The other girls rush over.

"Yes!" Ava says. "I knew—" She takes in my sling.

I shake my head. And seeing Ava's face drop undoes me all over again. This isn't just about my championship game, my chances in front of the scouts. This is her shot too.

I will not cry. I will not cry.

"Ava," I say, my voice coming out harder than I mean. "Team. We got here together. And we will win together. Just like when Sasha was out, and we felt her strength with us, I am going to be with you out on that field. You are not only capable of crushing these guys, you *will* crush them. We are winning. All we have to do is hold it. And I'm going to cheer every hit, push, flick, slap you got."

Dylan screams, "We got sticks!"

"We got balls!" Ava hollers back.

"Don't you call us baby dolls!" we yell.

Call us sugar?
Call us honey?
Just don't cry when you get muddy!
Hit 'em high.
Hit 'em low.
You can't stop our savage flow.

Ava throws her arm across my shoulder and whispers in my ear. "I'm going to pretend we can win this without you."

I smile and try like hell to keep the tears from leaking. "You can. Absofockinglutely."

Coach and I walk back to the bench.

"I am petrified about this second half, Cap. But I'll tell you, I've never been prouder of you than I am right now."

I squeeze my eyes shut and nod. Because if I say thanks, there's going to be a flood.

I find Mom and Dad in the stands and smile at them so they see I'm okay. They blow me a kiss. I take the bench.

I try not to think about the UNC scout who's watching other girls instead of me. I try not to think about my parents and the Rebels and Big Bob and Aunt Eileen who came to watch me play, and instead they're stuck watching me warm a bench. I try not to think about the stick in my hand that won't see another game for ten months. I try not to think about the way my muscles ache to run out and join my team, my friends.

And then I stand.

I refuse to sit this game out.

At the whistle, I scream. I scream so loud Coach steps a few feet away.

From here, everything looks different. I can see the way Sasha still hesitates when another player's stick comes off the ground. The way Bella plows through and forgets to pass. The way Quinn does everything to avoid a reverse hit. The way Cristina's so fast she overruns into the corner. The way Liv defers to everyone. The way Nikki crowds space. The way

Kiara's so busy watching the ball she forgets to keep an eye on the player. The way Michaela sometimes hides from the ball. The way Dylan rushes in. And the way Ava rushes out.

But I also see all the things that make them great. And I realize that it's not really about the individual flaws or strengths. It doesn't matter that Liv is the fastest or that Dylan is the fiercest. What matters is that together, we're faster and fiercer. And that's what makes us better than every team we've played this year—win or lose.

The game goes back and forth, nobody scoring. It's tight. Balon Bay has some great strengths, but I still think we're better. They dance it, but I don't think they feel it.

Then Dylan rushes out too soon and there's a tangle and . . . a foul. They get a penalty corner.

We crowd the box and Ava jumps twice and we can do this we can do this we can do this.

Balon Bay scores: 2 to 2.

Ava looks out at me and I run around to the back of her goal. "Don't let it psych you out, Cap'n. You are the most talented fockey goalie this dome has ever seen and this dome wants you to come back. It needs you to come back. Don't give up!"

She doesn't turn around but I know her well enough to know she's grinning. She crosses herself and hops up and down twice. Like she does.

I run back to the bench. Six minutes. Six minutes to make a change. "Bella! Pass back! Liv! Don't give it up. That ball is a human rights violation and you're the one it needs!

Sasha! Play angry, girl! Michaela! Don't you dare hide. Play like Harvard's watching!"

I catch Coach staring at me.

"Sorry, Coach. I got carried away."

She lifts her eyebrows. "You can get carried away like that all day long."

I turn to the crowd. "Let's go, Northridge." I pump my free hand in the air and the Rebels and my folks start to clap. Clap-clap, clap-clap-clap. Soon everyone's in on it. "Let's go, Northridge!" Clap-clap, clap-clap-clap.

I turn around to see Liv jab and force the Balon Bay player right into Nikki who steals it. Liv runs ahead and Nikki slams it to her. Sasha and Liv pass back and forth and knock it to Quinn who gets it to Cristina.

I can't see from here and Balon Bay blue seems to be everywhere but then I hear that beautiful smack against the board.

GOAL.

I scream. I jump up and down. Coach goes to grab my shoulders then she remembers my wrist and she grabs my left fist and raises it high and it's mad awkward but I don't even care and all of us on the bench are jumping and yelling and whistling.

Because we won.

After everything. We focking won.

FORTY-SEVEN

IT'S A LONG NIGHT IN the ER, and I am beyond beat when I get home. The next morning, I sleep in. My body aches all over, in places I didn't even know could hurt. My hips and back like always, but also my hands, my cheeks, my throat, my wrist.

But we won.

I'm sure I lost all the scholarships. Nobody wants someone who bails on their team in the second half.

But strangely, I feel okay. I feel lighter than I have in months, maybe years. Besides, I'll get another shot at States next year.

We won.

I push myself up to sitting and take a moment for my body to adjust. I pull out my phone, ready to mindlessly scroll, then I remember I deleted the app. I re-download it.

Wow.

There are so many reposts. So many new entries under our hashtag: *#BoycottDDO*. There are hearts and fire emojis and raised fists. There are girls I've never seen before sharing their stories. There are plans for mani-pedi parties yesterday afternoon.

Yeah, there are nasty comments too. But there aren't nearly as many as I'd feared. And the ones that exist are getting called out.

Maybe Reilly will go to jail after last night. Maybe not. Given everything we've experienced, I doubt it. But now everyone knows who he really is. Everyone's talking.

Finally, we changed things.

I choose clothes based on how easy they are to pull on one-handed: loose sweats. I don't bother to change my shirt.

I ease toward the stairs. Dad comes to his door, his face all worried.

"Hi," I manage. My voice is scratchy from all that screaming. I have no idea how Coach has a single vocal cord left.

"Hey, tiger." Dad hasn't called me tiger in forever. "Mom's at work, so you're stuck with me. How are you feeling?"

"Weirdly good?"

He smiles. "You were"—he shakes his head—"amazing last night."

"Thanks," I say. "Too bad I only got to play the first half."

"No," he says. "I mean, you were amazing the *second* half. You were great when you played. You were. You were deliberate and explosive. But you know what makes the greatest players great?"

I shake my head.

"They bend the game to their will. And you did that on the field. Which is incredible. But in all the games I've ever been to, I have never seen a player do what you managed to do *from the sidelines*."

Heat rises to my cheeks. "Really?"

"Really."

"Well, they played so well. They—"

He nods. "They did. But you were a big part of that. Can I hug you?"

I turn my big-bandaged wrist and sling away and offer a side hug. "Come at me."

He pulls me tight and I hug him back. "I love you, Dad."

"You too, sport." He pulls back. "Want me to make you some breakfast?"

I shake my head. "Nah. I can ..." I look at my arm and realize this may be harder than I thought. "Are you up to it? Because maybe I need help?"

At the kitchen table, he parks next to me, a bowl of coffee ice cream for him and s'mores ice cream for me. I scoop with my left hand. It feels new.

"All four food groups," I say.

"Damn straight. Helps, right?" he asks.

"I think it does. My wrist feels better already."

My phone vibrates.

AVA: Did u hear from SU?

AVA: I did. THEY WANT ME.

AVA: well for visit or whatever

AVA: Zo?

AVA: Why aren't u answering meeeeeeeeeeeee

"Oh wow," I say.

"What?" Dad says.

"Ava heard from SU."

Dad elbows me. "Just open your email."

I do. There's nothing there. I check my junk mail. Nothing.

I put it down. I shake my head.

It's one thing to think something won't happen. It's another to know it.

I pick my phone back up.

ME: Congratulations!!!
ME: 😎 😄 🔥 💯 🎉 🎉 🎉 ❤️ 💧 🎉 🎉 🎉 😄 💯
ME: Nothing for me.
AVA: . . .
AVA: . . .
AVA: Coach will write.

I heart the message and put my phone facedown.

Dad and I spend the morning watching sports. He plays some music off his blog. We invent a game where we sit on the couch and use only our left hands to toss pens into a mug on the coffee table.

It's exactly what I need.

After lunch, he nods at my phone. "Check your email again."

I shake my head. "It's that Schrödinger's cat thing. If I don't check it, there's still a possibility that I'll get an email. If I do check it, all my scholarship dreams die forever."

"Wow," he says. "That's a lot of pressure on a cat."

I glare at him.

"Open. It."

I pick up my phone and hover over the email button. Because I wasn't kidding. There are a thousand possibilities that still exist as possibilities if I don't actually look. But this whole weekend has been about seeing. Seeing things fresh, seeing things fully, and seeing things real.

I open it.

There's one from Coach.

Zoe.

I'm so proud of you. So, so proud. Do let me know if you need assistance with the case against that boy. I'll be in communication with your parents about that. But I want you to know that I am on your side. Always. I hope your wrist is on the mend. We need it in good shape for next year!

For now, though, I have some good news to pass along. The recruiters wanted to do some double-checking about the circumstances of that boy's attack, but you'll see they came to the right conclusion. We can talk about all of it more next week.

I sit up straighter. She's included a note from the recruiter.

Dear Miss Alamandar,

Thank you for your interest in UNC Chapel Hill's field hockey program. We are always looking for young women who are stars on the field as well as in the classroom.

I was already impressed by the detailed video and testimony sent to me by Eileen Allen.

"What the—"

"What?" Dad asks.

"Aunt Eileen talked to them for me?"

"Ohhhh. Maybe that's why Eileen's old college roommate was there. Joan? Jill?"

I just stare at him. "*Now* you tell me?" Dad starts to answer but I shush him. "Let me keep reading."

. . . She was a phenomenal collegiate field hockey player, and her in-depth assessment of your abilities bears out the testimony of the video she sent.

This was further borne out by your performance tonight. I was deeply impressed by your talent, skill, style, and drive. What really stood out to me, however, was the way you handled adversity. After breaking your wrist, you didn't give up and sulk. You remained a captain to the end and rallied your team to victory. It was a sight to see.

We would like to invite you to Chapel Hill to meet our coaching staff and team. You will get one-on-one time with coaches, play with the team, and spend the night with members of the team. Someone from our office will be in touch shortly to set up the arrangements.

Sincerely,

Jane Hodgkins

Assistant Field Hockey Coach

UNC Chapel Hill

I'm about to tell Dad everything when I see there's more.

Dear Miss Alamandar,

*We were very impressed by your performance at the State Champi-
onships last night. We loved seeing a local team win the trophy in our
home Dome. You exhibited strength and intelligence, as well as skill
and grit.*

*We hope you will consider coming to campus to meet our team
and coaches. You will get a taste of what will await you at SU with
some practice sessions, time with our coaches, and an overnight. Someone from our office will contact you soon.*

Sincerely,

Sarah Meyers

Assistant Field Hockey Coach

· *Syracuse University*

"I am not a patient person, Zo," Dad sings. "Please for the
love of Michael Jordan tell me what—"

I pass him the phone.

He starts to read. "Wow," he says. "Oh, wow." Then, "Oh,
Zoe, wow." And then, "Wow!" And, "Wow wow wow."

He places the phone gently on the table.

"Wow," I say.

"Yeah."

"I gotta text Ava."

He nods.

She doesn't put up with my texts for long. Soon we're
screaming and jumping and screaming but it's hard holding
my phone with my left hand, so I just put her on speaker and
Dad shakes his head while we scream and scream and scream.

It's the afternoon when my doorbell rings. On the other side of the door is Grove holding a giant white box with blue lettering.

"Oh," I say, "tell me that's from Geddes Bakery."

He grins. "I aim to please."

"How did you know?"

He shrugs. "Magic?"

I tilt my head at him. "You asked Liv, didn't you?"

"Yes. Yes, I did."

I laugh. I point to the porch swing. And the three of us—Grove, me, and the box of baked yummies—get comfortable.

I open the bakery box. Just the smell alone is enough to make everything better. It's filled with half-moon cookies. "Oh, you did good," I say, pulling one out. "Tell me about Regionals."

"Tell me about States," he says, grabbing a cookie.

We munch on cookies and he tells me about all the plays, how close the game was, and how it felt to walk away winners. I tell him everything that happened on our field.

He looks at me and puts his arm across the back of the swing, his fingers grazing my shoulders.

"We don't have to talk about the fact that your arm is all wrapped up, but we can. If you want." He bites his lip. "Reilly do that?"

"How'd you—"

"Dylan posted pictures of Reilly flat out on the floor in zip ties."

"Right," I say. I forgot about that.

He grits his jaw.

"I don't want you to get all testosteragey and promise to kill him for me or anything."

He half smiles. "I make it a mission in life never to get testosteragey. Besides, it's pretty clear you can fight all your own battles." He strokes my shoulder. "I just want you to know I'm happy to fight them beside you. If you want."

I put the box on the floor and move closer to him. "Is it okay if I kiss you now?"

He smiles. "Yes. Yes, it is."

He tastes like sugar, and snow, and I smell the laundry detergent on his shirt and the shampoo he must've used, and I pull my knees up into his lap, and he wraps his arm around me and even though I have this clunky splint, it's a perfect kiss. And maybe it would taste just as sweet if everything hadn't happened the way that it did.

But I don't think so.

FORTY-EIGHT

"OH WE ARE TOTALLY GETTING matching field hockey canes when we get old," Liv's saying as we slip and slide up the snowbank that divides the parking lot from the beach.

"Absofockinglutely," I say, using both hands to scamper up the hill. My wrist came out of its cast a few weeks ago, and I still haven't gotten over how good it feels to have it back.

When we reach the top, we stand tall along the mini-mountain, waiting for our eyes to adjust to the bright moon-light flashing off the crisp white surface.

Two feet of snow buries the summer sand of the beach. I'm the first to leap off, and my boots crunch through the top layer to the fluffier snow beneath. Soon, we've all jumped, and we boot-stomp our field to flatten it.

We plant our goal flags and paint the narrow strip of skin between our eyes and scarves with glow-in-the-dark face paint. This time, instead of the snow-colored white ball, Ava surprises us with a glow-in-the-dark green one. We race onto our homemade field, taking our positions, like we do.

We dribble and drive, push and pass, turning the flawless

field of snow into something a lot less perfect. We fall flat on our faces and get snow down our necks. We play hard and topple over one another into the snow. Every time Sasha falls, she has to make a snow angel, and every time Dylan falls, she tackles whoever brought her down. We chant our chants, each side trying to drown out the other, each side making up new rhymes for new moods.

Finally, we collapse against one another on the snow. A few of the girls run back to the van to get the firewood, and we make a fire—not quite like the bonfires of the fall with their towering logs and giant flames, but I like it better. There's room for all of us to crowd around it, and the logs are low enough that I can see everyone's faces lit up across the circle.

We laugh and talk about school and fockey and crushes and food. Always food.

I follow an ember as it flies away from the logs and shoots itself up, up, up into the cold night until it finally disappears.

I look across the circle and meet Ava's eyes. She rocks back and smiles.

I stand. "Parkour anyone?"

We kick snow over the fire, which has melted away a ring around the logs. We race toward the playground. It's a little small for us, but we make it work. We tumble and roll and fly and jump all over it, making it ours.

Like we do.

AUTHOR'S NOTE

This is a work of fiction, but sexual assault is all too real. There are many important young adult books that follow the courageous journeys of survivors of rape. In *Dangerous Play*, I wanted to explore the insidious and pervasive effects of sexual assault and rape culture, even when a rape isn't the focus. I wanted to examine what happens to a group of girls and their community when rape culture goes unchecked.

Consent culture is the opposite of rape culture. *Yes* is a powerful word. Active consent ensures that each individual has a voice, that each individual values the voice and desires of their partner. That is why there is active consent in every romantic interaction between Zoe and Grove.

I gave Zoe a bigger team than she realized she had. Zoe's friends and family showed up, listened, believed her, sympathized with her, and allowed her to tell her story in her own way in her own time. When someone we care about gets hurt, it's hard to know what to do. Those are all good places to start.

It took time for Zoe to find her voice. That's because there is no "right" timeline for finding your voice. *You* should get to decide when to talk, to whom you will speak, and what it is you want to say. Those are weighty decisions and they are yours to make.

I worked as a sexual violence peer counselor for several years and we used to say: your worst experience is your worst experience. Like Zoe, some survivors question whether they have a right to be upset if their attacker didn't rape them. You absolutely, unquestionably have that right. You did not deserve it. It was not your fault. You are allowed to have feelings, you are allowed to give those feelings voice, and you are allowed to seek help. I hope you do.

If you or someone you know wants more information about sexual assault, please visit www.rainn.org or call their National Sexual Assault Hotline at 1-800-656-HOPE (4673).

ACKNOWLEDGMENTS

This book has a twenty-four-plus-person cast, but it took many more to bring it into existence.

First and always, to my students—past, present, future. And to all the teachers and librarians who give their students a safe place to try on ideas, practice civil dissent, and learn deep as if their lives depend upon it, because they do.

To my agent Roseanne Wells, who demanded that this book be as strong as the girls who populate its pages and helped me get it there. Forever thanks for jumping into the game with me, Cap'n. Thanks, too, to Jennifer De Chiara, Betty Anne Crawford, and Kim Guidone.

To my editor Mekisha Telfer of Roaring Brook Press, my coach, who asked the perceptive questions that led me to play my best game. Thanks for helping Zoe, and me, find the right words. To Aurora Parlagreco for the stunning design, and to Laura Callaghan for the jaw-dropping, fist-raising cover art. Thank you, too, to Cynthia Lliguichuzhca, Avia Perez, Susan Doran, Tracy Koontz, Kerry Johnson, and the entire team at Roaring Brook Press and Macmillan.

To Pam Neimeth and CARES for being a refuge and a training ground for what it is to be a woman activist in this world. To the brave people of the #MeToo movement: This book began well before I heard your stories, but I'm so grateful that when you bravely spoke up, so many finally listened.

343

To the original Rebels, my mom's consciousness-raising group: Sheila Berger, Lois Chaber, Gloria DeSole, Judith Fetterley, and Joan Schulz. I spent my childhood eavesdropping on your feminism and friendship, and it shaped my life.

To Erik "Obi-Wan" Canavan for the superhero talk while you were turning me into one.

To my MVPs: Steph Liberati, Coach Maggie Kennedy, and Bri Stahrr, and also to Sarah Bisesi, Coach Megan Caveny, and Julia Loonin—all gifted athletes as fierce on the field, turf, and court as they are in life. Special thanks, too, to Coach Joe Burke and Coach Pat Kennedy.

To those who answered my questions at all hours, but especially David Babikian, Erin Becker, Christa Desir, Jackie Hayman, Daniel Henderson, Keri Levin, Susan Macomber, Samantha Olds, Toni Santoferrara, Nicole and Genaro Sepulveda, and Cathy Wool.

To my careful readers, especially Miriam Barquera, Jiton Davidson, Tarie Sabido, and Bianca Viñas. Thanks also to Kim Purcell, Joseph Wiederhold, Ellen Yeomans, my first VCFA workshop led by Uma Krishnaswami and Nova Ren Suma, and Mary Quattlebaum. Thanks, too, to Eleanor Brown, Denice Turner, and the Writing Table, where this book began.

To my writing/publishing friends: the BCBs (Salima Alikhan, Gene Brenek, Rachel Purcell), the Saratoga Writing Group (Bre Grant, Rachel Krackeler, Barb Roberts), Eddie Gamarra, Rachel Gambiza, Gail Hochman, Laura Jackson, Melanie Jacobson, Jessie Janowitz, Erin Nuttal, Shannon Rigney, Anne-Marie Strohman, Erin Summerill, Lakita Wilson, and Elisa Zied. Thanks, too, to Holly Green, Tirzah Price, and the rest of the #The21ders.

To the inclusive and creative VCFA community especially the

Tropebusters, the Revisionaries, and my VCFA advisers David Gill, Amy King, Mary Quattlebaum, and Cynthia Leitich Smith, who each gave me tools to do this story justice.

To Meg Wolitzer, my steadfast and generous champion. You were the first person to tell me I should write for young people. As always, you were right.

To Amber Lough for being my first and forever crit partner. All kinds of grateful for that blissed-out moment in the YMCA parking lot that led to you.

It's impossible to write a book about the power of friendship without having had the experience of many amazing friends in my life. To the friends (not already mentioned) who have been my cheerleaders along this very long road: Julie Barer, Luke Cusack, Jill Erlitz, Denis Guerin, Astrid Koltun, Rachel Person, Rachel Simmons, the Tobrockes, and Jody Ziebarth. Most of all, to Amy Spitzer, a talented teacher, reader, writer, and remarkable best friend.

To my supportive, extended family: the Aaronsons, Fanellis, Hendersons, Husseys, Iaconnos, Nevilles, Newmans, Perrinos, Ratcliffes, Sepulvedas, Tetros, and Zampiers.

To my dad, Jack Kress, who imbued in me a fierce sense of justice that's never gone away. You are my partner in optimism, and there's no one with whom I'd rather get my hopes up. To my mom, Susan Kress, who taught me that every word and every woman holds power. You've been my role model as a teacher, writer, feminist. Listening to you read and discuss the biographies of words was one of the best experiences of my life.

To my children, Mazie and Max: for most/all of your lives, I've been chasing this dream and you've been among my most enthusiastic, patient, and insightful supporters and readers. It means the world to share this with you both. To Brody, for bringing the funny, the real, and the love to my stories and my life. Nobody can make me laugh as hard and as often as you. You are the heart of every romantic moment I write.